Six Mornings
on Sanibel

a novel by Charles Sobczak

Read below why readers love *Six Mornings on Sanibel*:

"This book is beautiful written and takes me back to Sanibel...I was saddened when the book ended. I wanted it to continue...What an incredible writer!"

-Vickie A. Hoelzer, Bonita Springs, FL

*"A terrific story! I hope that this is not the last novel that Mr. Sobczak will write...I would heartily recommend each (visitor) get a copy of **Six Mornings on Sanibel** and have it as required reading before passing through the toll bridge on the way back home to the frozen north."*

-David & Paula Harvey, Maryland Heights, MO

*"It was better than **Tuesday's with Morrie**."*

-Rusty Farst, Sanibel, FL

"Thank you for a beautiful, simple book that each and every reader will find a piece of themselves through your characters and lessons that only Nature, the fish and tides can teach so well."

-Judy Huggard, Cape Cod, MA

*"Reminded me a little of Hemingway's **Old Man & the Sea**."*

-Bonnie Thomas, Moline, AL

*"I laughed, I wept, and experienced a myriad of other emotions while reading **Six Mornings on Sanibel**. It was worth interrupting the reading of a Grisham novel I was half way through. **(Six) Mornings (On Sanibel)** is a splendid picture of life as many of us know it."*

-Lowell Thomas, Fort Myers, FL

"Last September I was lucky enough to spend not six but seven mornings on Sanibel. It was one, if not the best, book I have ever read."

-Bob Jacob, Christchurch, ENGLAND

"I love the premise for a story that may make you take stock in your own existence."

-Kevin S. Randolph, Medina, MN

Read below why critics love *Six Mornings on Sanibel*:

"Superficially seeming to be about a bunch of guys who spend mornings fishing on the Sanibel pier, it turns out to be a moving story that twines fishing and life, personal loves and personal losses. Read it and weep."
-Anne Johnson, *The Pelican Press*, Sarasota, FL

"A strong bond grows between the men as Carl, the philosopher-fisherman, and Richard take to heart the fiber of each tale. Richard begins questioning his life, his failed marriage, his spoiled children and his values. Each of Carl's stories of vanity, friendship, greed and survival deeply affect Richard, who begins to change. Sobczak captures the essence of Sanibel and the lives of his characters poignantly."
-Harold Hunt, *The Cape Coral Breeze*, Cape Coral, FL

"Sobczak shows keen insight into the issues men face: the surprising depth of grief common among men who lose a spouse; the socially rewarded drive to sacrifice ourselves to our jobs and money; the self-destruction common among men who have trouble expressing their feelings. The alternate presented in the book - a "follow your bliss" and die with grace approach is one the surely resonates in this day and age...Six Mornings on Sanibel is getting raves from readers for a good reason and I'll echo them I like the depth, the characters, the sense of place and the writing."
-Kyle Eller, *Budgeteer News*, Duluth, MN

"After you have read and enjoyed this book, it will be one you will want to place on the bedside table of you house guests to enhance their pleasure in discovering another side of Sanibel."
-Priscilla Friedersdorf, *The Island Sun*, Sanibel, FL

"Charles Sobczak's success story is the kind that most writers dream of living, but only a few experience. It is the tale of a classic merge onto the road of reaching readers, which many believe originates only in New York, but as this budding novelist knows can begin at home."
-Liz Flaisig, *Fernandina Beach*, Fernandina, FL

This is the seventh printing, January, 2012.
Printed in the United States of America by Whitehall Printing, Naples, FL

Published by: Indigo Press LLC
2560 Sanibel Boulevard
Sanibel, FL 33957

Visit us on the web at **www.indigopress.net**
ISBN 978-0-9676199-5-8

Cover photo by Charles Sobczak
Cover layout and design by Charles Sobczak & Bob Radigan
Book design for the 7th printing by MaggieMay Designs

Acknowledgments

In the end, no one writes alone. Stories are told to you by your distant cousin, Diane, from Los Angeles and they somehow find their way into the manuscript. Friends pour over the text and advise accordingly. Drafts are redone, edited and re-edited. Nothing comes easily. Still, some people contribute far more than others and their efforts should not go unheralded.

I would like to thank my wife, Molly Heuer for her lifelong support of this dream and our two sons for staying off the computer just long enough to allow me to write this book. Thanks also to the comments and editing of John Jones and Patricia Greenwood, who worked so hard on the early drafts of Six Mornings. Others who have been so helpful and encouraging include Scott Martell, Steve Beck, Marilyn Gary, Jennifer Thomas, Kip Buntrock, Norm Ziegler for his copy editing, Bob Radigan for the cover layout and design, and all of the people who have read my columns over the years in the *Island Reporter* and *Islander*. Never to forget Shirlene Grasgreen, whose tears inspired me to continue.

Also by Charles Sobczak

Novels:

Way Under Contract — A Florida Story

A Choice of Angels

Chain of Fools

Non-fiction titles:

Rhythm of the Tides
Selected Writings by Charles Sobczak

Alligators, Sharks & Panthers
Deadly Encounters with Florida's Top Predator-Man

Living Sanibel
A Nature Guide to Sanibel & Captiva Islands

The Living Gulf Coast
A Nature Guide toSouthwest Florida

Chant

It is the sound of sleep.
These eternal rhythms. The chant of surf.
How it soothes and becalms us.
A slow melody of waves and sand.
An oceanic whisper.

It is the song of the sea.
Curling. Uncurling.
Furling. Unfurling in primordial harmony.
How it wraps itself around us,
Embracing our soul in sweet allure.

It is the chorus Gregorian.
A thousand, thousand voices all together
In this ceaseless chant of eternity.
Monks in deep blue robes singing
This white capped song of God.

It is dreaming awakened.
The gentle hand of the ocean as if
Forever caressing the tired land.
Listen to it call to you.
Enthralling. Inviting. So alive.

The chant goes on, and on, and on, and on
In ceaseless repetition.
Before these words gave tribute to her.
Long since they will perish.

The chant of the surf washing against
The mystic shorelines of this,
Our lonely earth.

Charles Sobczak,
April 1997

A Long Time Ago

The pain would come later. The pain would come by nightfall, throbbing and silent like pain always is. Until then, if he could somehow work the barbed hook out, or clip it down to where it didn't affect his casting, Carl would keep fishing. They were on a good bite and he didn't want this little incident to ruin his morning charter.

A ladyfish, thought Carl to himself; it had to be a ladyfish. Not an hour earlier, as they had left the dock, Carl had gone into his well-rehearsed monologue on the dangers of ocean fishing. Most of his charters came from the Midwest, places like Duluth, Springfield and the likes of Toledo. Up there, they fished for freshwater species. Tossing their lines into pristine lakes where the most dangerous creatures were leeches and an occasional angry muskie.

Here, in the seas that surrounded Sanibel and Captiva, the waters held plenty of trouble. Carl had run through his standard list of dangers less than an hour ago. As he sat there, with his left hand wrapped in a bloodied towel and a lure impaled in his numb index finger, he realized that he should have paid more attention to his own lecture.

"It's not like lake fishing, mind you," Carl would always start in. "This here ocean's a whole different ball game. You've got to be a hell of a lot more careful down here. There are fish out there that can make a meal out of you to start with, but the big sharks are the least of your worries fishing back here in the bay."

Carl would go on to tell his charters about his catfish incident ten years earlier. He would mesmerize his two middle-aged customers with tales of unpredictable ladyfish, biting Spanish mackerel, and barracuda with razor blades for teeth.

"About two years ago, no, three years ago now, I was taking

a small mackerel out of the water just outside of Redfish Pass when a cuda decided to have my fish for lunch. He came along going twenty miles an hour and took three fourths of that fish in a flash of silver and blood. All I had left in my hand was the head. Had he missed that strike just a few inches higher, my hand would have been severed clean off."

His two anglers listened attentively. They were fascinated with stories like this. Tales of stepping on sting rays, getting pricked by pinfish, jabbed by porcupine fish and stung by jellyfish. Carl told them about freshly hooked tarpon jumping into boats and entire crews jumping out. Jumping straight into a chum slicked ocean to get away from two hundred-pound tarpon thrashing about wildly on the deck. Ankles and legs breaking like twigs. Stories of seventeen-foot hammerheads and hungry bull sharks, toothy kingfish, and broom stick pinching stone crabs.

"But remember, the two most likely suspects today are the plain old catfish and the wily ladyfish. Both of them have to be handled with the utmost of care."

If Carl had only listened to his own advice. One of his anglers had hooked a good size ladyfish ten minutes earlier. The ladyfish is the smallest member of a family of fishes that includes the magnificent tarpon. It resembles a miniature tarpon - long, thin and colored a brilliant silver. When hooked, ladyfish explode with energy, jumping and tossing themselves around frantically. Most of the time, they throw the hook on their own, long before the angler has a chance to boat them.

This one did not. As Carl reached over the gunwale of the boat to undo the hook with his long-handled pliers, the ladyfish took to the air one last time. As it did, it shot straight up toward Carl, ramming one of the lure's treble hooks deep into the knuckle of his left index finger. The ladyfish, over twenty inches long, was now hanging from Carl's hand, sinking the hook in deeper with every erratic wiggle.

Carl quickly grabbed a towel and wrapped it around the ladyfish, holding it tight with his right hand. He could see that the fish was barely hooked, and had he made his last jump without impaling Carl's finger, he would have thrown the hook. Working the fish gently, he removed it from the lure. He bent over the side and let the ladyfish go.

Both of his anglers had seen the accident unfold. Blood was now streaming down his left arm, mixing with the saltwater and dripping onto the white fiberglass deck.

"Are you OK?" one of his fishermen asked. "Is there something we can do?"

Carl laughed and said that there was. "You can remind me to listen to my own advice. Not an hour ago I warned you that the ladyfish was one of the most dangerous fish in the ocean. Now look at me, with this Mirrorlure dangling from my finger like it was some kind of Christmas ornament.

"Thanks, but I'll take care of it. I'll just have to take a minute to think it through."

"Shouldn't we head back in? You should have that looked at as soon as possible. Do you want us to take the boat back for you?" offered the other angler.

"No need to rush off. We've got a damn fine bite going here and I'm not about to let a little treble hook spoil your fishing. I'll just cut off the hook and deal with it when we get back. For the moment, it doesn't hurt all that much."

Carl Johnson was like that. His customers came first. It was his mistake for not netting that ladyfish in the first place and he didn't want to ruin a morning of fishing because of it. It was that kind of attitude that made him one of the most sought after guides on the islands. Besides, he reasoned, it was only a half-day charter. He didn't have a booking in the afternoon so he could take care of it then.

With his right hand he reached down into the top of his bright orange utility box. He always kept a large pair of wire cutters in that box along with his flares and backup hand-held radio. This wasn't the first time he had cut off a hook, nor would it be the last.

There was that morning when that horseshit fly fisherman from Baltimore stuck his streamer in Carl's right ear lobe. It hung there like an angler's earring. Carl had to cut that one out and thread it through. The fly fisherman wanted to head back in immediately and on that occasion Carl was more than happy to oblige. He had been ducking this amateur's casts all morning.

Or the time one of his anglers yanked a gold spoon out of a mangrove limb so hard that it shot straight back and impaled him in the shoulder. That barb was in so deep that a doctor ended up cutting it out. They fished the entire afternoon with that spoon stuck in his charter's shoulder. Landed some damn fine snook too, if Carl remembered right.

Carl put the cutting edges of the pliers on the top of the treble. Only one of the three hooks had gone in. Upon examining the wound closer, he could see where the other barb had scratched his finger but missed sticking him. He now had the wire firmly in the grip of the pliers. He wiggled the treble hook. Luckily, it had missed the bone. The barb was buried too deep to consider pulling the hook out. That would be too painful and way too damn bloody.

The best thing to do at this point was to shear it off right where the wire split off from the other two barbs. That would leave him half an inch of wire to work with later when he got back home. Marie, his wife, would help him get it out. She would wash it out with peroxide and insist that he have it looked at before it got infected. Fish hook wounds always get infected. She would smile at him in her wonderful fashion and, without ever actually saying it, remind him to be a little more careful next time. God, she was a gem.

When the kids got home from school and heard about it, they would both want to have a look at it. Rusty, his boy, would want all the gory details: how it happened, where it happened and how much it hurt. Emily wouldn't want Carl to undo the bandage but she would remind him, in an echo of her mother, to be more careful next time. They were both good kids. Island kids.

Carl's right hand closed down hard on the wire. It was a good sized treble and his first attempt at cutting it did little more than make a crease in the wire. On his second squeeze the cutters made it through. He set the lure down and started to retie a brand new red-and-white Mirrorlure on his angler's line.

"Are you sure you're going to be OK?" asked one of his customers.

"I'll be fine. My wife will bring me in for a tetanus shot and some antibiotics later. I've got the entire afternoon to take care of this. Now let's find us some redfish to take home."

Knowing that there were far too many ladyfish in this area, he started up his twin engines and readied the boat for a move. He knew of a good spot up behind Chino Island that held plenty of redfish. The tide was just starting to fall so the fishing would be great all morning. The sun lumbered up above the Australian pines and spread out across the broad grass flats of Pine Island Sound as they raced across the open water. Carl laughed to himself as he worked the throttles and listened to the steady hum of his two engines.

"A ladyfish. I should have known."

In the Courtyard

The wind was whipping through the urban forest that was planted decades ago to landscape the courtyard. Oaks, maples and chestnut trees sprang out of metal grates and towered overhead, shading the park benches and fountains below. In the fall a wind this strong could strip the trees of their leaves, but it was early summer and the leaves were young and healthy. They were not about to let go.

Mr. Richard Evans, his associate, Mr. Bret Harding and two other men made their way through the war memorials and the pigeons toward a quiet, out-of-the-way corner of the courtyard. Three of them carried dark black briefcases. Only one of them was not a lawyer.

The smells of summer were in the air. The smells of cornfields and fertilizers, flowing rivers and rain. It was June in Peoria and the afternoon thunderstorms were already drenching the fields that encircled this small Midwestern city.

Evans didn't take any notice of the sweet fragrances of summer. The wind was annoying him, whipping what little hair he had left and making a mess of his tie. He would have preferred to have this meeting in the air-conditioned hallway of the courthouse but he knew better. This was a private matter and they needed the seclusion of the courtyard to make it work. Richard had asked the judge for a fifteen minute recess only a few minutes ago. It was as good a time as any to get it over with.

"What the hell's all this about?" asked the one person who wasn't carrying an expensive briefcase of his lawyer, Lance Miller.

"I don't know anything more than you do. Your wife's attorney asked for a private meeting outside and I agreed. I'm sure we'll know what Evan is up to soon enough."

Robert Hines, the man without a briefcase, was getting a

divorce. He had filed three months ago on the grounds that he and his wife had irreconcilable differences. He wanted everything. He wanted the restored Corvette, the house and his Lincoln. He didn't want to pay any alimony and he was hiding as much income as possible out of his business, just in case. The kids were grown and out of the equation. Two days into the settlement trial, it was obvious to everyone concerned that Mr. Hines was winning.

Evans, a senior partner at The Peoria Family Law Firm, had been retained to represent the needs of Mrs. Hines. Judy was a good woman and had been a wonderful wife and mother. No one in his right mind would leave a woman like her because of irreconcilable differences. Evans knew that there was more to the story after his first interview with Mrs. Hines. Men divorce bitches for irreconcilable differences, not women like Judy.

Evans put his huge divorce machine to work for his client the following morning. This meeting was the outcome of months of that machine grinding away. That well-maintained device was about to grind Mr. Hines' divorce into sawdust.

As they paused beneath a dark green oak, Evans spoke up. "I suppose you are all wondering why I've requested this meeting?"

"Of course we are," replied Lance.

"Well then, I'll get right to the point."

Evans nodded silently to his younger associate, Mr. Harding. Acknowledging the signal, Bret proceeded to walk over to a nearby bench and set down his black leather briefcase. He punched in his private combination and opened the briefcase. From it he pulled a plain brown manila envelope. Closing his briefcase and leaving it on the bench, he brought the envelope back over to Evans.

"Is this what you mean by irreconcilable differences, Mr. Hines?" Evans handed Mr. Hines the manila envelope as he spoke. A cold wind swept through both Robert Hines and his attorney as he reached out for the envelope. This wind was stronger than the one that was racing through the courtyard forest and a thousand times colder. It was a winter wind, straight down from the arctic.

"What's in this?" asked Lance.

"Just open it," said Evans.

Robert's hands were visibly shaking as he turned over the

manila envelope and undid the brass clasp. He knew what might be in it, but he prayed it wasn't.

The silence between the four of them was so intense that it made everything in the universe grow silent and calm. A moment of suspension, where time itself holds its breath and the shadow of surrealism falls across the landscape. An ominous, distorted shadow, as if painted by Salvador Dali himself.

Robert opened up the envelope and reached inside. In it there were four five-by-seven black and white photographs. They were of him and his recently hired saleswoman in a series of compromising positions. These were the irreconcilable differences.

"Goddamn you, you son of a bitch!" Robert pulled back to take a swing at Evans. As his huge right arm reached back, Lance dropped his briefcase and took hold of him. They didn't need an assault charge added to their collapsing case.

Richard had stepped back a half a dozen steps. He had been hit by an angry husband or bitten by a screaming wife too many times before not to take note of Robert's right arm. Mr. Hines was in the construction business, and he could have easily flattened Richard Evans with a single punch.

"What does your client want?" shouted Lance across the distance between them.

Evans reached into his pocket and handed a note to Mr. Harding. Harding walked it over to the two men standing in the wind. The Lincoln was on the list, as were a dozen other requests totaling a quarter of a million dollars.

"This is extortion," said Hines' attorney.

"Don't call it that, Lance; it sounds so criminal. Let's just call it exhibit 'G'," replied Evans.

In the background Hines was swearing in the fashion that only someone from the construction business can. He had calmed down some, but given the chance, he would have gladly rammed a forklift through the chest of that fat bastard Evans. He kept wondering how in hell they had taken those photos. He knew it didn't matter. He knew that he was had.

Lance, his floundering attorney, knew it too. It was clear that there would be no negotiation. He handed the list to his client and watched him pale as he read through it. It would certainly curtail his plans for his Caribbean cruise this winter with his top saleswoman. He would sure as hell miss the dark blue Lincoln.

"If we accept, do we get the negatives?"

Evans nodded. Nothing would remain. This meeting would not have occurred, the photos, the wind in the trees, none of it would exist if Mr. Hines agreed to convey the items on the list. There would not be any exhibit 'G'. Mr. Hines would simply have a sudden change of heart and Mrs. Hines and would sign the revised settlement agreement within the hour.

Standing twenty feet apart, Mr. Miller and his client conferred for a minute while Evans and Harding stood by patiently. Evans knew they had won. They knew that their detective firm out of Chicago, with their 800 mm lenses and their relentless pursuit of the truth, had been worth every dime of their overpriced services. If these four photos made it in front of Judge Trenton, Mr. Hines might look at half a million. He was hopelessly caught in his own goddamned zipper.

Evans had seen this story unfold a hundred times before. Cheap motel rooms where the blinds don't quite close. Sixty dollars a night and $100,000 a marriage. It wasn't always the man, either. It was the wife with the pastor, the husband with the babysitter, the both of them with whatever shape their private infidelity required. That's why the other party came to The Peoria Family Law Firm and asked for Evans. That's why his clock ticked at seven dollars a minute. Evans was the best divorce attorney in Peoria, bar none. The terminator.

Nothing more was said. Within a few minutes, Lance glanced over to Evans and nodded. That was sufficient. They had an agreement. Evans wouldn't hand over the negatives, which were tucked away in the inside pocket of his $1,200 suit, until everything was signed. The judge would ask why the change of heart and what everyone had talked about over recess but no one would break their silence. Judge Trenton, having been an attorney once himself, would know better. Not wanting to stir the pot any more than need be, he would tacitly join in the conspiracy. It was easier on everyone.

As they reached the back door of the courthouse, Evans was wheezing from the short walk. He paused at the bottom of the stairs before going in, taking a minute to catch his breath. Just then, Mr.

Hines and his attorney, both of whom had been following safely behind, walked past Richard.

"You pathetic, fat pig!" said Robert as he stepped beside Richard. With that, he spat on his suit. It was a vicious, disgusting act that consummated the spirit of the deal. Richard knew that he would simply wipe it off before going back into the courtroom. That's why he had worn his black suit this morning, thinking that if something like this were to happen, it wouldn't show.

Attorney Evans had been spat on dozens of times in the past. It was where he earned his living, in the blood-splattered courtrooms of family law. It was who he was. The bill he would send to Mrs. Hines next week would top $30,000. She would pay the invoice without giving it a second thought. If he felt like it, Richard could have thrown this suit away come Monday and bought two more just like it with Mr. Hines' hard earned money. For Evans, winning was everything.

Evans and Harding walked up the stairway and back into the county courthouse. The air-conditioning felt fabulous. To the victors go the spoils.

Arriving

One

Carl put down the telephone and smiled. God how he loved that man. Dan and Carl had been friends for over sixty years. Friends since the fifth grade, when Dan's family moved across the river from East Moline into Davenport.

Carl was Danny's best man when he married Yolanda four decades ago and Danny was Carl's best man when he wed Marie a few years later. Through the trials and tribulations of child rearing, the strains and tugs of their marriages and, most recently, the loss of Carl's wife a year ago, Dan was always there for Carl. It was the kind of friendship few find but everyone searches for.

Dan Jackson had called to make small talk. Nothing important. He called every couple of weeks just to shoot the breeze and bring Carl up to speed on the grand-kids. Aaron, Dan's eleven-year-old grandson, was in a school musical last week and had one of the lead roles. "That boy sings as well as Yolanda," Dan would add.

Carl would let him know how the fish were biting down at the pier and how his two kids were doing in Atlanta and North Carolina respectively. It wasn't what was said that mattered. Dan called just to be a friend, to help Carl pass the time now that Marie was gone. It was what friends are.

Dan was still living back in Davenport. He had retired from the munitions plant on Rock Island ten years ago, after working there most of his life. Unlike Carl, Dan Jackson had never gone on to college. College wasn't his style. He had knocked around doing odd jobs for a couple of years after high school. He bought a hot car and cruised the strips of Davenport in the grand tradition of small-town nineteen year- olds. Somewhere along the line he landed a part time position working nights at the munitions plant. That was the same year he had met Yolanda Venageras.

He fell madly in love with her. Yolanda was an attractive, dark-skinned woman of Mexican descent. Her family had originally come to Iowa as migrant workers to work the vegetable crops in the summer. Yolanda's father had stayed on at a local farm and through the years had worked up the ladder into being the general manager. When Dan met Yolanda, she was studying nursing at the junior college. They were made for each other.

With a new marriage and their first child on the way, the offer to become full time at the plant was too good to refuse. He took the position immediately. Dan stayed on at the munitions plant for forty-two years. He and Yolanda went on to have three children of their own, two girls and a boy. Now they had seven grandchildren as well.

The Jackson family seldom left Iowa. They had come down to visit Carl and Marie only twice over the years. Dan never cared much for traveling unless he was motoring up to northern Wisconsin for a walleye expedition. The vast space between them didn't affect their friendship. There were always birthday cards, Christmas cards and the long-distance phone calls.

During their rare visits south, Carl would take off the entire week to spend fishing with Dan. They called themselves the "fishing fools." The two of them, and sometimes the boys, would be up each morning at dawn and back at dusk. Catching snook, grouper, and sharks. In short, anything that would bite. Dan had always loved to fish, and the excitement of fishing the ocean was a far cry from the carp and catfish of the Mississippi River.

Growing up in Davenport, Danny and Carl spent many an afternoon with their feet soaking and their bobbers floating in the muddy Mississippi. They loved to go down to the river and try their luck at fishing. After high school, the summer before Carl went off to Iowa City to college, they even managed to get in a walleye trip up to northern Minnesota. They had always been "fishing fools."

Danny had never really given up the sport, but Carl had. There was a time when he was lucky to wet a line once every five years. Those were the years back in Davenport when he worked at Riverside Savings and Loan.

Between raising their two children, mowing the lawn and paying the mortgage, there was never enough time to fish. His favorite rod and reel and all his tackle remained piled up in a corner of their storage shed out back. Spiders used the guides as anchors for their webs. Webs that stood for years collecting insects and flies that looked like many of the lures that were rusting away in his tackle box. Once, maybe twice, during those years Carl and Danny found the time to dust off the cobwebs and head out for a lazy afternoon alongside the river.

It was never Carl's wife, Marie, who kept him from fishing. She loved for him to take some time off and head out to try his luck. It was Marie who had bought her husband most of his rods and reels over the years. She knew how much it meant for him to be out there, on the water, having a beer and watching that big river flowing back toward the sea. Marie knew that it was important for him to spend time enjoying the company and conversations of his friends. To spend some time relaxing. It wasn't Marie who stopped Carl from fishing. It was Carl: Mr. Carl Johnson, the Loan Officer.

He had gone to that place where so many young men go during those formative years. He had become responsible. Carl was serious about his job. He didn't have the time to waste any more. Time was important to him and fishing had lost its priority. Fishing was a waste of time.

All that changed with their trip to Sanibel thirty years ago. Friends of theirs from Milwaukee had told them about Sanibel and insisted that they drive down to discover the sea shell island for themselves. Back then, the drive from Davenport to Sanibel was a three-day ordeal. None of them were looking forward to it.

As Marie, Carl and the two children made that final stretch across the newly built causeway, the long drive didn't seem to matter any longer. The calm, clear water that danced beneath the causeway spoke to Carl that late afternoon in March. What it said to him forever changed his life.

"This place is magical," said Carl as they slowly made their way across the three long concrete bridges of the causeway, the tires rhythmically sounding out the expansion joints along the roadway.

"It is beautiful Carl, very beautiful," confirmed his wife.

"Look, there's a dolphin," cried out their youngest boy, Rusty.

Amid the currents and eddies of a rapidly falling tide and the sunlight-rippled surface of the water, swam a solitary bottlenose dolphin. His grey back arching with every dive, his fluted tail fin the last to disappear. They all watched in amazement as this sleek, powerful mammal swam beneath them in the ocean. It made one last dive and vanished. Carl felt as if the ocean was talking to him that afternoon. Unexpectedly, he was willing to listen.

Carl was the model father. He had taken up the burden of responsibility with all the enthusiasm of America in the fifties. He was doing his best to provide for his family, to live the American dream. A nice home with nice children in a nice town.

But it wasn't Carl Johnson. The job at the bank was slowly killing him. There were always problems. Tedious, insidious little problems that, once resolved, were instantly replaced with new, equally important and insipid ones. After years of resolving variations of the same theme over and over again, the problems had a queer sense of familiarity to them. Carl hated being so familiar with these problems, so entwined in them. It was his job to solve them, but he longed for a finality that never arrived.

That afternoon, being just over 46 years old and terminally frustrated with his job at the bank, Carl was ready for a change. Marie had insisted that they take his rod and his tackle box along and do some fishing in the ocean during the week they had to spend on the island.

"You don't even need a license," Marie added. "Just go buy some shrimp at the Bait Box, drive down to the fishing pier, and take some time off, Carl. Remember, you're on vacation."

Carl, Marie, and their two children took the next thirty years off. They never drove back to Davenport, not even to collect their belongings. Carl arranged for their furniture to be packed up and shipped down within two weeks. Their friends from Milwaukee, the Hansens, were shocked when they got the letter from Marie explaining what had happened. When the first week had passed, Carl started to talk about how deeply he had fallen in love with this island and how he dreaded the thought of going back to the bank. After several days of hearing this, Marie looked right at him and said, "If that's how you really feel, then let's not go back."

They didn't go back. Deep down, Marie knew that Carl's

job was slowly, methodically, destroying him. She felt that they had very little to lose by deciding to change their life-style and staying on Sanibel. She had a heart-felt intuition that it was the right thing to do for their family and their marriage.

Carl and Marie had met at college. Marie was from Dayton, and had decided to go to Iowa State for her degree in liberal arts. She was a fine woman, with long black hair, high cheekbones and warm, brown eyes. She could have been a model with her natural good looks but it wasn't her style. Marie loved living simply and she loved her family. She knew that the move would put a strain on everyone, but Marie felt that it was the right thing to be doing. The children were upset by the decision.

"But Mom...," Rusty would go on and on about his friends in junior high school and what would they do down here on this boring island? Emily, the youngest, was less distraught about the move. Emily loved the beach and the warm weather. She was in fifth grade at the time, and she had always been less social than Rusty.

"Besides," Emily told her mother, "if they want to, my friends can always come down and visit."

By the end of the second week the move was in full swing. Carl had arranged through one of his many friends in real estate to have the house sold and all their furniture, clothing and household items shipped down. Back in Davenport, their home was in one of the nicest areas of town. It had a lovely view of the Mississippi River, so finding a buyer took only a matter of weeks. Marie, in the meantime, had scoured the local papers for a suitable home to rent. They knew that they were in no position to buy yet, since buying would entail jobs and income and a thousand unanswered questions. Carl Johnson had been a loan officer at Riverside Savings and Loan for years, and he knew when it was time to rent.

After they had settled in, finding a nice house just off of Donax, the tough decisions came. They both had to decide what they wanted to do to earn their keep on this remote barrier island. Marie wasn't sure, but she had always wanted to open a small store of some kind, and she started investigating that possibility. Carl quickly turned to his long-lost love of fishing. He had decided to become a fishing guide. With the sale of the house, coupled with the savings they had, they now had six or seven months to get their new lifestyle in order. They would have to make some adjustments, but they all did so willingly. Except for Rusty. Rusty was thirteen at the time, and he would have been angry and difficult anywhere in the world. Puberty was behind most of it. Rusty eventually got over it and, like his sister Emily, he grew to love southwest Florida like a native.

Marie opened a small kitchen accessory store in one of the local shopping centers. Carl began fishing. They both loved what they were doing and it was exciting to be starting anew.

Carl would readily admit that he was a lousy fishing guide for his first few years. Getting a Coast Guard six-pack license back in the mid sixties was easy. Anyone who took a fancy to fishing could set up shop as a fishing guide. The test was short and simple, and all you really needed was a boat that held water, some life jackets, and some rods and reels. The first six months he worked out of the canal house they were renting on the east end of the island. He had bought a small seventeen-foot Boston Whaler and equipped it for inshore fishing. He and Marie went to various condominium complexes and motels handing out their newly printed brochures. They were trying to drum up business.

The trouble was that Carl didn't really have a clue how to catch ocean fish. By default, he became a catfish guide. He was quick to learn that catching catfish was better than catching nothing. So when the snook bite was off, or the redfish had lockjaw, he took his customers to his secret catfish hole and started hauling them in.

The catfish that swim in the waters around Sanibel, Carl quickly learned, come in two varieties: awful and worse. The awful variety was the hard-head catfish. They are small, completely inedible creatures of the lowest order. They are voracious eaters and will devour just about anything that comes their way, from shrimp to chicken livers. They are charcoal grey to black in color, with a hint of brown and a whitish belly. Hard-head cats average about a foot in length, and, like all catfish, have a mucous-covered skin and a strong, fishy odor. They are not considered edible, Carl learned, even to someone who is starving.

Worse still are the gafftop sail-cats. They are known as gafftop catfish because both the dorsal and the two pectoral fins just behind the head are elongated. On a big fish, one weighing over five pounds, these fins can extend out over six inches. Covered with a bacterially infested slime, these barbed fins are poisonous daggers in the hands of an inexperienced angler.

Carl avoided those dangerous, dart-like-fins by cutting the line if the fish were hooked anywhere but on the very edge of their big, ugly mouths. He wouldn't let the customers near the catfish. They never failed to listen to him because before he reached his catfish honey hole he would tell his customers his famous story about the four-thousand- dollar catfish.

"Ya see," Carl would start in, "there's a chance that we might hook up a catfish or two here. They love this hole just as much as the big gator trout I was telling you about earlier. There's nothing wrong with catching catfish. Those big gafftops can put up one heck of a fight. But before we get started fishing here I have to tell you a story. It's about a catfish I once caught, and it will help you give them the respect these fish deserve."

The novices were all ears. Storytelling was what made Carl a great guide. It wasn't the fishing, and it wasn't his fancy boat or his expertise, it was his ability to tell tall tales that made his reputation grow in the small circles of Sanibel Island. Carl could spin a yarn. His deep, melodic voice never failed to captivate his charters. Carl's clients loved to kick back and absorb his stories of powerful fish and humbled anglers. More than anything else, that is what kept them coming back. They loved their precious few outings with him over the years. Carl was a storyteller, and everyone loves a well-told story.

Back then, when he was just starting out, Carl's favorite story was his tale of the four-thousand-dollar catfish. Right after the house up in Davenport sold, Carl started looking at boats. He had easily passed his Coast Guard licensing requirements and he was ready to start guiding. He had decided to purchase a twenty-four-foot Mako, with a center console and twin Evinrude 150s for his first boat. Two days before he put the order in on the Mako, he went up to the end of Dixie Beach Boulevard, located on the northern side of Sanibel, to try some shoreline fishing. He had just purchased six new rods and reels for his business and like any kid with a new toy, he was dying to give one of them a try.

It was late one afternoon when he drove up and started fishing. He wasn't three blocks from the Woodrings' old homestead overlooking Tarpon Bay. As usual, Carl was catching catfish. On his very last cast, he happened to hook into a good-sized gafftop sail cat. While he was reeling it in, being somewhat angry at himself for catching nothing but catfish again, he gave that fish a big tug, hoping to yank the hook right out of its mouth. At the same instant, the gafftop decided to jump. With the four-pound catfish completely out of the water, and Carl giving it a tremendous pull, that sail cat decided to sail. It sailed directly into Carl's thigh.

The pain was overwhelming. Carl, standing there in the knee-deep water with a four-pound catfish impaled into his right thigh, did everything he could to keep from passing out. The dorsal fin of this catfish was about the same diameter and half the length of a small crochet needle. The catfish was flopping around, with its long dorsal fin imbedded in Carl's leg an inch and a half. It was like having a doctor doing arthroscopic surgery with a darning needle and no anesthesia. This particular doctor had the shakes and his instruments were covered with an infectious slime. This doctor was a distraught catfish and it hurt like all hell.

Carl didn't know what to do. He knew he had to get to a hospital as soon as possible, but the thought of driving twenty miles with this ugly fish attached to his thigh wasn't going to work. He waddled back to shore, sat on the bank and tried to pull the damn catfish fin out of his leg. He couldn't do it. The ends of each elongated fin were covered with hundreds of small barbs that make pulling out the imbedded fins all but impossible. Besides that, every time Carl pulled he ran the risk of putting one of the two pectoral fins into his hand. That would be just great, imagined Carl - both his hand and leg impaled on the same catfish!

Using the fillet knife from his new tackle box, he cut off the barb. He left about half an inch sticking out for the doctors to have something to work with once he got to the hospital. Then he tossed the catfish back into the bay. The catfish swam away as if nothing had happened. The catfish had a custom dorsal fin and a free shrimp dinner. Carl had a long drive ahead of him.

Carl's problems continued. His leg was slowly growing

numb. He didn't want to stop and tell Marie and his children what had happened. It was too embarrassing. He decided to drive himself straight to the hospital. The nearest hospital was Lee Memorial. That was in downtown Ft. Myers, and it took him over an hour to get there. By that time, between walking back to the car and working the gas pedal with his right leg, the half-inch section of catfish fin Carl had left out for the doctors to grab had vanished. It had worked itself into his thigh.

Carl stumbled into the emergency room looking terrible. His khaki pants were covered in blood and slime, his legs were wobbling and his face was pale and distraught. The triage nurse took one look at him and rushed him into surgery. She thought he had been shot.

He should have been shot. It would have been easier and less expensive. In fact, there was a rough-looking biker from North Ft. Myers who had come in with a gunshot wound about the same time as Carl. He was out of surgery in half the time. Bullet wounds are easier.

After cutting open his pants leg and listening to Carl's story, the doctors realized that Carl had been stabbed. Stabbed by a catfish. Robbery was not a motive, despite the fact that the catfish made off with a shrimp.

The operation took over an hour. It ran him better than $4,000. There it was, the $4,000 catfish. When they removed the poisonous barb from Carl's leg, little did those doctors realize that they were also removing a twenty-four-foot twin engine Mako from his guiding business and replacing it with a far less expensive seventeen-foot Boston Whaler.

As he pulled up to his catfish hole and turned off the single engine on his Whaler, he would show the tourists his scar. It didn't look like much, but his clients were careful with the catfish they brought in from that moment on. For the first few years, they were always catching more than a reasonable amount of catfish.

Over the years Carl became better and better at fishing. After awhile he learned how to avoid the catfish and actually hook up the trout he had wanted to catch from the outset. After he mastered the trout, he perfected redfish. Soon after that he learned how to catch the elusive snook, and eventually all the fish that encircle Sanibel. With the combination of his ability to tell tall tales and catch plenty of fish, he soon became one of the most sought-after guides on the island. Some folks swore that Carl could actually smell the fish.

The years turned to decades and the fishing kept getting better and better for Carl. His days were spent on the water and his nights were spent at home, enjoying his friends and family as the years slowly whittled away. When it rained, or the wind blew too hard to get out, Carl would spend hours down in his workshop oiling his rods, fixing odds and ends on the boat, or catching up with the latest articles out of Florida Sportsman magazine. Life was good. The children grew up and eventually headed off to college, married and moved on. Rusty ended up in North Carolina and Emily in Atlanta. Life was a dream, a wonderful dream interrupted only by an occasional catfish or two.

Then, about five years ago, Marie became ill. During a routine checkup, her doctor had discovered some lumps in her breast. It was cancer. What followed was that awful roller coaster that is defined by the elated highs of remission and the frightening valleys of recurrence. A roller coaster ride whose grim excitement is made even more heinous by radiation treatments and the nauseating drugs of chemotherapy. A ride riddled with days of vomiting, weakness, and pain.

Near the end, Carl, after his long, wonderful romance with the ocean, had to stop fishing. Marie needed him. Carl started to turn down charters. He loved his wife more than the sea, and he loved the sea more than most men could ever know.

Marie was dying. The cancer, like the tides, ebbed and flowed over the next four years but, in the end, it took Marie away from him. The sadness that swept over Carl was like a storm surge of black, dirty water. He didn't understand what he had done to deserve this. His heart was a torrent of anger, denial, and depression. What made it worse was that she was no longer there to comfort him.

To cover the mounting expenses, Carl sold his boat. By this time, his boat was that twin-engine Mako he had once lost to a catfish. His clients, most of whom had stayed with him from catfish to tarpon, missed Carl and his fishing stories dearly. There was little they could do. A few of them sent some money to help with the expenses after the funeral, but it wasn't enough. Nothing could have been enough.

Carl was too old to start over, and with Marie gone it wasn't the same. He held a rummage sale and sold off most of his fishing gear. He started referring his clients to other, young and eager guides. It was over.

For the first three or four months after the funeral he didn't fish at all. He stayed at home. He had kept three fishing rods and one box of his tackle, although he didn't know why. He was certain his fishing days were over.

It wasn't meant to be. About seven months ago, one of his old clients from Cincinnati called him to say that he was sorry about Marie. Carl was glad to hear from him. He was glad just to hear the phone ring. His client went on to say that they were down on Sanibel on vacation and had just recently heard about Marie's untimely illness and passing away. He also mentioned to Carl that the snook were going wild down at the fishing pier.

"Maybe you should dust off some of your old gear and come on down here," said his old client and friend. "It would do you some good to get out of the house."

In all his years on Sanibel, Carl had never once fished at the pier. He had driven his boat past it a thousand times. In the spring for tarpon, sharks, and cuda, and in the fall for kingfish, grouper and Spanish mackerel. But Carl had never once tossed in a line from that small wooden dock. He told his old client from Ohio that he wasn't interested.

His client insisted. Knowing that his old friend wouldn't let up until he said yes, Carl packed up his gear and met him down at the pier the following morning. His friend was right: the snook were biting, and biting hard. As the sun rose over Ft. Myers Beach to the east, Carl and his former customers from Cincinnati had the time of their lives. Marie was there too, telling him in the language of the surf that this was a good place for him to be. That this was right.

From that morning forward, the Sanibel fishing pier was where you could find Carl Johnson. He was back on the ocean, laughing, tying Albright specials, uni-knots, and hooking up. Sharing the company of other anglers again, telling his stories and basking in the Florida sun. It gave him a new found sense of joy. He became himself once again on those weathered wooden planks of the fishing pier.

Over the months that followed, that stout, blue-eyed old

man from Iowa relearned his cast-net techniques, spooled up new monofilament on his few remaining reels, and re-found happiness. The fishing pier was his new boat. It was a boat anchored firmly at the eastern tip of Sanibel, its wooden pilings embedded in the limestone below.

Marie's death still cast a shadow over Carl, and there was no denying that. They had shared almost fifty years of life together. They had watched their children grow up and have families of their own. It was never going to be the same without her, and Carl knew it. But at the fishing pier, in the company of fellow fishermen, neighbors and tourists, he didn't seem to feel as lonely. His plans were to be down there again tomorrow morning, watching the tides change and waiting for a snook to hit.

The radio alarm went off at 5:30 a.m. sharp. Not that it mattered. Carl was already up and fixing himself a bowl of cereal when he heard the music coming from his bedroom. He didn't recognize the piece they were playing this particular Sunday morning. It was organ music, and Carl had an aversion to organ music. He went back into the bedroom and turned off the radio.

Carl had been dreaming again the night before. A variation on a dream that he had had a hundred times before. He was way out to sea amid a flock of seagulls and terns. But he wasn't adrift in the water or in a boat. He was just there somehow, watching hundreds of birds flying and diving around him. It was a clear day, and the ocean was calm. It was a pleasant dream.

As he finished breakfast, he realized that he would make it down to the fishing pier long before sunrise. Darkness was an ally to someone having to throw a cast net. In the dim world of twilight Carl could easily see the schools of baitfish along the beach, but they, in turn, could not see the thin monofilament of his six-foot cast net as it fell over them. The darkness was his ally.

Carl parked his old station wagon in the gravel lot and walked down the wooden boardwalk toward the pier. He carried his tackle box, his two rods and his bait bucket filled with his cast net. There was only the faintest hint of morning on the horizon as he stepped up on the pier. Only one other early morning angler was there to share his solitude.

He walked up to his favorite spot without saying anything to the other angler. He didn't recognize him and figured that he was probably just another tourist. He set his rods and tackle box down and walked back toward the beach with his net and bait bucket in hand. It was the perfect time to net up some fresh baits for the day.

Carl's six-foot cast net made a quiet splash as it hit the water above a school of whitebait. It settled quickly to the bottom, entrapping the minnows beneath it. They were all three to four inches long.

"A good size to use," mumbled Carl to himself as he pulled on the handline, causing the weighted lead line on the bottom of the small net to cinch in and securely entrap the fish. There were three dozen fish in the net as he lifted them out of the water.

He quickly walked back a few steps on the beach and lowered the end of his cast net into a five-gallon plastic bucket. The bucket was filled with the saltwater he had scooped up just before making the cast. Holding up the handline with his right hand, he bent over and grabbed the brail of the net with his left hand. By lifting the brail, the lead line dropped to the bottom of the bucket. The net stretched up and open. As Carl lifted and shook the cast net most of the bait fell out and into the saltwater. A few of the minnows fell on the sand. Some remained gilled in the fine mesh of his cast net.

Carl bent over and picked up the minnows that had fallen on the sand, tossing them back into the bucket. Most of them will still make it, he thought to himself. A few won't. He didn't bother picking the gilled minnows out of the mesh of his net. None of the gilled minnows would survive. He would take a break before leaving and remove them later, when he was finished fishing for the day.

From the fishing pier the other angler had watched Carl tossing his cast net. He had never seen anyone throw a net like that before, at least not in Cincinnati. He could tell the old man had done it before. A thousand times before. Although Carl had grown heavier with age, he still had a strong, solid look about him. He had always had large, powerful legs and a big, wide chest. If he had stood taller than his five-foot seven height, he could easily have made the varsity football team back in Iowa City. But he wasn't tall. He was stout and strong, built for endurance.

It was in Carl's face that his story was told. Although it was deeply etched by years of exposure to Florida's tropical sun, it had retained a softness. There was a feminine quality to his deep wrinkles, like a photo of an arroyo taken in a soft focus. His eyes were blue. Years ago they were as blue as the Gulf Stream. A deep and impassioned blue, full of vigor and joy. That intense blue had faded over time and now his eyes were cloudy with the pastels of aging. The passion was still there, but it was tired and distant. The blue of his eyes that first morning belonged more to the sky than the sea. By now, Carl Johnson was an old salt, and a handsome one at that.

The tourist who watched him throw the net was impressed with the strength and rhythm of this old man on the beach. His thick hands and his strong legs served him well. He was dressed for the heat, wearing a pair of clean tan shorts and a plain white T-shirt. On his head he wore a sloppy old cotton hat. It was there to try to keep the sun from carving any deeper into his countless crow's feet.

After shaking the water out of his net, Carl picked up the heavy five-gallon bucket in one hand and held his cast net in the other. Once back on the pier, he poured all the minnows and the saltwater into another bucket that had been riddled with small drill holes. Tying it off to the railing of the pier, he lowered the bucket over the side and watched the rope quickly grow taunt in the incoming current. He would ready his rods then come back to get his bait.

Carl looked around and surveyed the surface of the ocean that encircled him. It was calm and the light was gathering. He could feel that it was going to be another hot and humid day in south Florida, but he didn't mind the heat. He just hoped that the redfish would show and that he would be lucky enough to catch a couple. It was all he asked for at this stage in his life. It was all he needed.

Two

"Cancel the reservations, there is no way on God's earth that I can find the time to fly down to Santa Bell in the next few weeks. No way in hell, Helen, and that's final!"

"It's called Sanibel, Richard, not Santa Bell. And I can't cancel the airline reservations this late, they're non-refundable," said Helen.

"How much are we talking here?"

"Four tickets, first class..., let's see, that's about five grand." Helen had booked them two weeks ago, knowing that by making them non-refundable she had an outside chance of getting Richard to go. Money was his Achilles heel. Richard hated losing money, or paying for tickets he wasn't going to be able to use.

"If I can continue this case, I could pick up an additional ten grand in billing. I don't give a damn about the tickets. Cancel the trip."

Helen quickly changed tack. She realized that the money issue wasn't going to work. She started weeping, turning the tears on faster than a cold-water shower.

"I just wanted us to spend some family time together. You never get a chance to spend any time with your boys. Before too long, they'll both be off to college."

Helen knew immediately that the crying was working better than the non-refundable approach. She could see it in his eyes. Richard hated to see his wife in tears even more than he hated losing money. Somewhere, buried beneath the rubble of a thousand divorce cases, Richard still had the remnants of a heart.

"I'll see if Harding can close out the trial. Where the hell is this Santibel anyway?"

"It's in Florida, Richard, just south of Tampa."

Helen quickly turned off the tears and started to tell Richard about Sanibel. He was looking through the Money section of USA Today as she spoke, only occasionally responding to her story with a listless "yeah" or "uh ha."

Helen had heard about Sanibel from Wanda. Wanda was Helen's best friend. She was a typical suburban busybody. Dyed hair, cosmetic surgery, and an empty nest. Her husband was a senior executive down at the local Caterpillar plant. Wanda had far too little to do and way too much time to do it in. She was always coming up with something or other. More than once, Richard wished Jack would get transferred out of Peoria, taking his wife, Wanda, with him.

It was Wanda who had suggested the ill-fated Yellowstone trip. That sojourn occurred a little over three years ago. It also came about amid a river of tears and a need for so called "quality family time." Whatever the hell that was.

The trip out to Wyoming was a disaster. They had rented an enormous Winnebago that gave them nothing but trouble from Des Moines west and back east again. They ended up spending a total of two days at Yellowstone National Park and nine days in small town motels along the way waiting for their motor home to get repaired. "It's the carburetors," the mechanics kept telling Richard.

"Bad carbs," was the standard diagnosis by a series of gum-chewing, red-necked mechanics across the plains. "Bad carbs will do it every time," one of them added insidiously.

"Well," continued Helen. "Wanda had just read this fabulous article about Sanibel Island in the St. Louis Dispatch and it sounds so intriguing. They have this big wildlife sanctuary and great restaurants and a beach that's just covered in shells...," Helen went on speaking.

Richard kept looking down at the stock report and wondering why they made stock symbols so God-damned small. Who the hell can read these things?

"Wanda wanted her and Jack to slip away for a week, but you know how busy Jack has been lately. Wanda did take some time to make a few phone calls and look some things up on the Internet. She found this great rental condominium named Seaside. It sits right on the beach. Don't you think it sounds fantastic?"

"Yeah."

Microsoft was down again. Damn, thought Richard, I wish the

feds would leave Gates alone. Their anti-trust lawsuits were wreaking havoc on his 1,000 shares. Let's see what General Electric's doing.

"So I called the rental company and booked a week in late September for us. It's a belated thirty-ninth birthday present from me. I only had to pull the boys from school for three days because of teacher conferences and they're really excited about the trip. It will still be summer down in Florida and this condo has a big pool right outside of our apartment. You know how Tyler and James just love to swim," said Helen to essentially no one.

Richard had conceded to the vacation easily. Although he would have been the last person in the world to admit it, he needed a break. Aside from a few weekend trips into Chicago or business trips taking depositions around the country, he hadn't taken any time off since the Yellowstone fiasco. This time they would fly. At least jets don't have carbs.

Richard finished his fourth English muffin, stood up, grabbed his briefcase, and headed out to the garage. Helen kept talking to him about the island right up until he closed the garage door behind him. Her monologue was a blur. He would let Bret Harding know that he would have to settle the Brown vs. Brown case. They might even consider going to mediation with it. Richard Evans hated mediation with a passion. In divorces, winning is everything. No one really wins when you go to mediation. Everything is divided up just too damned equally, thought Richard as he fired up the Cadillac. Family law.

Richard Evans wasn't always like this. Ten years ago he didn't weigh in at 297 pounds, chain smoke Camels, and drink top-shelf Scotch with a vengeance. Ten years ago, recently married to Helen and fresh out of law school, he was a totally different person.

When he first entered law school up at Northwestern, he had lofty dreams of teaching law at a university someday. Back then he believed in the integrity of the law. He had graduated summa cum laude, filled with all the ambition of the Hammurabi Coda of Babylonia. Impassioned with the pursuit of truth, justice, and equality. Noble ideas filled his vision of the future, echoes of the Magna Carta, the Declaration of Independence, and the inherent rights of all mankind.

The stock market took a 500-point nose dive the week after

Richard's graduation. It was the same market he had just invested his entire postgraduate nest egg in. Richard might have believed wholeheartedly in the honor of the written moral code, but for the moment, his thoughts were elsewhere.

He was broke. Newly married to Helen, who was already pregnant with Tyler, he didn't have the luxury of waiting out the next economic recovery for his chance at landing a teaching position. He had to waylay his lofty goals and focus on the mundane for the moment. He had to get a job.

As fate would have it, there was a notice up at school that The Family Law Firm of Peoria was looking for a young graduate student or lawyer to do case studies and research for the firm. Lacking any other viable opportunities, and too damn broke to consider anything else, Richard applied for the position. With his grades and talent, The Family Law Firm of Peoria hired him after their first interview.

Richard turned out to be good at doing case studies, filing briefs and searching for precedents. Extremely good. After being with the firm for just over a year, he was asked to take a case. It involved a couple with little in the way of net worth who had filed for divorce after just six months of a poorly planned marriage. They were a young couple, and lacking any apparent assets to cover their billing costs, none of the senior partners at the Peoria Family Law Firm wanted to handle them. One of the senior partners knew the young lady's mother and had agreed to take the case on as a favor. Richard was getting bored with clerical work, so he thought he might as well handle an actual divorce.

From first appearances it looked as if it was just your ordinary "they married too young" parting of the ways. The husband, who had betrothed his client when he was only twenty, had started fooling around with his old high school sweetheart. Their marriage had rapidly gone from bad to worse. Both kids wanted out. Besides two late model subcompact cars, a household of miscellaneous furniture, and a small joint bank account, there wasn't much to argue about.

A week before the first hearing that changed. In a conversation with his client about the settlement, the young, distraught wife mentioned something about a trust fund her young husband had. It was set up for him by a wealthy uncle from Bloomington. Richard, upon further inquiry, discovered that the trust fund was worth 1.6 million dollars. Pay dirt! The fund was set up in such a way that the young husband would have half of the 1.6 million in his possession, tax free, on his 21st birthday. That was three months away.

Richard quickly advised his client, the distraught bride, that she would be far less distraught after the divorce if she and her estranged young husband could endure another 90 days of matrimony together. He showed her the arithmetic to prove just how beneficial tolerance of her husband's indiscretions could be.

She took his advice. Richard stalled masterfully. They continued, they appealed, and they waited. In the final settlement, the young wife ended up with $300,000 out of the fund. Richard had converted a typical "they married too young" case into a little more than $50,000 in legal fees.

The senior partners were impressed. Evans was in. He proved that he could divorce them up with the best of them. Richard could now hunt with the wolf pack.

That's how he got started. He slowly drifted away from his useless idealism of the integrity and dignity of humanity's written codas into your standard small town "drag the divorce out as long as the assets will cover your action" attorney. Over the years he had learned every disgusting means of extracting blood out of spouses, and henceforth, out of his clients. Now he was the best divorce lawyer money could buy in and around Peoria. Richard could rape and pillage every asset and find every buried dime his client's spouse was trying to hide. He would bring in sleazy detectives from Chicago to take clandestine photos of all the infidelities in Peoria. There was always more infidelity in the world than there was grainy, black and white film. That was the beauty of family law.

His success came with a price. To compensate for how disappointed the idealist deep inside of him felt, Richard had taken to chain smoking Camels, inhaling Dewars by the liter and compulsively overeating. At thirty-nine years old Richard Evans teetered on three hundred pounds, was totally out of shape, and had a net worth pushing three million dollars. Given his present rate of decline, there was no chance in hell that he would ever live long enough to spend all of the dirty money he had so cleverly earned.

It was money he had amassed by turning once loving couples into vicious, rabid dogs in the marble hallways of the Peoria County courthouse. Couples screaming at each other during recess, swearing and spitting like venomous cobras. It was blood-stained coinage Richard had earned from liquidated real estate, stock holdings, and long-drawn-out custody battles over the sad, sad children of divorce. It wasn't any wonder Richard sometimes felt he had six catfish spines stuck in him. He craved strawberry cheesecake and chocolate malts with a passion.

His wife, Helen, loved it. She liked what all that dirty money could buy and she enjoyed spending it as quickly as Richard brought it home in his thousand-dollar briefcase. They lived in the best part of town, up on Elm Street. He drove a new Cadillac Brougham and she had a BMW convertible. They had both their children in private school and they spared themselves no luxury.

Being smart enough to recognize what a walking heart-attack victim looked like, Helen had taken out a two million-dollar life insurance policy on Richard six years ago. It was a sure bet. A winning lotto ticket.

Helen had once loved Richard and not just his money. Now she found him barely tolerable. She would never leave him, since she knew how good he was in divorce court. He would leave her penniless, and the thought didn't sit well with Helen. That meant no Cuisinart, no Nieman Marcus and no fun. She would rather live with her chain smoking walrus than go penniless. So their marriage was down to an arrangement. He would mount her every so often and she would tolerate it for the luxury of a purse full of credit cards and a wrist full of tennis bracelets.

The children were spoiled beyond measure. Richard never had any free time for them. Every issue was solved, not by conversations or understanding, but by buying them something expensive enough to distract them for another few months. The two boys had more toys and sports gear than do most Wal-Marts. They were drowning in a sea of toys. They had a huge playroom in the basement complete with pinball machines, air hockey games, pool tables, race car sets, the latest Nintendo 64, and, in short, everything imaginable.

Everything but love. Helen was too busy watching soap

operas, attending bridge games and ordering useless bric-a-brac from her expensive, mail-order catalogs to pay any attention to the kids. Catalogs that seemed to specialize in overpriced, useless items that were sent explicitly to rich, dysfunctional families. Too busy ordering more non-necessities for the empty household they shared.

Richard didn't really know his boys. He was too fat to do anything with them for more than a few minutes at a time, and he was too busy to spare them the time anyway. Every night he would come home from work with stacks of cases to go over to get ready for trial the next morning. Every morning he was up at dawn, drinking coffee and devouring donuts while examining what the market did the day before. Once a week, religiously, he would deposit another five-figure paycheck into one of their accounts.

To try to compensate for his lack of time with his family, he would spoil them. Money, thought Richard, cured everything. He had truckloads of money, that paper-thin American elixir. Dirty divorce money at that.

The familial arrangement had evolved into this balanced pattern of behavior that kept everyone looking perfectly happy. The kind of facade-like happiness that sits well with the neighbors. Most of the other families along Elm Street were propped up with this same, net worth exterior. Just below their thin veneer of material joy, they were all equally miserable. The same was true on Oak Street, Piedmont Road and Heather Lane, for that matter. At least the lawns looked good.

Richard pulled into the parking lot of their office building and turned off the radio. The morning news was good: there was talk of lowering the interest rate to help stimulate the economy. He reminded himself to call his broker and see if there was any play he might make in the stock market to capitalize on the rate drop. Opportunity knocks.

He grabbed his briefcase and headed to the elevator inside the lobby. Once up to the sixth floor he checked in with their receptionist and went into his spacious office. It was your typical successful attorney's office. An overabundance of dark red mahogany, rows of unread law books and plush leather chairs. Once seated, Richard rang up Marilyn, his private secretary.

"Marilyn, get Harding in here ASAP!"

Marilyn noted that Richard had forgotten to say please. She was used to it by now. She picked up the phone and dialed the interoffice number to Harding. He was back at her desk in less than five minutes. Harding had become Richard's whipping boy. He was a well-paid whipping boy. Marilyn paged Richard.

"Harding's here, do you want him to come in now?"

"Send him right in."

Harding went in and sat down in one of the two dark leather chairs that sat strategically in front of Richard's huge desk. Harding had a legal notepad and pen in hand. He was always ready, willing and able.

"Richard, my goddamned wife has gone ahead and booked us on another 'family time' trip. This time she and that dizzy girlfriend of hers, Wanda, are sending us down to Florida. Some island down there called Santibell. We leave in two weeks."

"What about Mrs. Brown's case, isn't that slated for trial on the twenty-sixth?"

"Sharp, Harding, real sharp. That's why I called you in here this morning. You're going to have to take it over for me. Settle it yourself. If you want, you can take the whole mess over to mediation for all I care."

"Mediation?" Harding was in shock. He knew how Richard felt about negotiating out a settlement. It cost the firm a bundle in lost hours when their cases mediated and Richard hated the county's chief negotiator, Mrs. Sparks, more than she hated him.

"Only as a last resort. I think we can still find something on that son of a bitch Mr. Brown between now and the trial. But if we can't, it might be easier just to hand it all over to Mrs. Sparks and let her cut up the cake. In any event, get on it right away.

"Also, what do you know about this place called Santibell? Have you ever heard anything about it? I don't have a clue as to what in hell I'm supposed to do for a week down on some barrier island in Florida." Richard was being honest for a change.

Harding paused for a minute and thought. He had heard of Sanibel. His uncle and aunt used to go there back in the '60s. It was...? Uncle Clarence. Yes, it was Uncle Clarence and Aunt Eva.

"My uncle and aunt used to go down to Sanibel a long time

ago. My uncle Clarence was one hell of a fisherman. Now that I think about it, he used to go on and on about how good the fishing was down there. They fished for redfish and sharks and they used to catch the hell out of them if I remember right. They loved the place but had to stop going after Eva's knee surgery."

Richard thought for a minute. Fishing? Hell it wasn't so bad. He could park himself on the beach or charter a boat or something. It would help pass the time. Give him an excuse to get away from his family.

"Shit, I haven't fished since junior high school. I used to enjoy it, but that was one hell of a long time ago. Still, have your uncle give me a call for some pointers."

"He's dead."

"Sorry, how about your aunt?"

"Ditto."

"Well, I'll just have to pick up some gear when I get down there. In the meanwhile, get right on the Brown case and keep me posted."

"When do you leave?"

"In two weeks; we fly out and back on a Saturday. Luckily, it's only a week this time. Not like that miserable Yellowstone trip a few years back."

"Is that all?" asked Harding, who had dutifully noted the entire conversation down.

"That's all for now."

Bret Harding got up and headed back out the door. Just before he opened it, Richard added one more comment.

"Did they have any children, your aunt and uncle? Maybe they would remember something about their parents' fishing trips to Sanibel?" "I'll look into it, Richard."

As he closed the door behind him, Harding was glad Richard was taking some time off. Evans was a workaholic of the highest order. He put in sixty, seventy hours a week and ate more pasta for lunch than any man he had ever known. Bret had noticed that in the past few years Richard had developed that labored, heavy breathing that his uncle had just before developing emphysema and dying. His uncle was seventy-four at the time. Evans hadn't turned forty.

It would be a welcome respite for everyone at the firm to have Evans out of the office for a week. They could relax and slow down for five wonderful days. Evans, since becoming a senior partner, could be such a royal asshole. Bret smiled as he shut the door to his office. He laughed out loud as he sat down behind his desk, hoping that if Evans did go fishing the sharks might eat him.

On second thought, he knew that they wouldn't so much as take a nip out of him. Bret remembered his favorite lawyer joke and chuckled to himself. That's why sharks won't eat divorce attorneys - professional courtesy.

The flight down was uneventful. Richard hated the turbo-prop that took the family over to St. Louis, but that wasn't anything new. The minivan was waiting at the airport and the drive from the airport out to Sanibel was equally without fanfare. Once on the causeway, they all remarked how lovely the island looked.

As Helen drove, Richard kept looking to the east to try to catch a glimpse of the fishing pier. As requested, Bret Harding had done some legwork for Richard on Sanibel fishing spots. Harding was good at legwork. He had called one of his uncle's boys, his cousin Eddy, to find out where his mom and dad used to fish back when they were going down to Sanibel. Eddy mentioned something about a fishing pier on the eastern tip of the island. He remembered that you could just barely see it from the causeway as you headed in.

Richard could see it. It didn't look very big. Harding said that they used to get all of their shrimp and tackle at a little shop called the Bait Box up on Periwinkle Way.

After unpacking and settling in at the condo, Richard decided to head down to the tackle shop to buy his fishing gear. The young clerk working that day must have thought that this big guy was made out of money. Richard bought one of everything.

He didn't have a clue what any of the lures, leaders, sinkers, popping corks, nets, hooks, or frozen Spanish sardines he purchased were to be used for. That didn't matter. After picking out an attractive shirt with an embroidered tarpon on it, and a matching teal hat, he walked out of the Bait Box looking the part. To Richard Evans, looking the part of a fisherman was all that mattered. Some $447.85 later, attorney Richard Evans felt that he had successfully bought his way into the angler's world.

"So what's biting down at the pier these days?" Richard asked the clerk as he handing him his Platinum VISA card.

"I hear that the big ocean-running reds have been hitting pretty good. The bite seems to be best first thing in the morning," said the young clerk.

"What do I use for bait?"

"Oh, those frozen Spanish sardines will work, or you can stop by in the morning to pick up some shrimp. Where are you staying?"

"A condo called Seaside."

"That's not far from the pier. I'd stick with the sardines and if you don't have any luck with them, come back after we open at seven and we'll fix you right up with some live shrimp."

"Thanks."

"Hey, no problem. And good luck tomorrow."

The clerk watched Richard hobble back to his minivan. He had seen hundreds of wanna be anglers come in and try to buy their way into the sport. Most wouldn't catch a thing. This guy, looking like a manatee out of water, had little chance of landing one tomorrow morning either. Catfish. That's what this guy will catch tomorrow. Catfish.

After a great dinner at a place called the Timbers, Richard set the alarm for 6:00 a.m. and hit the hay. It had been a long day and he was tired. Helen and the boys would have to fend for themselves until lunch time. The boys were used to having their father gone. They wouldn't even notice.

When he woke up, he made some coffee and ate four large apple fritters for breakfast. He was used to getting up early and heading out to the office to prepare for court, so the plan to fish all week set well with him. He put a sandwich and some Cokes in a small cooler and headed out toward the east end of the island.

As the sun grappled its way up and over the horizon, Richard

Evans found himself walking slowly down the wooden dock to the small fishing pier on the very eastern tip of Sanibel. It was a warm, calm day in late September. Richard was wheezing as he walked.

He lit a cigarette just before stepping onto the dock. This is living, he thought to himself as he stepping up onto the pier. The smoke from the burning Camel lingered in the moist, calm air behind him like a thin trail of fog. This is living.

The First Morning

One

Dawn arrived with a sense of the spectacular that first morning. There was an uneven row of worn out thunderstorms hanging just to the west of the fishing pier. As the sun rose above the condominium-laden skyline of Ft. Myers Beach, the shafts of sunlight reflected off the high tops of those towering clouds. In that rarefied light, the air took on a bright, golden hue. It was a stunning color, not unlike the light of sunset reflecting off those same, active thunderstorms the evening before. Only this light was more refined, more mystical in nature.

The waters surrounding the point of the island were alive with millions of tiny, silver shiners. Carl knew that this was a good sign. Bait meant food. If there was plenty of bait around, there were fish nearby. There were plenty of shorebirds, feeding on the schools of bait. The beach was lined with them. There were egrets, with their long sinuous look, smaller snowy egrets, and a couple of great blue herons. They were all wading along the beach, feeding on the pilchards that swam in too close.

These were birds that had completely lost their fear of man. Birds that had spent their entire lifetime dodging tourists and shellers in search of lettered olives and lightning whelks. They no longer flew off or panicked as strangers approached them. They just strolled out of the way for a minute. Then strolled back. They were domesticated wildlife, peculiar to places like Sanibel.

Richard noted their tameness as he got close to the beach. One of the largest blue herons he had ever seen waded just to the north of the ramp leading up to the pier. Richard knew how the herons and wildlife around Peoria reacted to an approaching stranger. Most of them had been shot at before. They kept their distance. They were always ready and quick to take to the wing. This great blue heron didn't even move as this large man waddled up the pier.

Instead, it took a long, studied look at Richard's plastic baggie full of frozen Spanish sardines. The heron looked at the sardines, then looked up at Richard, then back down once again at the thawing fish. He knew that a few of them would soon be a part of his breakfast. To the heron, this tourist was an easy mark.

Richard went up to the covered section of the pier, about a third of the way down, and set all of his brand new gear down on one of the wooden benches along the outside edge. He looked around. There were six people fishing on the pier. They were scattered intermittently around the T at the end of the pier. Carl Johnson was one of them. There were buckets dangling from long lines tied to the wooden railings and gently swaying back and forth in the incoming current. They were full of bait: shrimp and shiners, grunts, finger mullet and pinfish.

Next to him, under the shelter of the covered section of the pier, were two five-gallon plastic jugs filled with saltwater. They were filled with bait, and the minnows in the buckets were being kept alive by little battery operated aerators that kept up a constant hum, like the sound of old electric shavers. The anglers had sealed their buckets shut with tight-fitting plastic lids. They knew from experience how brazen the island herons could be.

Richard noticed several stringers hanging next to the buckets. Two had fish on them. One stringer had a very large fish on it. It was a species he had never seen before. The fish was long and narrow, with a white belly and a dark black stripe down the entire length of its side. This fish was forty inches long and it looked to Richard to weigh at least twenty-five pounds. There was a second stringer with two beautiful bronze-colored fish on it that were five or six pounds each. They looked sort of like carp, he thought.

All the fish looked sad. Their slender bodies were swaying in the incoming current like the branches of willows sway in the light winds of summer. They were captured animals, tethered to the weathered railing of dock by a long stretch of nylon rope. At some point in time the angler who had caught them would lift them up and toss them into a cooler, or lay them in the back of his pick-up and drive off.

He looked down at the stringers once again. He realized that these fish were far larger than those he had caught the last time he had been fishing back up in Peoria. That afternoon three years ago they had managed just three two-pound walleye and a couple of scrawny perch. By comparison, these fish were monsters.

He started working on his gear. There were packages to open, lines to spool and then thread through the rod guides. He had leaders to tie, sinkers to affix, and it all had to be done by someone who hadn't fished in years. He was becoming self-conscious about the task before him. His fingers felt thick and uncoordinated, like bowling pins.

The regulars on the dock took turns glancing over to him. To them, he was just another touron. A touron is a mixture of equal parts tourist and moron. Richard Evans, sitting there for an hour, threading, re-threading and fumbling with his line, chain smoking and looking like a beached Jewfish, looked worse than your average touron. He looked ridiculous.

Richard looked like a touron with more money than sense. Judging by the inordinate amount of the fishing tackle he was busy taking the price tags off of and the time spent unwrapping lures out of the vacuum-sealed packages, the pier regulars were right.

Finally, he was ready to begin fishing. He reached down and took out a six-inch sardine from the Ziplock baggie and nervously stuck it on the hook. He walked about half way up the pier and went to toss it in the water. With the weight of the four-ounce lead sinker he had tied on, it sounded as if someone had thrown a rock into the ocean. The sardine sank quickly to the bottom.

Carl was laughing to himself as he watched Richard fumbling about. He remembered his first few days of fishing some thirty years ago. He recalled what it was like to fish the wrong baits, at the wrong times, and in all the wrong places. He remembered catching all those catfish. Carl was laughing because he knew that Richard, fishing with those oily sardines, was on his way to his first catfish. It would only be a matter of time.

By now, the sun had labored its way high above the horizon. It was starting to warm up. Although the sunlight was still slanted, it was easy to sense that it was going to be another hot September day in south Florida. Fall had merely teased everyone the week before, with the wind shifting for two days out of the northeast. It was still too early for fall to slide this far down the peninsula. The subtropical jet stream had bullied the early cold front back into Georgia and the cool weather was over. It had been in the mid-nineties every day since. Today was to be no exception.

The pier gang had drifted in by now. The pier gang was a loosely knit bunch of locals that fished the pier religiously. They were regular passengers on this T-shaped bus that went nowhere and back every day on the changing tides. Some were retired, like Carl, with ample time on their hands and no stomach or insufficient funds for owning a boat. There were the construction workers enjoying a day off. Big, brawny kids standing around with Coors Lights in their hands at 8:30 in the morning, always ready to party. There were golden skinned Latinos, and scruffy, unemployed, and unemployable men with bad teeth and a penchant to profanities. There were a few women who came down and fished the pier but none on this particular Sunday morning.

On a good day there might be a dozen of the pier gang fishing. All of them hanging out in the northern section at the end of the T. Standing around, leaning on the old wooden railing with their beer bellies and their well-used rods set on clicker. They were all waiting for the big strike. Swapping stories about what happened down at the pier last week when George or Mike wasn't down to see it. What a frenzy it was! Talking about last week's football game.

"The Gators should have won that game yesterday, goddamn it!" said one of them to no one in particular.

The pier gang. Drinking beer and smoking cigarettes until their allotted fishing time was up or the bite was down to a distant memory. Country boys taking a day off.

Carl was amused by them. To the untrained eye, it appeared that Carl was one of them. He wasn't. He usually fished on the other side, the south side of the pier, and he didn't like to drink beer before noon. The fact that Carl kept his shirt on was enough to keep him out of the ranks of the pier regulars. The regulars fished without shirts. It was like the division of basketball teams back in junior high school: skins and shirts. The pier gang was always the skins. Carl, the tourists, the occasional local, and the rare Florida Marine Patrol Officer were the shirts.

As far as the fishing went, the skins always won. They won

because they were there so often. When one of them failed to make it down to the pier, he would be brought up to speed immediately by a fellow pier gang member. That way, each of them knew when to expect the bite, and what to use to make sure they were going to get hooked up. Except for the chronically unemployed in the group, most of them had fairly good tackle. Their fishing pier skills were well honed. They deserved to win.

On the shirts team, only Carl and the Sanibel locals had any chance of taking a round. The tourists stayed on the bench. Richard was pure bench material. This huge, overweight, chain-smoking touron was standing there, with his brand new rod and reel in his hand, waiting. Waiting for his first big catfish run.

Twenty-five minutes later, a catfish finally took Richard's sardine. Richard, who had been leaning hard against the wooden rail, mesmerized by the rushing tide beneath him and the Florida sun warming his back, was startled by the tug on his rod. He panicked. He gave that rod such an enormous yank that had that catfish been anywhere near the surface, Richard would have looked exactly like Carl did some thirty years ago; impaled, and headed for the hospital. But the big sail-cat was deep below the surface. The hook quickly pulled through the sardine and became firmly embedded in the side of his ugly mouth. The fight was on.

Richard had set the drag too light. The catfish, as it swam off down current, was pulling line out at an alarming rate. He reached over and tightened the drag a bit and the fish halted seventy-five yards out. Now to reel him back, thought Richard.

The hook was well set. Richard was not. He was doing everything wrong. He was reeling against the drag, spinning the line into a hopeless tangle. He was pulling hard when he should have let the fish run, and letting the fish swim about lazily when he should have been bringing him in. Five minutes later Richard had worked the catfish to within netting distance.

That is when Carl decided it was time to tell this novice his $4,000 catfish story. Carl picked up one of the pier gang's nets and walked over to give this hapless angler a hand. Carl knew that whoever he was, he wouldn't know how to de-hook a sail cat. Carl had seen too many injured tourists leaving the pier in agonizing pain. So Carl left his pinfish dangling in the water, with his one big rod and one smaller rod tied with old shoelaces against the railing, and walked over to Richard with the net.

"Can I give ya a hand?" Carl asked.

"Sure. I've got a really big fish on here," answered Richard. Neither of them had seen the fish, but Carl, just by watching the pattern of the rod tip over the duration of the fight, knew it to be a catfish. Catfish have a distinctive head shake that makes the rod tip bounce in a familiar pattern. Carl had fished for so many years that simply by eyeballing a rod tip for a few seconds he could tell the angler what was pulling on it down there, in that salty abyss.

When Richard finally got it up close enough to the surface for Mr. Johnson to confirm its notorious identity, indeed, it was a catfish. Richard remarked, "Wow, what in the world is that?"

Richard had seen catfish before, but never a gafftop. Their heads are far larger than most catfish and the three elongated fins make them look like some kind of sea monster. To a divorce attorney from Peoria, it looked surreal.

"It's a gafftop-sail catfish," answered Carl, quickly adding, "I'll forewarn you now that you'll have to be damned careful with it once we get him up on this dock." With that warning, Carl leaned over the top of the railing and, holding the long-handled net in his hand, quickly scooped the catfish up. With the unbroken rhythm of a professional, he pulled it straight up, clearing the railing and onto the wooden floor of the pier.

"Don't touch it!" insisted Carl. "I'll go get my hook removers."

Richard heeded the warning. He knelt down to get a better look at this grotesque looking animal lying on the planks of the dock. It looks like it's from another planet, thought Richard. The top of the fish was a solid, charcoal grey. Along the sides and near the belly the grey turned to a bronze coloration. On the bottom of the fish, on the belly, the bronze faded to a dirty white. The two pectoral fins and the primary dorsal fin were six inches long. The big catfish kept grunting. It looked like something you would expect to catch in the canals of Mars.

By this time the fish had flopped around enough to completely slime the bright green netting. Its long sharp fins had become entangled in the nylon mesh. It kept making an awful, grunting noise, like a tiny pig. It was disgusting. To make matters worse, it had partially regurgitated the sardine. Besides all of that, the fish stank. At this point, Richard was not so sure about this fishing tip Harding had given him. It might be better to spend some extra time with those strangers that were his family instead. He was wondering if the Bait Box would take all his tackle back and give him a refund.

"Stand back," said Carl, taking command of the situation. The pier gang wasn't paying much attention at this point. They had watched the first minute or two of the fight, amused at seeing this big fellow, now panting and out of breath, battle so heroically against a slimy catfish. That was enough entertainment for the moment. Now they were disinterested. They knew from the rod tip motions, just like Carl, that it was a catfish. They didn't care about catfish. No one in their right mind ate them, and they were always such a nuisance to get unhooked and untangled from the net. The pier gang didn't want to have anything to do with this fish once it was ready for netting. They all turned around and faced east toward the awakening sun. They were going to ignore Richard completely.

Carl figured as much. If it were a big snook that this tourist had caught by accident, or a hefty redfish, one of the skins would have been there helping. They would have helped Richard land the fish, measure it, and one by one the rest of them would have come over to congratulate him on such a fine catch. They found time for the winners. Catfish, and the tourons who hooked them, were losers. Carl had to go this one alone.

Carl bent down and picked up the long-handled dip net. With a quick flip, he dislodged the six-pound catfish from the net. The fish was still hanging by one of its slimy pectoral fins, but with a couple of terse shakes, it fell free to the deck.

"There," said Carl, "that part is over. Now let's get him unhooked."

Carl grabbed his six-inch set of stainless steel hook-outs and carefully reached over and grabbed the shank of the hook. Picking the entire fish up carefully, wary of every sudden wiggle or squirm, he brought the fish over to the end of the pier and flipped the fish up and over the pliers. He gave the pliers a few quick jerks and the catfish dropped back into the brine below.

"Can you eat those things?" Richard asked.

"If you were starving," replied Carl.

Few people ate catfish, either hard head or gafftop. There was a small contingent of tourists who insisted that gafftop sailcats were delicious. No one took them seriously. Cleaning them was dangerous, and because of the gooey slime that covered their bodies, it was disgusting as well. Carl was right. "If you were starving." Richard Evans didn't meet the starving criteria.

"Have you ever fished down at the pier before?" The question was merely an ice breaker. Carl already knew the answer.

"No, this is the first time I've ever fished in the ocean," replied Richard. He knew that he was talking to someone who had fished the ocean for years. He knew it from the way this old man had handled the catfish.

"Well, welcome to the Sanibel fishing pier. My name's Carl," said Carl while reaching over to shake Richard's hand enthusiastically.

"My name's Richard, Richard Evans. I want to thank you for helping me net and unhook that fish just now. Those are really ugly fish. Why did you say they were dangerous?"

Carl went on to explain his early days of fishing around Sanibel. He told Richard his infamous catfish tale. It wasn't the tale that was drawing Richard in. It was Carl's voice. Carl had the voice of a storyteller. It was the voice of nuance, timing, and sincerity. Timeless and warm, it was the voice of the elders telling the young warriors how to conduct the hunt. Where to throw the spear to fell the beast. How to cure the meat for winter. The voice of time that was gathered into this soulful resonance. Richard was immediately entranced.

Carl had always been a great storyteller. It was his storytelling, not his disposition to catching catfish, that had established Carl as a popular guide from early on. His clients, friends, and everyone who had ever known Carl loved to hear him speak. Carl had a Mark Twain aura about him. Although he had never acquired a southern accent, the melodic drawl of the south had crept into his voice just enough to lend it a native charm.

Richard was soon laughing aloud at the part about the guy with the bullet wound getting out of surgery in half the time. The two of them were hitting it off wonderfully. The sun was lumbering its way toward the top of the sky.

After finishing the catfish story, Carl asked Richard if he might not want to come over and fish with him down at the end of the pier. Carl had some extra minnows to share, and if they got lucky, they might latch onto a passing redfish.

"I would be delighted," said Richard, quickly accepting the offer. As he turned around to walk back and get his tackle box from under the covered section of the pier he looked straight into the eyes of a great blue heron. Richard remembered that he had left his sardine baggie open. He looked down at his bag of bait. There were three left. He had purchased a dozen yesterday at the tackle store.

The great blue heron looked up at Richard. He knew that he was about to get shagged off. It was too late; the crime had been committed. In Richard's displeased glance, the great blue heron lost its sense of majesty. Its long graceful lines were thin veneer for its sleazy behavior. The elegance of this bird was a deceit. The heron was a petty thief, and Richard had left his wallet out.

Carl was amused by it. Carl was intimately familiar with the underhanded tactics of the local egrets and herons. He laughed as Richard bolted toward the heron, his big arms and small hands waving in the air to scare him off. The heron, in calm defiance, casually lifted up and flew off. He didn't mind being shagged off. He was stuffed.

Richard gathered up his tackle boxes, the rest of his bait and his small cooler full of Cokes. Waddling up the pier like an elephant seal with legs, he soon joined Carl at the southern end of the T. They talked for hours. They talked about fishing and Illinois, about football and hurricanes. Casual conversations, filling the time like the tide fills the basin of the back bay. It was a rare conversation. Like two old friends finding each other again after a decade apart. It felt good.

The redfish never showed. There were a few more catfish hauled in by the tourists, and the pier gang brought up a handful of undersized snook, but overall, the fishing was poor.

By eleven, Richard knew it was time to make it back home for lunch and see what his wife and boys wanted to do for the remainder of the day. Carl was going to stay, no longer having a wife or a family to return home to. Before Richard left, he asked Carl if he would be coming to the pier again tomorrow. Richard said that he wanted to catch one of those beautiful bronze-colored fish he saw drifting on the ends of those stringers near the shore.

"They call them redfish, Richard," said Carl. He explained to Richard that he fished the pier nearly every day and would be delighted if Richard could join him in the morning. In fact, he'd bring some extra bait if Richard would bring some extra Coca Cola. The bargain was struck. They would both be at the pier at dawn. Dawn of the second morning.

Two

Richard felt great. He went back to the condominium that Sunday morning wanting to tell Helen about the huge catfish he had caught down at the pier. He wanted to tell her about meeting Carl, about how interesting a person he was, and how they were planning to fish again tomorrow. He was disappointed to find out that he had to wait his turn. Helen was on the phone with Wanda back in Peoria, telling her how absolutely perfect Sanibel was.

"The beaches are just covered with shells and my husband has just come back from fishing and..." Richard sat down at the dining room table and waited for her to hang up. He knew that it might be a while.

"I tell you, Wanda, it's everything you said it was. Hopefully we'll get down to the beach later today and try to swim some laps in the heated pool. I'll call you later this afternoon; Richard just came back from fishing and he looks like he's anxious to tell me all about it. I'll call you again later." She put down the phone. Back up in Peoria, Wanda was relieved. She hadn't said more than two words during the thirty-minute call. Richard was glad; he had expected a much longer conversation. Helen had a co-dependent relationship with the telephone.

"So, Richard, did you catch the big one?"

"Sort of. It was a big catfish. We threw it back. Carl said that nobody eats them," he replied.

"Who's Carl?"

"He's an older fellow, I would guess him to be in his seventies. His face has this classic weathered look to it and he tells the best damn fishing stories. For years and years he was a fishing guide here on Sanibel. He really knows his stuff. We've set up a rendezvous back down at the pier tomorrow morning again. He says that the redfish might be running by then."

Richard carried on about Carl and his conversations with him for the remainder of the morning. He was clearly excited.

Helen wasn't impressed. She listened inattentively. Richard's voice came across like the voice of a narrator on a television show she wasn't interested in watching but didn't feel like bothering to get up and turn off. If Helen had held the remote in her hand, she would have put Richard on mute.

After ten minutes of feigning attention, she asked Richard to take the kids to the pool or something so she could do some shopping. She didn't like the heat. The heat was tolerable, but only while she was busy looking over the various offerings of the local boutiques. There, in that air conditioned comfort, everything was as it should be. A platinum VISA card and an island full of boutiques were all Mrs. Helen Evans ever needed.

Helen took the rental car. She noted it had a fishy odor. It was a horrible smell, thought Helen as she drove off toward Periwinkle, the island's main street.

Richard fixed the kids peanut-butter-and-jelly sandwiches for lunch. He fixed three for himself, with extra butter. After eating, he decided to take the boys to the pool. He parked himself beneath the shade of a cabbage palm on a chaise lounge that strained beneath the load. He had picked up an issue of the National Enquirer that Helen had bought that morning when she was getting their groceries over at Bailey's, the local grocery store. As the Florida sun pounded the sand, he casually flipped through the Enquirer.

It was your typical issue. There had been recent sightings of UFOs and Elvis and still no arrests on that child murder case in Colorado. All he read were the headlines. The stories were irrelevant. It didn't matter if any of this garbage was true. Richard knew it wasn't. It was entertaining.

As the afternoon wore on and the shadows on the pool grew long and cool, Richard dozed off. He could hear the screams of the boys as they swam, shoved, and argued in the pool, but he was asleep. He was tired. He was used to getting up at 6:30 a.m., but the one hour time change made it 5:30. That was early, even for a workaholic. The nap felt wonderful.

Lying there, in that straining chaise longue with nothing but his size 52 trunks on, Mr. Richard Evans was a pathetic sight. His body was too large and too pale to be exposed to the view of the world. He looked like a sumo wrestler without hope for a match. He didn't look successful, or wealthy, or powerful. He looked odd. His upper arms and thighs were puckered with hundreds of dimples formed by a career of cellulite. His light-brown hair was thin and balding, his face smooth and pudgy. He looked like an overweight child. A child raised on a diet of cheeseburgers, chocolate shakes and ripple chips. High-stress food to feed his high-stress lifestyle. A curious by-product of family law.

Eventually, Tyler and James got into an argument they couldn't resolve. It was over who could use the one diving mask that didn't leak. James came over and shook Richard. As he shook him, even as mildly as the boy did, Richard's body reverberated like a bowl of thick, vanilla custard. Richard loved custard, especially a flambeau. After hearing the details of the case, Richard ruled in James' favor. Tyler handed the good mask over. The boys swam for about fifteen more minutes after which, at Richard's insistence, they were all to head down to the beach. None of them had yet been down to the beach.

They walked across the long wooden boardwalk to the sand. The first thing they noticed was that the beach was awash with shells. Millions upon millions of them. Richard had heard about the shelling on Sanibel from his friends. Standing on the beach, with a waning sun tumbling from the sky, the mounds upon mounds of shells beneath him took him by surprise. Most of the beach shells were fragments. Many were still whole but they were chipped and cracked. A few of the smaller ones were perfect. All of them were unlike anything they had ever seen back in Peoria.

As if in a trance induced by these mounds of empty mollusks, all three of them started filling the small pockets of their swimsuits with an assortment of whelks, clams, and scallop shells. Then they became disinterested. Tyler and James commenced a game of Frisbee. Richard didn't join in. It was difficult for him to chase around, and he was preoccupied with thinking about the morning. What was it that made him feel like this?

The sun finally dove head first into the ocean. The air cooled quickly. Richard was sitting on a small bluff that the waves had carved from the beach, just up from the breaking surf. The boys were playing off in the distance, throwing their plastic discus back in forth in the faltering light. A flock of white ibis started working their way toward Richard. They probed their long, curved orange beaks deep into the wet sand that lay exposed as each wave withdrew back into the sea. They looked like farm chickens. Beach chickens with thin, banana-curved beaks and matching orange legs.

The ibis were more skittish than was the heron that snatched Richard's sardines earlier in the day. Richard had no way of knowing that some of the good-ole-boys up in Pine Island and down in Goodland still shoot them. They call them "Chokoloskee chicken." This flock of ibis had been shot at before and had good cause to be nervous. They kept their distance and flew well around Richard as they continued down the beach toward the vibrant colors of the sunset.

Richard was thinking. He was thinking about his life as the surf began chanting to him. He hadn't noticed when the song took hold. It was a slow, melodic chant, like a chorus of medieval monks. The song was new to him, but pleasing. His life, the life of this pale, overweight divorce attorney, was misplaced here. He felt the dichotomy and the distance between him and this natural world. For a brief instant, he wanted to overcome that distance. He sensed that there were secrets hidden nearby, tales of wisdom, whispering to him but a few yards away. He could hear them, but they spoke in a language that was foreign to him. A language he had long since forgotten.

"Richard! RICHARD! You've locked me out of the condo!" Helen stood there, twenty feet behind him. There were two big shopping bags in her arms. They looked heavy with the quarry of well-scanned plastic. Richard could tell in an instant that Helen was pissed off. The boys came running back up the beach, hearing Helen's flustered voice from a distance. Neither of them offered to take a bag. They were too busy with themselves to consider either of their parents. That's how they had been raised - perfect models of selfishness.

"Richard, could you pleeease get off your big butt and come open the condo for me. These bags aren't exactly light!"

"Sorry honey," said Richard as he slowly got to his feet. It felt odd for him to be getting up off the ground. He wondered when the last time was that he had actually sat on the ground. He sat in three places: his Cadillac, his Lazyboy recliner, at home and his black leather chair at the office. That, and restaurants, he added as an afterthought. As he walked over to pick up his beach towel and help Helen with the packages, he took one last glance back toward the surf. The chant was gone. It was just the sound of water hitting a shoreline now. That is all it ever is, thought Richard as he walked with Helen and the boys back up to their beach front condo. That's all it ever is.

Three

Carl went home late. He had brought an apple and some salt peanuts with him for lunch so there wasn't any need for him to leave the pier early. The redfish swam in around noon and the bite was strong for almost three hours. Carl had caught and released nine. Maybe ten. He had lost count. It didn't matter.

The pier gang had a royal time with the run. When the school finally arrived and the fish started biting, only a handful of the regulars were still fishing at the pier. They must have landed over fifty reds. Every member of the skins had caught their limit five times over. Some of them gave their extra redfish to a tourist or an islander not having any luck. Even the tourists had hooked a couple of decent fish at the peak of the action. Most wrapped around the pilings and broke off. One of the tourists actually landed and netted a redfish, but it turned out to be too small to keep.

It was a great afternoon, thought Carl. Too bad Richard had left so early. He would have really enjoyed himself. Maybe tomorrow. There was always tomorrow.

The house was dark when Carl pulled up in his old station wagon. It was dark most nights since Marie had passed away. It made him sad as he pulled up. He never thought about her much when he was at the pier. As he pulled up their driveway, he thought of her once again. She had been his life.

Marie and Carl were married more than forty-seven years when God took her away from him. For a while, Carl was angry with God about it. He was angry because God had left him alone. Alone was a place foreign to him, a land he was unfamiliar and uncomfortable with. As he pulled into the driveway and turned off the ignition, all of these feelings came rushing back to him like the storm surge of a hurricane. All the denial, the anger, and the loneliness overwhelmed him in a momentary flood of emotion. As quickly as that dark wave came, it vanished. He would not drown in it any longer, like he did for months on end after the funeral. He refused to feel sorry for himself any longer. Things just happen in life and no one, least of all God, can be blamed.

Carl knew that he should sell the house. He knew it would help. Coming back to an apartment on Sanibel wouldn't bother him as much as coming back every night to this big, empty house. In an apartment, he wouldn't come back home every evening expecting that light to be on in the kitchen. A light that she would never flip the switch for again. He wouldn't remember coming in through the garage door, taking off his old sneakers, and smelling something baking in the oven. Something delicious. That was all behind him now. But something held him back from selling the house.

He kept telling his children that the reason he was hanging onto the place was to have the extra bedrooms available for them when they came down to see him. It was a lie. They had not been back home since the funeral a year ago. Carl knew it was a lousy excuse to keep the house but he used it anyway.

"That house is just too much for you, Dad," Emily would say over the stretch of telephone lines between Sanibel and Atlanta.

"Now that Mom's gone," she would add.

Naw, thought Carl. This is where I belong. Besides, it won't be that much longer. He methodically got all of his fishing gear out of the back of the wagon and carried his rods and tackle boxes one by one back into the garage. There wasn't any room in the garage for his car. It was full of assorted freezers, lawn tools and miscellaneous boat junk.

The garage was a mess. It looked like he was about to have a large rummage sale that would never happen. All he needed to do to make it happen was to paste price stickers on everything, and put a sign up on the corner. A tag sale. He chuckled as he reminded himself that he'd have the garage sale the same week he sold the house. Next year, he added, laughing quietly to himself. Next year for sure.

He went in to make himself a TV dinner and see what was on the television. He flipped through forty or fifty channels and decided there wasn't anything worth watching. There never was. Finally, he eased back on his big recliner and picked up a book. He liked historical novels, an occasional mystery, and everything that had ever been written by Hemingway. Tonight, he was reading *A Farewell to Arms*. Carl couldn't remember how many times he had read that book any more than he could remember how many redfish he had reeled in and released that afternoon. Neither number mattered.

Carl fell asleep reading Hemingway in his big easy chair. Around 2:30 he woke up to go to the bathroom. He took off his old worn clothes and crawled into bed. He checked his alarm to make sure it was set for 5:30 a.m. His alarm was always set for 5:30, but he always double checked it. It was a ritual. I hope the bite comes a little earlier tomorrow, he thought to himself as he fell back to sleep. Then that attorney fellow can catch his redfish.

The Second Morning

One

"Don't touch it, Sidney! Don't you dare touch it!"

The tourist woman was standing next to the flat fish yelling at her husband to stand back. She was hysterical.

"Look at it, Sidney. It's some sort of mutation or something. Maybe it's from all those chemicals they've dumped into the ocean. All that fertilizer from the sugar cane fields. Look at it closely. It's horrible. Both eyes are on the same side of its head."

"But Rosanne..."

"Don't you dare go near it, Sidney! It might be radioactive or something. Maybe we should call the police."

It was a flounder. One of the two tourists who had been fishing at the pier when Carl arrived had caught a flounder. It was a big flounder at that.

Ralph hadn't arrived with his landing net yet. Lacking the net, the middle-aged touron from the Midwest had hoisted the flounder out of the water and lowered it back down onto the splintered wooden deck of the fishing pier. When it touched those damp planks, it started flopping around like an excited pancake. In the dim light of dawn it looked bizarre, covered with small brown dots across the back and ivory white skin on the belly. But the eyes on that flounder were what disturbed the tourist who had hooked it. She thought it was the fish from Dow Chemical.

Carl walked up to her. "It's a flounder, ma'am. That's the way flounders look," he told her calmly.

"You mean it's not a mutation?" she asked.

"No. It's perfectly normal. And if you're interested in taking something home with you, they are an excellent eating fish," said Carl.

"Rosanne, that's what I was trying to tell you a minute ago," added her husband, Sidney. He bent down to take a closer look at the flounder. The fish had stopped flopping around. It was tired.

"Well, I don't care what it is. I'm not about to eat it," concluded Rosanne. "It looks too weird for my taste buds."

"Then we'll let it go," said her husband.

"Fine then, let's throw it back," added his wife with a sense of finality.

"I'll unhook it for you, ma'am," volunteered Carl.

Carl took out his long, stainless hook removers and knelt over the fish. He grabbed the shank of the hook with the device and picked up the fish with the hook still firmly lodged in its mouth. Holding it out over the water, with a quick jerk of his hand, he flipped the entire flounder over his wrist. The hook became dislodged at once. The flounder fell back into the ocean.

"That was incredible. The way you just unhooked that fish," said Sidney.

"Just don't try that trick with a catfish. He'll nail you every time," said Carl as he walked back toward his spot and waited for Richard and the rest of the pier gang to start showing.

Carl enjoyed the tourists that fished at the pier. They were a constant source of entertainment. They did everything wrong. Losing fish after fish, holding their spinning rods upside down and reeling them in backwards. Setting their drags so tight as to make the spool and the reel fuse together, so when the fish hits, the line snaps with a loud crack. Or on the other extreme, having the spool on so lightly that when the fish hits, the spool pulls off and falls into the sea. The novices offered a thousand variations on how not to land a fish.

On the rare occasion that a tourist actually brought a fish in, the fun continued. The next scene in this comedy of errors was listening to the onslaught of mis-identifications that followed. Most of the tourists were from the Midwest, a few were from up East, and a few from Europe. Towns like Dusseldorf and London. None of them knew what these subtropical ocean fish looked like.

He had seen them call snook everything from saltwater bass to albacore tuna. Redfish had been identified as carp, lizard fish, spot tails and Spanish sea trout.

The only fish the tourists consistently identified correctly were the sharks. Sharks were hard to miss. Once on the deck, a wildly thrashing four-foot blacktip shark could clear the pier of panicking tourons in seconds. They would scurry toward the safety of the land en masse. The tourons did not want to be devoured by a tiny shark incapable of anything worse than the bite of a golden retriever.

Sharks and stingrays. The tourons were almost as afraid of stingrays as they were of sharks. The difference was that after the big stingray stopped flopping around, the tourons would all make their way back toward this strange creature to have a better look. They knew from *National Geographic* specials that stingrays don't have the razor sharp teeth of sharks. All stingrays wield are their lethal stingers. "I think it's in their tail somewhere...," you could hear them say as they cautiously worked their way back toward this auburn-colored fish drying out on the hot wooden planks of the dock. "It's deadly poisonous," one of them would add reassuringly.

Carl noted that the tourists were always fascinated with stingrays, skates, and rarely, when one was landed, a guitar fish. Why shouldn't they be? They were pure Hollywood in design, looking like creatures custom fabricated for the next sci-fi thriller. Carl sometimes wondered if stingrays felt the same about the circle of humans peering over them. Odd looking creatures they were, with noses, arms, and standing upright. Always making these strange vocalizations.

The tourons on the pier were fun. Carl never laughed out loud as they made their ridiculous or they all scattered back to shore because of a harmless nurse shark. He did chuckle on occasion. The skins, on the other hand, laughed out loud. You couldn't help but hear them. Trying to keep from spilling their beers while doubling over with laughter. Pointing. Loudly recounting the tale throughout the day until the person responsible for losing the fish, embarrassed and humiliated, quietly slipped away. Carl thought it was cruel. Everyone is a beginner at one time or another, he thought to himself. Everyone makes mistakes.

Carl's alarm had gone off at 5:30 a.m. earlier that same morning. He awoke to the sound of an obscure jazz saxophone player on the public radio station he always had his radio alarm tuned in to. At 5:30 in the morning this nervous saxophone was too much for an old salt to handle. He would leave it on if it was one of his favorites, like baroque recorder music, or a piece by Mozart. "But not for this crap," he mumbled quietly to himself as he reached over to turn off his clock radio.

There was never any telling what would be playing on any given morning. The programming was left up to the tired announcer. Carl was amused by the thought that only he and the sleep-deprived announcer were listening to the radio at 5:30 a.m.. He reached over and hit the mute button. Now only the announcer was listening.

Carl got dressed. He elected to wear the same clothes he was wearing yesterday. They didn't smell all that badly and Marie was no longer there to complain about them even if they did. Besides, he thought, if I decide they're dirty, I'll have to wash them. I don't like doing laundry, he reminded himself.

Laundry was something Marie used to do. As a couple, they had divided the household chores along traditional lines. Marie did the dishes, the laundry, and the grocery shopping. Carl took care of the routine maintenance of things, fixed and washed the cars, and painted the house on an "as needed" basis. The only exception to this arrangement was the lawn.

Marie loved to mow the lawn and do the yard work. She had several beautiful flower gardens, and kept the orange and grapefruit trees in perfect health. She loved the physical aspect of yard work. She loved to clip the hedges, pull the uncountable weeds from the flower beds and rake leaves. The mahoe, or the sea hibiscus as they were also known, provided Marie with plenty of leaves to rake.

Carl felt that yard work was too hard for a woman. He had offered to hire a yard service year after year. Marie would have none of it. It was a passion of hers that she would never relinquish to anyone. Carl conceded. He often wondered if the cancer didn't have something to do with all those chemicals and pesticides she was exposed to. He could only guess at that.

Carl went into the kitchen and fixed himself some eggs. He decided not to bring a lunch down to the pier today. He would either go over to the nearby East End Deli for some of their black beans and rice or come home and make a sandwich. He might even take a short nap after lunch. The eggs and a couple strips of bacon would hold him over. Carl knew that his doctor had warned him about his favorite breakfast, but he didn't care. He liked bacon and eggs. They might not be good for my heart, but they're good for my soul, he would say to himself while savoring every guilty bite. His heart was not as strong as it once had been, but his soul had never been stronger.

He finished breakfast and picked up the kitchen, stacking the dirty dishes in the sink beside the others. Then he went out to the garage to start reloading his gear into the station wagon. He had never had a rod or reel stolen in the decades he had been fishing on Sanibel. "Why take any chances?" Carl mumbled to himself while slamming the tailgate of the station wagon. As he pulled away and started driving down to the fishing pier he looked back over the dimly lit yard. He was disappointed with what he saw. The yard missed Marie as much as he did.

When Carl stepped onto the old wooden deck, Richard wasn't at the pier yet. Only the two tourists who had just caught the flounder were there when Carl arrived. The kid at the Bait Box must have told these tourists to get to the pier early to find a good spot. The two tourists took his advice to heart.

Carl went back to his spot and watched the sun get out of bed above the condominium-lined horizon of Ft. Myers Beach to the east. It was breezy down at the pier. The fall is like that on Sanibel - breezy. About ten minutes later, Jose and Ralph stumbled down the boardwalk and up onto the pier, laden down with bait buckets, all their tackle and a cooler full of Budweiser. Ralph had converted an old golf cart into a tackle shop on wheels. Where the golf bag used to sit, he had fashioned a small box that held his bait bucket. Above that were some rubber straps that held his tackle boxes and in front of the whole thing were three white plastic rod holders. It was his own invention and it looked homemade. It served its purpose and that was all Ralph cared about. Looks were not his concern.

Jose was Cuban-American. He fit his stereotype. He wore several gold chains around his neck, a thick gold bracelet and three or four gold rings, depending on his mood. He was a fairly young man, in his mid-thirties. He had classic Hispanic good looks, with dark, romantic eyes and a big, inviting smile.

Carl often wondered what Jose did for a living. Not that it

bothered him any. Jose had excellent equipment, and a twelve pack of cool ones with him every morning. But Jose never appeared to have a work schedule. He had a beeper and a cell phone in his tackle box, and you would see him wander back toward the beach shortly after his beeper would sound once or twice over the course of the day. Whatever he did, thought Carl, he was damn good at it. On any number of occasions Carl had thought to ask Jose how he made his money but never did. It's none of my business anyway, Carl had always concluded.

Jose was a skins player. He never wore a shirt, except in the early morning hours when a chill was still hanging in the air. Once the Florida sun muscled its way to forty-five degrees, the shirt came off. Jose had beautiful, dark-brown Latino skin and a strong, muscular build. He kept his jet-black hair pulled back into a tiny pony tail at the back of his head. He was a damn good angler. That was enough for Carl.

"Morning, Jose. Good morning, Ralph," said Carl as they both walked up the pier and found a good tie-off place for their bait buckets. "Any luck yet this morning Carl?" asked Ralph as he set up.

"Just those two tourists back down the pier a bit. The lady caught a flounder. She thought it was some sort of mutation. They threw it back," said Carl.

"You're kidden' us, right, Carl?" said Jose in his slight Hispanic accent.

"No, Jose. I'm serious. The lady was freaking out because both of the fish's eyes were on the same side of its head. She thought it was from toxic waste or nuclear fallout or something."

"Too much," commented Jose, shaking his head in disbelief.

Over the next fifteen minutes a few more tourists showed up to wet a line. A few locals also found a spot for their middle-aged bellies to rest against the railing. No one had hooked up. Richard was running late. That didn't surprise Carl at all. Richard didn't look like the type that was accustomed to getting up at dawn.

Ralph suddenly hollered over to Carl, "Jose's hooked the big one, Carl!"

Indeed, Jose had. Jose was holding on to his big spinning rod for dear life. The immense fish on the other end of the line was splashing and darting around in a flurry right next to the pier. The pull was so strong that Jose had to rest the butt end of the rod against the railing to keep the tip up. It was a dangerous technique to use. Carl had seen many a good rod snapped in half after being pulled down against the railing. Rods are not designed like crowbars, and they will often break in two where they touch the railing. Jose was lucky. His rod was holding.

It was a mean old snook that had been fooled by Jose's pinfish. No sooner had Jose started to make some headway on the fish than it wrapped him.

"Ping!" They all knew that sound. It was the sound of the line parting as it touched the barnacle-encrusted piling. Jose had lost. On a snook that big, almost everyone loses.

"It was a monster, Carl," said Jose in frustration.

"Yeah, it sure was, Jose," added Ralph.

"That was the big one all right," certified Carl.

It happens all the time. The truly giant snook at the fishing pier don't bite that often. They are only caught during the dark of the night. Or, if conditions are just right, at sunrise and sunset. Some of them are enormous. Four years ago Ralph caught one that was almost fifty inches long. It weighed forty-two pounds. Once a snook this size hits a line, it immediately heads back under the pier to wrap the thin monofilament around the pilings. That is what happened to Jose's fish, and a thousand more before it.

Once the line gets wrapped around the pilings, everything is lost. Through the years of being submerged in these tidal currents, the old wooden pilings have become covered with barnacles, clams, and mussels. The smooth, pressure-treated wood it used to be is turned into a surface of razor blades. The second the fishing line touches these pilings, even 100 lb.-test line, it is instantly frayed away. It parts and the big fish is free.

The old timers and the skins have devised several methods to avoid this. They don't always work. The tourists and infrequent pier anglers fare far worse than do the regulars. Almost every snook over eight or nine pounds manages to pile-wrap the tourists. Throughout the day, depending on the number of hook ups that occur, there might be as many as twenty or thirty fish getting away on the pilings. If the fish is a true monster, it doesn't matter who's handling the rod. If the big snook or bull redfish weighs over twenty pounds, and that fish makes a dash for the pilings, it's over. Knowing this one unchanging rule is as much a part of fishing the pier as is knowing that the herons and egrets will steal your bait. The skins knew these ground rules better than anyone.

Carl stood on the beach and made his second cast with his cast net. For some reason, the baits in his first cast weren't doing well, and Carl wanted to have fresh ones in his bait bucket when Richard arrived. Carl had come full circle with cast nets. He had started with a six- footer thirty years ago. Then he graduated to an eight-foot net. Not long afterwards, he began throwing a ten-foot cast net. Eventually he was able to throw one of those sprawling twelve footers that weigh forty pounds and engulf an entire school of threadfin herring in a single toss.

Now, he was back to throwing a small, six-foot cast net. The twelve-footer had become too heavy for him. Besides, there was no need for such a large net at the pier. A well-placed six-foot net would bring you all the shiners and minnows you might use for the next three hours. After that, you could just walk over and make another cast. It was easy and your baits always stayed fresh.

After tossing a perfect circle, he pulled the net back in slowly. It was full of two-and three-inch whitebaits, mostly pilchards or scaled sardines and a few threadfin herring. Good bait, thought Carl.

"Hey, do you two need any extra bait?" Carl hollered over to Jose and Ralph.

"Thanks, Carl, but we're all set. We brought pinfish," Ralph hollered back.

Ralph was a character. He had retired years ago and was now in his late sixties. He had sold his boat five years ago. After fishing at the pier few times, he decided it was easier and cheaper to fish there then it was to keep his boat. Ralph didn't live on Sanibel. He commuted across the causeway every day from South Ft. Myers. He used to be a school bus driver back up in upstate New York. He and his wife, who was a former teacher in the same area, had retired to Ft. Myers ten years ago. His wife's name was Eileen, though no one had ever met her or even seen her. She didn't mind letting Ralph come down to the pier to fish all the time. Ralph loved it, and he was the only other person who fished the pier as much as Carl. He was a feisty old fart. He always brought a long-handled net with him and he was willing to let anyone at the pier use it to bring up their catch.

Ralph had that high, crackly sort of voice and a piercing laugh that feisty old farts tend to have. He and Jose would stand there for hours, drinking cold Budweisers and bullshitting. They liked the north side of the T. They were good friends, Ralph and Jose. Angling buddies.

Ralph was a skin, but he shouldn't have been. He had pale, wrinkled skin that looked even worse beside Jose's dark Latino skin. Ralph didn't give a shit. He never tanned. Instead, his chalk-white skin simply burned, eventually turning a bright reddish-pink. Ralph had one of those bumper stickers on his car that said, "I'm retired, what's your excuse?"

Ralph never took care of his gear or his net, because he didn't care about his equipment, either. He gave all of his fish away to his neighbors back at the trailer park. Eileen hated fish. The fishing pier was his local bar. The beer was cold, his drinking buddies were fun and full of bullshit, and every once and awhile he would hook onto a monster. Ralph liked keeping things simple.

Carl pulled up the net and unloaded as many baits as he felt he might need into his other five-gallon bucket, the one with all the holes drilled in it. After dumping in the minnows, he quickly stepped back up on the pier, tied the bucket off on the railing and threw it over the side into the steady current. With the water washing through the holes, his bait would stay healthy for hours.

With his net put away, and his bait bucket full, Carl started fishing again. That was when Richard showed up. Showed up smiling. For a few hours he was going to be able to forget about family law and waste some time fishing with his new-found buddy. Richard was happy. He looked ridiculous, smoking a cigarette and waddling down that small pier. But he was happy and that was all that mattered.

"Hi, Carl!" Richard exclaimed as he approached Carl. He felt wonderful, like he had just lost sixty pounds.

"Howdy, Richard!" replied an enthusiastic Carl. "Are you ready to do some serious fishing?" Carl was glad to see that Richard was keeping his word about showing up this morning. "Did you remember the Coca Cola?"

"You bet I did, Carl. Did you bring the bait?"

"Just netted us a bucketful of fresh ones. You might as well feed the rest of your frozen sardines to the great blue heron, Richard - you won't be needing them today."

They both got down to the business of doing some serious fishing. Carl and Richard tacitly understood that "serious" fishing is a classic oxymoron. By their very nature, they are polar opposites. It's like saying you're going to have some desperate fun. Fishing should never be serious. If it is, it isn't fishing.

"Would you like an ice-cold Coke?"

"Don't mind if I do."

Carl told Richard about the flounder that was caught and released earlier that morning. He did so in a hushed voice. Carl didn't want the two tourists, who were still fishing nearby, to overhear him. The skins would have told the tale to Richard through a megaphone, had they witnessed the event. That's the way they were.

Since the pier was still fairly empty, Carl and Richard chose to fish with four rods instead of two. Ralph and Jose were still down at the end of the dock, and until the latecomers began arriving there was plenty of room on the pier for the two additional poles. They put on some half-ounce sinkers just above the swivel, tied on about three feet of forty-pound test leader and, cast out to the north. The tide was still swift, and the lighter sinkers would keep the small white minnows at the ideal depth.

Carl and Richard settled back and quietly drank their Cokes. As the caffeine started to kick in, they started conversing. The sound of two voices on that windy pier fit this landscape well. It was the sound of two new friends getting to know each other. It was a beautiful sound, the sound of that second morning.

"Whatever brought you down here, Carl? This island seems like paradise to me."

Carl paused for a few minutes and answered slowly. "Well, I guess fate brought me down here. But paradise, Richard, well...that's where you make it. I used to tell my charters that it never rains on Sanibel and you never grow old here, either. I guess I was wrong about both."

"Were you always a fishing guide?" continued Richard, intrigued by this old man he was now beside.

"No, I wasn't always a guide. Back up north in Iowa I was a loan officer at a local bank, Riverside Savings and Loan. Our family came down here on a two-week vacation just over thirty years ago. After the first week my wife, Marie, and I decided to sell everything back in Davenport and stay. It turned out to be the longest damned vacation any banker has ever taken - thirty years, two and a half months now and still counting."

"Does Marie like it here?" Richard asked. Richard was beginning to feel self-conscious about his string of questions. He was cross-examining Carl. It was a bad habit of his, one picked up from years of trial work. Carl didn't mind. He knew that Richard was curious about him. Besides, thought Carl, the fish weren't biting.

"Marie passed away about a year ago from cancer," said Carl.

"Oh," said Richard, ashamed now for asking.

Carl could sense the awkwardness in Richard's voice, and he quickly added, "It was for the best. She was suffering so."

"I understand," concluded Richard. "And I'm sorry."

Just then Ralph yelled over to the both of them, "Hey ya'll, come on over here and look down below the T."

By this time the sun had risen in the east, slowly climbing the multicolored stairway of daylight toward zenith. The slanted beams of the sun had wedged their way below the dock and pried deep into the dark waters below. Ralph was pointing to a huge school of snook illuminated by those shafts of sunlight. They were swimming idly in the incoming tide.

Richard's jaw dropped. Every fish in that school was a lunker by Peoria standards. He had never seen so many fish swimming together in his life. They were exquisite. The school was suspended three feet below the surface, just behind one of the pilings. They seemed to be floating, as if adrift on liquid air. To Richard, they seemed free, unbound from the physics of gravity. Free from the exhausting weight of responsibility.

From the angle where Richard and Carl were viewing them, they could observe the fish perfectly, their fins gently flapping into the current. The long black stripes that ran the length of their slender bodies added to their effortless grace. The larger snook would hang motionlessly behind the piling, while the smaller fish would curl and drift off, only later to reappear, sometimes above, sometimes below the rest of the school.

There must be at least two dozen, thought Richard, as he looked down and admired them. What a magnificent sight to behold.

Just then one of Richard's rods, which had been left on a clicker, started screaming off. It was a big fish. It was a snook! Richard was in a state of panic as he reached over to engage the drag and set the hook. He had buck fever. After admiring that school of twenty-pound snook, he was unprepared to deal with the reality of catching one. He flipped the reel into gear and took the reel off the clicker mode. The fish had been running so hard when Richard slammed on the brakes that the snook had hooked itself. That was good. Richard had completely forgotten about setting the hook. Now the battle was drawn.

Carl kept quiet. It was Richard's fish to catch or lose, and unless Richard asked for it, it was best to just stand back and watch. Fortunately, the fish hit one of Carl's rods. Carl knew that the line was fresh, the drags were new and the tackle had been tested a thousand times before. If something failed in the next few minutes, it wouldn't be the gear.

"Look, Carl, he's jumping!" exclaimed Richard. "Look at the line flying off your reel, Carl!"

Carl could see that this was going to be a long battle. At the end of the pier, Ralph had also hooked up a big fish, and he and Jose were absorbed in an exciting fight. Two or three tourists had noticed the flurry of action and walked up from the beach to get a closer look. They were forming a circle around Richard, like a circle that forms around a pro golfer on the 18th green. Only this circle of fans, in ragged cut-offs, two- piece swimsuits and T-shirts, didn't look like the crowds at Augusta. This was a circle of beachcombers and wannabe anglers. They would have been politely escorted off the greens had they looked this bad at the Masters.

Richard was doing fine. He was keeping the rod tip up and the tension on the line tight. He was doing everything he could to hang onto this trophy sized snook. After what seemed like an hour,

Richard had worked the fish back to the pier. Carl had gone down to grab the long-handled pier net that Ralph had brought. It was a community net. Anyone was welcome to use it. Ralph and Jose were getting close to landing their fish also, so Carl and Richard would have to act swiftly if they wanted to get their fish in first.

Then the inevitable happened. Richard's snook made a frantic dash for the pilings. Richard was doing fine as long as the snook was fighting downstream, but he didn't have the faintest idea how to handle the snook once it worked its way back in close to the pilings. Carl knew what to do. He knew that the trick to controlling a big fish at the pier is to lean way, way out over the railing with your arms extended as far as possible to gain leverage. The angler has to put as much pressure as he can to pull the snook back out.

Richard did just the opposite. He took the rod tip and lowered it as the snook dashed toward the razor edged pilings. It gave the fish more than enough line to wrap himself around one of the wooden pilings. Within seconds, the fight ended. The rod snapped back up with the parted line and Richard swore.

"Shit!" he said in an angry voice.

"Don't get mad, Richard, you did a good job," replied Carl, "the fish just had one more trick up his sleeve than you did. It takes a lot of experience to land a snook that size on this pier. Given a few more hook ups like this one, you'll get the knack of it."

Carl was trying to cheer him up. It's always hard for an angler to lose a large fish. Having a small crowd looking over your shoulder when it happens makes it that much worse. Richard wanted to disappear.

"Hey, Carl, bring the net over here!" Jose shouted. "We've got this fish ready for the box!"

Carl grabbed the long pier net and headed toward the northern end of the T-dock with it. The group of motley tourists followed. Richard had missed the putt. It was time to see how the pros were doing. Richard pouted for a brief minute, put down his rod, and walked over to see the final minutes of the other fight.

"Go ahead and net him, Carl," said Jose, offering Carl the honor of bringing the trophy in, letting the sea captain scoop him up from the salty brine. Carl leaned over and as Ralph turned the big snook's head one last time, he engulfed the twenty pound fish in the net. With a smooth, unbroken motion he hoisted the huge snook up and onto the deck of the pier. The fish started thrashing madly about, working his way out of the net. He was gut hooked. Because of the long battle and the deep penetration of the hook, blood was coming out through his gills and mouth with every twist of its body.

Ralph put down his rod and quickly picked up a small lead-filled billy club. Without hesitation, he raised that heavy club and starting bashing it against the skull of the snook. You could hear the delicate bones crunching and shattering with each repeated blow. Thick red blood was pouring out of the fish's gills and from the deep depressions in the top of his head. The big fish stopped flopping and started quivering. It was now vibrating, shuddering, as the last few sparks of energy left its damaged body. In a minute's time, the snook was dead.

Richard felt sick. A little while ago, he had delighted in watching a school of these graceful animals suspended in the current, bending and flowing like sea oats in the winds of fall. And now this. This was disgusting. The cruel bludgeoning of this fish right in front of him. He was amazed that Ralph could be so vicious. He was shocked at how Ralph had slammed that club into this wild creature, now lifeless and still on the wooden planks of the pier.

Richard had always struggled with violence, bloodshed and death. These last few minutes on the pier had taken him by surprise. It wasn't fishing. It was murder.

Carl saw the look in Richard's eye. He knew what he was thinking. Carl had seen that look before. Ralph almost always clubbed his fish to death. Carl had seen that same look on unsuspecting tourists, other anglers and most often, on the faces of children. Carl didn't like the way Ralph and Jose handled their catch, but it was none of his business. Unlike most of the fishermen on the pier, they preferred to kill their catch and ice it down at once. Other anglers left them dangling for hours on long, nylon stringers.

People abhorred the cruelty Ralph showed. But it wasn't cruel, thought Carl. He knew that Ralph's club was merciful. Was it better to keep these beautiful creatures on a stringer all afternoon? Wasn't that like putting them on death row? Everything that was brought up to the deck of the pier and not released by the anglers was eventually going to die. Why not kill it quickly?

As Carl and Richard made their way back to their station Carl turned to Richard. "It bothered you, the way Ralph clubbed that snook just now, didn't it?"

"Yes. It bothered me. I've always had a hard time with bloodshed. I guess I never thought that fishing could be so violent and bloody. I'm glad my snook got away," said Richard.

"I understand. It's worse when Ralph catches them in the afternoon, when the pier is full of children. They don't like it either. Clubbing them like Ralph does, it's not all that bad for the fish. They die quickly and they are thrown into the ice chest dead. It's better than throwing them in the cooler alive. Then you have to listen to them thrash and twist about until their hearts give out. There is a kind of luxury in dying quickly. It's like having a switch flipped off on you rather than having the light slowly dimmed. I think there's an element of dignity to it."

"I'm not used to seeing any violence. In my profession I deal with a lot of anger, but by the time the divorce is under way the violence is usually over. I see medical shots of bruises and black eyes from abused spouses, but it's far removed from the act itself. It's just 'evidence' by the time I see it; 'Exhibit A' 'Exhibit B.' You know what I mean."

"What happens here on the pier is nothing when compared with what happens out there in the ocean," said Carl. "Look out there, Richard. Tell me, what do you see?"

Richard paused and looked around him. He looked over San Carlos Bay to the north. In the distance he could see the causeway. Between the pier and the causeway he saw the immense flow of water coming into the bay, with the eddies and tide lines weaving through the surge of seawater. He saw a flock of seagulls and pelicans diving. They were working over a school of baitfish that kept rippling across the surface of the water like a rain shower in the wind.

To the east he saw two small fishing boats running toward the open waters of the gulf. They were about a mile away, and although you could see them move, they moved silently. The rush of the wind was riding over the sound of their small outboard engines.

Looking toward the south and the gulf, Richard saw a shrimp trawler coming in. The boat was close enough to the pier so that he could hear the deep, guttural noise of its single diesel engine as it lumbered toward Ft. Myers Beach, its hold filled with pink gulf shrimp, iced and ready for market. Beyond the shrimp boat all he could see was open water. In Richard's mind he knew that this view ended at the condominiums and luxury hotels of Naples. From the pier he couldn't see those buildings. He was too low. From this vantage point all Richard saw was miles and miles of unbroken water. Near the horizon line, the blue of the water appeared to merge with the blue of the autumnal sky. They became one, ocean sky and sky ocean. Perhaps they had always been one.

"It's beautiful, isn't it?" added Carl in his deep, melodic voice.

"Yes, it is beautiful. What's this about, Carl?" inquired Richard.

He felt like their conversation had suddenly become so different, so philosophical. It was another layer of conversation altogether. A place he and Carl had never gone before.

"Because the ocean isn't what you think it is, Richard. Like all things, it is much, much more than the story told upon its surface. Every hour, every minute, the struggle for life goes on out there. Just beneath the thin blue skin of its surface, everything survives, and kills to survive, just as we do. The snook attack the schools of pilchards from below just as the pelicans and terns dive on them from above. The snook in turn are eaten by the bottlenose dolphin and the far quicker blacktip and bull sharks.

"The ocean is a watery graveyard of the living and the dying, just like the ground we walk upon. Even the beaches of Sanibel, littered with the remains of a million empty shells, remind me of the great circle of life. Those shells were all alive once. Predators, storms, and time itself took that life away from them. Now only their empty cases remain. As much as the beaches of Sanibel are every shell collector's dream, they are equally a graveyard."

Carl went on, "I've seen sights on that ocean that are impossible to describe. Mornings on the Gulf Stream with hungry schools of dolphin pushing schools of flying fish up by the thousands. Amidst the chop of that powerful current it is as if the waves themselves become alive, giving birth to the deep blue bodies and silver wings of a thousand flying fish. The brilliant gold-and-blue flash of the bull dolphin grey hounding out of the sea after their prey. While from above, a flock of frigates dive and take their portion of the feast.

"I've seen a single hammerhead shark attack a hooked tarpon not three miles off the beaches of Sanibel. Within minutes the light green color of the water was dyed a dark, blood red. The exhausted tarpon was taken in two bites. On the first bite, the seventeen-foot shark took the tail half off of the hundred-pound fish. The tarpon, exhausted from the long battle with my charter, was helpless. It was just too tired to flee. The hammerhead turned its head sideways, grabbed the back half of the fish, and shook it violently. It was still hooked to my angler's line, not twenty feet from my boat.

"As the front half of the tarpon slowly sank toward the bottom, the hammerhead circled back and devoured the upper portion in the second bite. The shark's razor sharp teeth sliced through the 125-pound monofilament leader like butter. My angler stood there in disbelief.

"The ocean is like that, prey and predator. Life and death. A drama that continues forever just below that endless plane of the surface. We see so little of it. We think we know what happens in that world, but we don't."

Richard was quiet. They both quietly cast their lines out and got back to fishing. Richard went back over to the cooler and got out a Coke for Carl and himself. The two of them leaned silently against the railing and stared toward the causeway.

Richard was mesmerized by the depth of Carl's voice, by the tales Carl shared with him. He was being let into Carl's private world, a place of quiet thoughts and a perspective far more complex than Richard would have imagined from this weathered old man. He glanced back over at Carl, his pale blue eyes sparking in the sun, a peaceful expression on his face, like an old monk.

Richard found himself transfixed by it all, by the metaphors that reached beyond the surface. Carl too was enjoying these moments with his new fishing buddy. It had been a long time since Carl had been able to say these things out loud. He used to talk about his thoughts with Marie, but Marie was gone. Carl never spoke like this to the pier gang. They were preoccupied with Gators football games and

Budweiser. Carl needed to talk as much as Richard needed to listen.

It was like one of those conversations people have when they sit beside a stranger on an airplane. They never bother introducing themselves, but in no time at all they find themselves telling a perfect stranger confidences that they wouldn't tell their best friend. For Carl it was an exorcism of sorts, an outpouring of all the sadness and silent reflections that had been within him since the death of his wife. He didn't want to stop talking about it. He wanted to explain the rhythm of it all, the closure of the circle. He felt compelled to continue.

Richard, on the other hand, wanted to do nothing more than listen. In his world of private investigators, depositions and lies, it was a welcome relief to hear this old man talk about truth. Truth, acknowledged Richard, just didn't belong in a divorce court. Richard, suddenly finding an unexpected moment of truth on this tiny fishing pier at the eastern end of Sanibel, wanted to immerse himself in it. He wanted the conversations to last until the sun perished. Only now did he realize how much he missed it.

"All of us face death," added Carl between sips of his Coke. "As distant and immune from mortality as we might think we are, all of us are tied into the rhythm of these tides. The long and inexplicable pulse of life and death. We do what we can to explain it, to deal with it, to protect ourselves from it, but it is always present. It moves through us like the wind across the skin of the sea. We know so little and expect so much. Yet, from the moment we are born, somewhere deep within us, there is the intuitive knowledge of our own passing. I believe that from that knowledge, and the mystery beyond it, all of human spirituality springs forth.

"That it is the mystery of life and death that remains the foundation of our centuries of temples, churches and cathedrals. Yet death is as natural as this ocean and all the living things within it. That from the end of life, more life springs forth. Forever. It is a story that has no ending, and maybe never had a beginning either. So much lies hidden beneath the surface of it all. More than we will ever know."

Richard did not reply. There was nothing to say.

Their conversation soon faded. Richard and Carl shared a candy bar Richard had brought with him and Richard told Carl that he would be back the following morning to try his luck again. They had a few more runs that morning but they were just little fish: two undersized mangrove snappers and a small sheepshead.

Tomorrow would be another day.

Two

Richard returned home that afternoon to more of the same. With a fading breeze shifting to the west and a warm, autumn sun sprawled across the sand like a permanent lawn chair, he found his boys inside the air conditioned condominium watching TV. Watching TV!!! They might as well have been vacationing in Chicago, thought a frustrated father. As long as they have cable, what difference does it make?

All you need is fifty-seven channels of the same preprogrammed bullshit. With the television on, like an electronic IV drip of pure morphine, they were fine. Give them endless commercials of a new mint fresh flavor and they became zombies. Sitting there, absorbing the ultraviolet glow of the cathode ray like bipedal tubers. After listening to Carl all morning talking about the marvels of the human spirit and the mysteries of the sea, Richard was not in the mood to join the zombie brigade.

"Let's go for a walk!" Announced Richard.

Helen overheard him from the kitchen, where she was preparing some microwave popcorn for the boys. She was in shock. For years she could not remember a time when he actually asked his boys to do anything other than those minimal functions necessary to appear to be a perfectly good father. Take them to basketball practice, birthday parties and an occasional pizza. But never in that decade could she recall him asking them to do something spontaneous with him.

"You aren't serious, are you, Richard?" She noted that the boys, unfamiliar with his new found sense of purpose, had ignored their father.

"Yes, I'm serious. And why don't you join us?"

Now Helen was aghast! Join Richard and the boys for a walk? Where to? Why? The idea was so unique to the framework of their relationship that Helen didn't have a response.

She mentally sifted through her marriage's standard operating procedure manual. Without finding anything in that worn booklet to help her decide what to do in a case like this, she said, "Sure, why not." She said it as if she were in a trance.

The boys, Tyler and James, failed to acknowledge any of this. They were growing roots into the couch and deep pile carpeting in an insidious attempt at human horticulture. They were watching reruns of Mr. Ed, or Star Trek, or The Simpsons. It didn't matter. They were watching television.

Richard, knowing that asking the boys to turn off the TV would prove as useless as asking them to fly, walked over and simply pulled the plug on the set. To his surprise there wasn't an immediate reaction. There was just a long, pregnant pause. They both remained in their respective Orlon soil and continued watching a blank screen. To them, it was like a slow-motion accident. They saw their father reach down and grab the cord, watching him pull on it until it was severed from its electric lifeline, and they noticed the screen go dark. They were both in shock from the impact. The television was the only one that had been killed.

"What did you do that for?" said James in an angry tone of voice.

"I did it because it's an unbelievably beautiful day out there and we didn't fly down here over a thousand miles for you two to lie around all day watching TV! You can do that at home. Now, right here and now, we're going for a walk." Richard had found a passion stirring inside of him. He didn't have a clue as to its origin or its destination, but he could feel it. The feeling pleased him immensely.

"I don't want to go," said Tyler, who was the older of the two and usually the first to start the rebellion.

"You're going," replied Richard emphatically.

The boys knew that it was going to be a difficult battle to win. They were smart enough to sense when it was best to dig trenches and when it was best to retreat. They looked at each other and saw only cowardice.

"OK," said Tyler with the tone of a vanquished warrior. "Where are we going to walk to?"

Richard had to pause a minute to think about that. In better than ten years he had never asked his family to go for a walk without having a destination prearranged prior to heading through the door. That is how his entire life was - organized. Spontaneity was no longer in his lifestyle's portfolio. What he said next baffled him as much as it did Helen, Tyler and James.

"Anywhere but here!"

With that, they all walked through the door of that condominium together. They were excited and afraid. They had never done such a brave and wonderful thing before in their well-rehearsed lives. They were taking a walk to nowhere.

They were taking a walk to everywhere.

Three

Carl stayed at the pier until after sunset. He didn't have anything to do except read the morning paper when he finally made it back home. By that time the morning's news was already twelve hours old. Carl pulled up the driveway and went through the same well-rehearsed ritual he had performed two hundred times before over the past year. He unloaded his fishing gear from the station wagon, knowing that in this neighborhood there was never any need to do so. "Why tempt fate," he mumbled to himself again as he walked back and forth to the overstuffed garage with his tackle box.

Once inside he opened the morning paper. Sometimes he would bring it in before he left for the pier, but this morning the delivery boy had been running late. It was still lying there in the driveway. In that thin plastic wrapper, the Florida sun had baked the white out of it, and as he unfolded the front page, the half that had been facing the sun looked prematurely yellowed and old. It looked like one of those newspapers people save for some reason: noting a national tragedy, a feature on a friend, or an obituary on page twenty seven. It looked as though it had been stored in someone's attic for a decade.

Carl folded the paper back up and carried it into the house with him. He knew it was more of the same. Political scandals, murders, distant wars fought over confusing issues and the opinion page.

Carl loved the opinion page. Opinions are like assholes, he used to say - everyone has one. Once, long ago, Carl was very opinionated. That was the reason he loved to read the letters to the editor. He enjoyed the maundering of the pundits who contributed their opinions to the editorial page. He was amused by it all, and he found a certain amount of truth in every perspective. They were all sort of right, and all sort of wrong, he would think to himself while he reflected on the various topics they would elucidate and expound upon.

Carl chuckled quietly to himself while reading them over and waiting for the microwave to finish his TV dinner. Salisbury steak, his favorite. It was odd that Carl never brought home or ate fish any longer. He used to love fish when Marie would fix it for him. Not any longer. He released all of his fish now. He had done so since the day Marie had been released. It made sense. He felt good about letting all those fish swim free.

Over the years, the ocean had been good to him. He had made his livelihood upon the sea and he felt a kinship to it that only a fishing guide or a man who has made his living upon the sea can fully understand. The sea had given Carl and his charters a thousand coolers filled with delicious fish over the years. Carl felt that his life upon it, and the fishes he had taken out of it, were his gifts from the sea. Now it was time for him to catch and release those same fish. To give them back. It was his way of saying thank you.

After finishing dinner he sat back in his favorite recliner. The old recliner had come to cling to the slumping contours of his body like a well-tailored suit. He flipped on the television for a few minutes. He never enjoyed reading the news in the newspaper but he liked to watch the news on TV. A picture can tell a thousand stories, he thought, and television news was a thousand pictures. As much as he loved to watch the news on TV, he despised TV editorials. He found them painful to listen to. They always came off so preachy, so "holier-than-thou- ish." People were welcome to write down their opinions, but never to voice them on the television set. It made perfect sense to Carl.

After watching the news on CNN for another half an hour, Carl turned the set off. He walked over to the refrigerator and poured himself a glass of white zinfandel. Turning off all but the kitchen night light, Carl came back and collapsed into his easy chair, like a tired, old lion. He sat there quietly for a few minutes listening to the night wind in the trees and the quiet rhythm of his own breathing. He was at home with himself. He started talking, in a gentle, whispering voice, to Marie.

Whenever he felt this at ease, when the sky was safely dark, and Carl knew that no one but Marie would hear him, he would talk to her like this. Sometimes for hours. He would tell her about what he caught at the pier that day. He would tell her that he was still having some pains in his left shoulder, or that he had just met a heavy-set divorce attorney from Peoria. He would just talk to her about anything that came to mind.

Carl told Marie that he had just heard from their daughter again. That she still wished he would come to stay with her and Rudy up in Atlanta. He told Marie, just as he had told his daughter, that he could never leave the ocean. That he did not belong inland anymore, away from the song of the surf and the sweet, elusive scents of the sea.

He spoke with her like this, in this quiet, saddened whisper, for over an hour, pausing on occasion as if waiting for her reply. Marie didn't reply. In his heart he could still hear her voice. The voice was not the tired, strained voice that befell her as the cancer wore through her, but the voice of his young, beautiful wife. Energetic, crisp, and alive.

Carl was tired. He walked slowly over to the bedroom and got ready for bed. There was a photo of Marie that he seldom looked at next to his bed. Tonight, because of the strange, sad state he was in, he looked at it for the longest time. It was as if he looked through the photo itself and into her very soul.

Death had not, could not take that part of Marie away from him. The depth and beauty of their love for each other did not belong to this temporal place we live and die in, this hurried moment in time. These creatures that we are, thought Carl, these physical bodies filled with pleasure and pain, are only an illusion. Our souls are all that matter in the end, and our souls are like the sea itself, liquid and endless. These thoughts comforted him. They made his loneliness less pressing, less of a cross to bear.

He remembered the words she had said to him, just before her passing. "We only lose our fear of dying when death finally takes it from us. Then we are no longer afraid."

Marie was not afraid in the end. She knew that it was her time and that she had lived a good life. She knew that her children were happy and that her husband loved her. Finally, she surrendered to the pain. God, he missed her so.

Carl checked to see if the alarm was set at 5:30 a.m. No one had changed it. No one ever would. Carl quickly fell asleep, dreaming of Marie.

The Third Morning

One

Carl began his story as the morning sun climbed toward the height of noon. They both moved slowly, as if in harmony to a deeper score.

"Irene started going mad. She took up religion. It wasn't religion in the traditional sense. It was a personal Lord that she had found. She didn't go to any of the island churches or involve herself with any religious organizations. Irene read her Bible and screamed at Art for his lack of faith. You could tell by the look in her eyes that it wasn't Jesus who was working within her. It was madness.

"From that point on, which must have been about six or seven years ago, their marriage started falling apart. Irene became a fanatic. She would go for long walks in the early morning, carrying that small black Bible in her hand, mumbling sections of memorized scripture. She looked lost and disheveled. Art, her husband, avoided her. He would spend all of his time in the small office underneath the house selling the last half dozen vacant lots they still owned in the development.

"The two older boys were away at college. The only one still at home was their daughter, Kathy. Kathy was still in high school. She wasn't handling her mother's madness well. A thin, attractive young lady through junior high, Kathy started compulsively overeating. She gained a ton of weight over the next few years. She became shy and reclusive, as overweight young girls often do. Irene didn't take any notice, her insanity being more than enough to occupy her time.

"Then came the sickness. Diabetes. Irene felt that she developed the disease because the Lord was punishing her for her decades of faithlessness. Art didn't know what to do. Kathy put on another twenty-five pounds. Irene's condition deteriorated rapidly. The insulin injections couldn't keep up with her failing health. Less than two years after being diagnosed with diabetes, Irene collapsed one summer afternoon and died a week later. They found out later that she had stopped taking her insulin. Needles were instruments of the devil, she had secretly confided to her daughter. The four remaining family members came together for the last time as family and they buried Irene just off island.

"Art went back to selling the remaining parcels and leasing out the occasional vacancies in his small shopping center. He didn't miss Irene much. She had come to think of him as evil. She was always preaching to Art about the second coming, telling him that his soul would burn in hell if he didn't straighten out and follow the Lord. Art never understood Irene's madness, or the reason for it. Art was a church-going man and always had been. Apart from being an ornery old cracker at times, he was a good person."

Carl took a sip of Coke and continued.

"A little over a year after Irene's funeral, Art started going out with Vanessa. Vanessa was a bank teller at the small island bank where Art kept his commercial accounts. Art had befriended her over the decades of depositing his rent checks and making loan payments. Nobody thought anything of it when they started seeing each other. There were a few comments about Vanessa being twenty years younger than Art, but no one took it to heart.

"Vanessa was a really pretty gal, a 'looker' you might say. She had long blond hair that hung straight down and ended just above her waist. She had a slender face with blue-green eyes. Back up in Iowa she would have what I would call 'Scandinavian' good looks. Although she was in her late forties, she still had an attractive figure and a charming personality. What she ever saw in old Art Nestor was a mystery to the rest of us.

"It wasn't until they announced their engagement some time later that the trouble started. Art's two boys, Art Jr. and David, were very upset with the news. Kathy liked Vanessa, so she didn't see any harm in the marriage. Art was happy. He had not really been with a woman in years. Irene's religious fanaticism and the illness that followed had convinced him that he was never going to find someone to love again.

"He never understood why Irene had gone crazy in the first place. Maybe it was the pressure of the move to the island. Maybe it was when her boys went off to college. Irene was always so attached to those boys. No one really knew.

"Vanessa was completely different from Irene. She went to the same church as Art. She loved to go for long bike rides, go out to dinner, and enjoy life. She wasn't crazy at all. She had been married once before, but that was long, long ago. She had never had any children.

"Through years of living alone, and managing her modest income at the bank carefully, she had purchased a few rental properties on Sanibel. Now, with the rental income and her promotions at the bank, Vanessa was doing quite well for herself. Art knew that her skills as a landlady could come in handy for leasing out the rare vacancy at the shopping center. Art never liked that part of the family business. He was just too darn cantankerous.

"They got married about a year after they started dating. To everyone's surprise, Art's two boys refused to come to the wedding. Kathy was the maid of honor.

" 'Vanessa's just after your money, dad,' said his son David.

" 'Can't you see that she's only a gold-digger? She's way too young for you. All she wants is for you to die soon so she can take over the shopping center and take our inheritance,' added Art Jr.

"Art was disgusted by their comments. Vanessa had quite a bit of her own money and some nice real estate to boot. She wasn't the type who would go in for what his two sons were now accusing her of. Maybe he and Irene had spoiled those two boys. He and Irene had always given in to their every wish. During their whole life growing up in Atlanta, then down here on Sanibel, they had the best of everything.

"When the final subdivision was approved by Lee County, back in the late '60s, they had sixty vacant lots to sell. With the money coming in, Art and Irene felt that they owed it to their children to give them whatever they wanted.

"They had a lovely house located a block from the beach. They put in a big pool, a huge playroom under their piling home, and much more. When they finally made it into high school and started driving, Art bought them each a brand new Chevy when they turned sixteen. Maybe it was too much, Art used to say. They had become nothing more than ungrateful brats!

"Their decision to not come to the wedding was unforgivable to old man Nestor. After the honeymoon cruise, Art came back and removed the two boys from his will. He disowned them.

"That's when the shit started flying. Art Jr. and David convinced their sister Kathy to join them in a lawsuit against their father. Kathy was reluctant to do it. After being pressured relentlessly by her two older brothers, she conceded to join them as a co-plaintiff.

"It was a difficult decision for Kathy. She liked Vanessa. She liked having a normal woman around the house. She had started to lose that extra weight and find some happiness in her life. She finished high school and took a part time job at a local boutique until deciding which college to attend. She didn't see Vanessa as money hungry at all."

Carl took another sip of Coke. In the distance, a flock of seagulls was bombarding a school of glass minnows. You could hear the gulls' screams in the distance. They inadvertently formed the ideal background to Carl's story. He continued.

"Her brothers kept calling Kathy and reminding her of the age difference between them. It was the fact that her two brothers were now cut out of the will that convinced Kathy to join them in the suit. They filed a motion to have the will overturned due to their father's mental incompetence. That and the undue influence of a third party, Vanessa. Art went ballistic. The little bastards. Art dropped Kathy from the will the next day. Vanessa was stunned. She was caught completely off guard by the antics of her new husband's family.

"Wanting to further simplify his lifestyle and spend more time traveling, Art decided to sell the shopping center. To the children, it was just more evidence of Vanessa's determination to liquidate the family's assets. When the center went under contract, the children filed an injunction to stop the sale, saying that their father was under undue influence and was not mentally stable enough to conduct the sale.

"Their father countersued. The lawyers involved were having a field day. They needed wheelbarrows to carry all the money they were making to the bank. Legal fees were collected from both sides of the family. The usual melee followed; court hearings, expert witnesses, psychologists, psychiatrists, doctors, detectives - they were all called in for this horrible, drawn out battle.

"The three kids banded together and spent every dime they had fighting for their inheritance. It was pathetic. Accusations of a prior relationship, of adultery with Vanessa long before Irene's death, started churning in the gossip mills of this small island. Everyone was fascinated and appalled by the rumors. None of them were true. At that point truth had nothing to do with it. It was the money talking. Money never sees eye to eye with truth.

"The legal battle began taking its toll on Art. He was seventy one when he married Vanessa and Art had been a heavy smoker all his life. Now, with his three children at him like a pack of wild dogs, and Vanessa sleepless and haggard over this legal nightmare she had never intended to create, Art's health started to fail. Two years after the wedding, Art passed away from pneumonia in Vanessa's condominium.

"The children were certain that their father had been murdered. They demanded an official investigation. There was one. Art had died of pneumonia. It turned out that Vanessa was a former registered nurse back up in Ohio. The investigation revealed that Art had received better care in the loving hands of Vanessa than he would have in any hospital.

"The two boys and Kathy ignored the coroner's report. Vanessa had murdered their father, had them all disinherited, and was now about to grab all of the money from the estate. With their father dead, they turned the lawyers on Vanessa.

Vanessa was lost. Every possible legal maneuver was made by the children to keep her from selling the properties. They froze the bank accounts and leasing incomes that rightfully belonged to her. They made her life miserable.

"To survive, Vanessa hired the best attorneys in town to act with counter suits against the children. She said that it was the hounding of their father, and not her, that caused his ill health and untimely death.

"This went on for six months. Vanessa, with her pretty smile and quiet, bank-teller demeanor, couldn't keep it up. One night in November, she took a bottle of painkillers left over from Art's sickness, ate them slowly one by one, laid down on the same bed where Art had passed away and went to sleep. She never woke up.

"In the end, the three kids got the money. They got the shopping center, the rents, the two vacant lots, and all the bank accounts. All it cost them was the love of their father and the life of a woman that loved him.

"You can call Sanibel Island 'paradise' if you want to, Richard, but it's not. It's just an island in the sun. People live here, die here, suffer here and find happiness here, just like they do in Peoria, or Savannah, or Kathmandu, for that matter. Don't be fooled by the palm trees any. They're just the tallest members of the grass family, and they don't mean nothing by it. You can be just as happy under a willow or an oak, or an evergreen for that matter."

Richard stood there, with his fishing rod in hand, trying to think of something to say. It was a tragic tale. Money. In his practice he had heard a thousand stories just like this one, but it was business. It was part of his job. Standing on this fishing pier with the slow, deep voice of this retired fishing guide resounding against the sound of the freshening wind out of the northeast gave this tale a different impact. Richard was open and exposed. He was standing naked in that breeze, ready to experience anew all the sad truths of the world.

He stood silent. He reached into his shirt pocket and took a cigarette out of his pack of Camels. It was difficult to light. There were questions he wanted to ask Carl, but he didn't have the nerve to ask them. The wind had more to tell him.

Tuesday morning had arrived windy. The breezes from the morning before kicked up and the big, white teeth of a wind-driven ocean were grinning angrily when Carl and Richard walked onto the pier. Although it was windy, it was clear. The combination of the warm sun and the steady breeze made it feel hot, like a convection oven.

On days like this, Carl loved being on the pier instead of being on his boat. The wind was kicking at fifteen to twenty knots and the sea was fast and choppy. On Carl's boat, this made for a rough, wet boat ride. He could remember working on days like this. Coming home to Marie after fishing a full charter in choppy seas, with his legs and lower back aching. His shoulders sore from working the wheel, constantly navigating to keep his boat on course.

None of that mattered on the pier. The wind could howl across the churned-up texture of the sea and the pier did not bob or weave. The waves never buried the bow, drenching everyone on board. The roll and pitch of the boat never knocked customers down, slamming them to the deck with their knees skinned and their patience worn beyond the point of repair. The pier remained steady and true. As reliable as the tides that poured back and forth between the bay and the Gulf. Constant, like those long, sensual sighs of the ocean.

Earlier that morning, Carl was the first to arrive at the old fishing pier and it surprised him. He wondered what could be up with Ralph or Jose. Didn't they want to fish the pier in this much wind? No, that wouldn't bother them. Carl recalled them fishing on windier days. While he was still wondering what might have happened to them, Carl went about the business of getting everything set up.

Within minutes, Chip arrived. Carl liked Chip. Chip was simply Chip, and Carl felt that seeing him show up this morning was a good sign.

"Hey, good morning, Carl! We going to catch the big kahuna today? The monster snookerfish?"

"Sure 'nuff, Chip," replied Carl whimsically.

Chip was a character. Carl remembered that Chip always had Tuesdays off. He worked a construction job through the weekends and had every Monday and Tuesday off. Tuesdays, Chip spent fishing. But for some reason, Carl remembered, Chip wasn't at the pier last week.

"Where were you last week, Chip? We missed you down here," said Carl.

"I took my boy up to Orlando for the day. He had some sort of teachers conference day off, so we all drove up to spend the day at one of those stupid theme parks. Man, I hate that plastic Disneyland shit. You know how it is - Carl, my boy loves it up there. It's only fair to give him a chance to enjoy what he likes now and again. We had a good time though, even if I don't much care for it. Were the fish hitting last week?"

"Not too bad, but no really big ones like the kind you like to catch."

"How'd ya'll do yesterday Carl, any big-uns?"

"Yeah, there were some big runs around mid-morning. Ralph and Jose nailed one over twenty pounds. This tourist I've been fishing with the last couple of mornings, Richard, he lost a real beauty when it wrapped around the pilings."

"Sure 'nuff had that happen before," said Chip while he set up his two rods and baited them up for big snook.

Chip was a meat fisherman. He fished 80 lb. test line on big, offshore boat rods. He often used a 6/0 triple-strength hook with a four-ounce egg sinker. To prevent those piling cutoffs common to pier fishing, he resorted to 125 lb. test leader. There was no drag on either of his reels and both of his rods were as stiff as broomsticks. When a big snook took one of his baits it was a straight up and down battle. A tug of war. A long run might take out two, maybe three feet of line. The entire fight might not last more than a minute.

Chip fished down and dirty for big linesiders. He probably had landed more snook over 40 inches long than any other members of the pier gang. It wasn't a pretty way to fish, but it was damned effective. Carl thought that Chip's fishing techniques bordered on the illegal. He liked Chip's attitude so much that he overlooked his angling shortcomings. Chip was always in a fantastic mood. Chip was the kind of person everyone wants to have fishing with them. The kind of person you talk to a couple of minutes and remember having met someplace before. Instant familiarity, that was him.

Chip looked the part of a Florida construction worker. He had a dark tan and a scruffy, unshaven face that was always on the verge of becoming a beard. It was as if his razor had about an eighth of an inch of lift to it. The best shave he could manage left his wide face with a dark brown stubble. His clothes were a pair of cheap shorts and dirty, construction-style T-shirts. The kind with the sleeves cut off and the collar ripped. His T-shirt was always covered in smudges of various stains and adhesives. He wore old cheap sneakers with no socks. He never wore a cap, nor did Carl ever remember seeing him put on any suntan lotion.

Although Chip was clearly a member of the skins, he seldom,

if ever, took off his dirty T-shirt. He had thick, dark eyebrows and short curly hair. He spoke with a well-defined Florida accent. Chip was a cracker, a good old boy. Like all Florida crackers, he had a heart as big as the peninsula and a smile the length of the Panhandle.

Ten minutes after Chip arrived, Richard finally waddled up the boardwalk that wrapped like a long wooden snake between the parking lot and the pier. You could hear the heavy footsteps of Richard approaching before he came into view. Even in the steady wind, Carl thought he could hear his labored breathing. Between the weight and the smoking, it was a chore for Richard to manage even a little walk. After the long walk the family took yesterday afternoon, Richard was exceptionally winded.

"Hi, Carl!" Richard said as he approached. "Windy day today, isn't it?"

"Quite a breeze up, that's fer sure Richard. It's hard to say what it'll do to the fishing. Sometimes those big old reds bite like crazy on windy days, but sometimes all you ever seem to catch are those damn catfish."

"How long have you been here Carl? Is there any bait in the bucket?"

"I've been here about twenty minutes now. Help yourself to some bait - there's a ton of fresh whitebaits in my livewell. I got them all on my first cast. There's plenty around."

They started fishing. Like the morning before, the tide was still coming in. In another few days, the direction would reverse itself. Every day, the tides on Sanibel run about 45 minutes behind the previous morning. Because of the delay, within a week's time the tides reverse. The incoming becomes the outgoing. Fishing for the large snook was fair on these long, incoming tides but it was better on the outgoing. By Friday morning the tides would flip. Carl, Chip and the rest of the regulars knew it.

Richard had no idea which tide was the best, or which was worst for catching fish at the pier. It didn't matter to him. Richard realized as he got up that Tuesday morning that he wasn't coming down to the pier to fish. He was coming down to the pier to spend time talking and listening to Carl. He liked these conversations with the old man. They were stirring something within him. He didn't know what it was, but he longed for it.

When he came home from the pier yesterday, he went for the longest walk in his life with his family. Despite all the complaining at first from the boys, they soon found themselves inexplicably happy. These feelings of happiness were foreign to Richard's family. Happiness felt odd to them, like shoes that didn't fit.

Richard and Carl set out their four rods. All of the lines were quickly drawn tight by the rushing current. The tides were stronger than the morning before, in part because of the following seas. The pressure of the wind was helping to drive the tides in. Because of that fact, Carl knew it was going to be an exceptionally high tide later that afternoon. The back bay would fill with seawater brought in by the quickly rising tide.

The redfish would follow the rising water, coming in from the beaches by the thousands to feed. Carl knew it would be a great day for fishing, and he was looking forward to some runs.

"Boy, is it windy today, Carl," said Richard. He was trying to get Carl started.

"Yup," answered Carl, not feeling quite awake enough to talk much. A couple more members of the pier gang showed up; Jose, and Becky along with her skinny husband, Paul. Jose headed over to his favorite corner at the end of the T-dock. Becky and Paul went to the south side of the T, opposite Jose. Paul never fished. He just stood around and chain smoked. They both lived on Sanibel. They had lived on Sanibel for so long that no one could tell you which came first, the island or Paul and Becky.

Paul should have died from lung disease before the causeway was built back in '62. He was one of those thin fragments of a person who are immune to the dangers of excessive tobacco smoking. He smoked three packs a day. Just like Richard, he preferred Camels. He looked like death warmed over. The sides of his cheeks had collapsed, like the face of a WWII death camp survivor. His hair was gone for the most part, and his eyes, his eyes were deep and sunken. Nobody knew the color of his eyes. They were hidden beneath a chronic squint. Paul didn't weigh a hundred and twenty-five pounds. He talked even less than he fished, and he never fished.

"Hi, Carl," Paul said as he walked by. He was carrying Becky's enormous tackle box. Becky fished. She fished for one kind of fish, and one fish only: gag grouper. The locals called them "blacks." To catch them, Becky used techniques different from anyone else on the pier. She used a single, nine-foot rod with a big spinning reel on it. With this oversized combination and a five-ounce sinker on the end of her line, she could toss her favorite baits, pinfish and grunts, fifty yards out into the deep, rocky hole just off the far end of pier. Those rocks held grouper.

This morning was to be no exception. She was rigging up to catch some grouper, which appear in gathering numbers every fall. Paul stood there, next to his hefty wife, Becky, chain smoking in the howling wind. He kept watching the water stream under the pier in its never ending ritual.

Soon after their arrival, the tourists began filtering onto the pier. Fishing tourists, with their three-day permits and their rods and reels rented from the Bait Box. Off-island tourists, with the K-Mart price tags still dangling from their rod tips like Minnie Pearl's new hat. They were the pier gang's primary source of entertainment through the day. Reeling everything upside down and backwards. Rigging everything with 100-pound leader, and ten ounces of lead. Their casts hitting the water with so many sinkers on the line that it was as if they were throwing bathtubs off the pier. Ready to conquer ten-foot sharks. Always catching catfish.

The real fun began when a tourist accidently did get a strike. Instant panic. Their voices would rise with shouts of joy and they would turn to anyone nearby saying "I got one, I got one," as if it was the last thing they had ever expected to happen. Then, as the battle continued, and the fish pulled and tugged to be free, the helpless tourist would do something wrong. He would either jerk on the rod repeatedly until the thin monofilament line parted, or try to hoist the fish out of the water, thereby allowing it to easily shake the hook. Sometimes he would leave the drag set so lightly that all the line would quickly vanish off the spool. Whatever the combination of errors, the fish got away.

The tourists who fished the pier, most of them from the United States, some from Canada, and many from Germany and England, had perfected the art of losing fish. The pier gang members, when a nice red or snook was on the line, would try to help out, but to no avail. The tourists were always too swept up in the fight to pay any attention to the well-meaning directions coming from Chip or Jose. One out of ten tourists fishing on a given day took home fish. The others, just as content as those who actually did catch fish, took home memories. The memories were larger, and you never had to clean them.

Just then a run of redfish swept under the pier. The school was on its way into San Carlos Bay with the rising water of the flood tide. Rods started to bend like the tops of the tall pines were bending in the wind. Chip hooked up, two tourists hooked up, Jose hooked up, and three of the four rods Carl and Richard had out had fish on them. The long, uneventful hour that had gone by was followed by a flurry of screaming drags and excited anglers. It was pandemonium!

Richard didn't know what to do. He rarely had to deal with catching one fish at a time and now he was standing there with two rods bent over at once, both rods whipping back and forth under the strain of two powerful redfish. What do I do?

Carl, on the other hand, quickly grabbed his rod and gave it a swift, decisive jerk. It imbedded the hook deep into the redfish's mouth.

"Which one do I grab Carl?"

"Both of them," replied Carl, laughing aloud as he said it.

Richard did it. He grabbed both rods and pulled back quickly, trying to set both hooks with the same motion. The rod in his left hand suddenly went slack. The hook had pulled. The redfish was free. The rod in his right hand was still bouncing wildly. Richard immediately set the other rod down to concentrate on landing his first redfish.

Carl was laughing to himself. The picture of this overweight attorney from Peoria holding up two rods, and trying to set the hook on both of them was comical. Carl knew that had Richard been able to set the hook on both fish, he would have lost both of them. It would have been entertaining to watch. Carl was secretly disappointed that the hook had pulled on the one rod.

It was a lucky break for Richard. At least he had a chance of landing one of them. Still, it would have been a hoot, thought Carl quietly to himself.

By this time, some of the redfish that had struck the other

lines at the end of the pier were being pulled up and over the railing. Jose's long-handled net was working hard. They were magnificent looking fish. Each redfish was painted in a palette of bronze, copper and gold. Several were thrashing and flopping about the deck of the pier in a vain attempt at freedom. They had big, strong heads and powerful shoulders, followed by a long, bronze-colored body. Each fish had a pale, white underbelly and a single, large black spot on the end of its tail. Their arrival on the deck and the sudden outburst of noise had brought several beachcombers and sightseers up to look at the excitement. The pier became crowded. The disposable cameras came out of hiding as locals and tourists alike were kept busy holding up the redfish for photos and accolades.

With all the tourists, beachcombers and anglers on the pier, it became unusually noisy. The pier came alive with comments and questions.

"What kind of fish is that?" "Oh, it fought like hell. It almost broke my line!" "Can you eat them?" "Stand back a bit, let me take your picture."

Some of the comments were in German, some in French, but most were in American. Some spoken with New Jersey or Tennessee accents thick enough to walk on. It was one of those brief moments when strangers suddenly know each other. One of those moments when the world becomes both smaller and friendlier.

There were still two fish in the water: Carl's and Richard's. Richard had just about worked his back to the pier. He was disappointed to discover how small it was when compared with some of the others that were caught. Jose, whose fish was still fresh and tumbling about on the pier, came over and netted Richard's fish. Richard's fish was 24 inches long. It weighed roughly six pounds.

Carl was working his fish hard. It was a big redfish and Carl knew it. That made Carl happy, since he still loved the deep, hard tug of big fish. They tested both his skill and his stamina. It was hard for Carl to hang onto a big fish for more than fifteen minutes. He became winded, and his left shoulder and arm would start to become numb, as if they had fallen asleep. Years ago, only the fight of the big tarpon could get him that sore and exhausted. Age had settled over him like twilight, and he knew that he could not handle the powerful fight of the silver kings anymore. This redfish was trouble enough, he thought.

When Carl finally managed to get his redfish back to the pier and it flashed across the surface for the first time, both Richard and Jose were amazed.

"Boy, Carl, that's a big redfish you've got down there," commented Jose, in his faded Cuban accent.

"It's got me tuckered out, Jose, that's fer sure," said Carl.

"Is he ready for the net, do you think?"

"In a minute."

Five minutes passed. The fish made several more deep runs but never wrapped the pilings. Jose leaned over the top of the railing and slid his net under the big redfish. He scooped him straight up and set both the fish and the net on the deck. The redfish was exhausted. Unlike the other, smaller fish that were still flopping around, this big fish just laid there in the net. His gills flared open, then shut, then open, then shut in a futile try to catch his breath in this thin, new ocean he was suddenly pulled into. This ocean of air.

"He must go thirty-five pounds!" Exclaimed Jose, delighted to see such a big redfish landed.

"Is this as big as they get?" asked Richard of Carl, curious as to how large some of these pier fish can grow.

"No, they get up to around sixty pounds in the open ocean, but here at the pier we seldom see them much larger than this," replied Carl. "Could you unhook him and send him back into the Gulf for me Jose? I need to sit down for a spell."

"No problem, Carl," answered Jose.

A few tourists asked if Richard or Jose could hold the big fish up for a photo before they threw him back into the sea. Richard was glad to oblige. A few quick shots were snapped, a few more comments were added to the hundreds of others that had been made in the last fifteen minutes, and Jose threw the huge redfish back into the sea. It splashed hard, realized that it was back in the ocean, and swam off instantly.

Carl had walked back to the small Tiki-hut about a third of the way down the pier toward the beach. It covered fifteen feet of the pier and offered everyone a welcome respite from the relentless Florida sun. He sat down and rested, letting the wind rush over him like a massage. It felt good to rest. He could hear his heart pounding inside him. He wished that he could tell Marie about this redfish when he went back home later, but he knew that he could not. At least not in person.

"Did you see that? I had two on at once, Jose." said Richard.

"Yes, I saw that. Why did you lose the one?"

"The hook pulled."

"One time I had three big snook on, back in the days when I used to fish three rods. It was a disaster. When I went to reach for the third rod that got hit, one of the rods that I had let go of was yanked up and over the railing. It disappeared into the sea," said Jose.

"Did you ever get it back?"

"Yes, but no one believes it when I tell that story," said Jose.

"You have to tell it to me," insisted Richard.

"I will tell it in a moment, but let me take care of my redfish first."

Jose did not bring a cooler with him that morning and, because of it, Richard was spared the onslaught of Jose's club. Instead, Jose dug a large, bright orange stringer out of his tackle box. He slid the redfish on the stringer, walked up next to Carl, and lowered it over the side. The redfish dangled on the end of that long, thin stringer like a hanged man. Perhaps Carl is right about the club, thought Richard.

Jose came back and stood next to Richard and started telling him the rest of his story. Carl could overhear them from a distance, but didn't bother coming over. Carl had heard this story a thousand times before. It was a great story.

"You see," started Jose, "it goes like this."

Jose told Richard what had happened that morning about a year ago. First the one snook hit. Then, a second snook grabbed his other line within a few seconds of the first strike. The pause in between had given him just a moment to set the hook on the first snook. When the second one hit, he grabbed that rod with his other hand and set the hook on that fish as well. Finally, about a minute later, a big snook grabbed his third line. With both of his hands occupied, he decided to risk it and set one of the rods down briefly to try to hook up the third snook. Big mistake. No sooner had he set it down than the snook made a tremendous run and the entire rig: the rod, reel, and the attached fish - went for a swim.

Jose was devastated and embarrassed. How could he have done such a stupid thing? He had gotten greedy, and that greed had cost him the third rod. Since Jose never fished with inexpensive gear, the value of the outfit was over one hundred and fifty dollars. That, coupled with the knowledge that Carl and Becky had both witnessed the entire fiasco, made him feel terrible. They had been busy catching fish of their own at the time, or they normally would have helped. They knew that what Jose should have done was to take out his buck knife and just cut off one of the three rods, or at the very least, tie one rod off to the railing and hope for the best. Setting a rod down with a big, powerful snook still attached to the other end was a sure way of losing it. Even the part-time members of the pier gang knew it.

Jose did manage to bring in both the other snook, but his spirits were at an all-time low. Right then and there he promised himself that he would never be that selfish again. "From now on," he looked up and spoke to God, "I will only fish with two rods and no more!"

Shortly after keeping the larger snook and setting the smaller one free, he put out his two rods and began fishing once again. About ten minutes later he got another strike. When he went to set the hook, it felt odd to him. There was a fish on the line, but it felt spongy and soft. Maybe it was a catfish, he thought. It was coming in easily and he thought that he would find out what it was soon enough.

Much to his surprise and delight, it was his rod and reel. Apparently his other line had accidently dragged across and over the other rod and had managed to snag one of the rod guides. Very, very carefully he pulled the other rod back up to the pier. Once it was safely back on the deck of the pier, he shouted with joy and let both Carl and Becky know that he had managed to retrieve his lost rod.

Then he felt a tug. Looking down at the spool he noticed that all of the line was out, and the only thing that remained was the loop that you make when you first spool up a reel with monofilament. Jose suddenly realized that the snook that had pulled his rod over the railing was still on the other end of his line, all 200 yards of it! What to do next, he thought. He couldn't reel the fish in because every time he tried to reel the loop would just spin round and round on the shiny aluminum spool. He needed some line to get it started and called over to Becky for help.

Becky quickly saw the problem. She reached over the tip of the newly recovered rod and pulled in some line by hand. After retrieving fifteen feet of monofilament, enough to get the spool wrapped with a few dozen turns of fishing line, Jose managed to start reeling in the snook. With so much line out it took him fifteen minutes to get the big linesider back to the pier.

It was a monster. It measured 38 inches long and weighed twenty-three pounds! Becky netted it for him and to show his appreciation, Jose, who had never released a keeper, tossed this big fish back into the gulf. Jose was glad to have done battle with such a fish. He was grateful to God for helping him get his outfit back.

"From that morning since, I have never fished with more than two rods," concluded Jose.

"You are kidding me, aren't you, Jose?" said Richard in disbelief.

"No, Richard, I am not kidding you. This is a true story. Ask Carl if you don't believe me, or ask Becky. They both were here to witness it," insisted Jose.

Richard yelled over to Carl, "Hey, Carl, did you hear any of this bullshit Jose has told me about the three rods?"

Carl got up and slowly walked back, recovered from his exhaustion. "Yes, Richard, I was here that morning and I saw the whole thing happen."

"Did he really catch the snook on the end of the rod that had gone overboard?"

"He caught it, and, unlike Jose, he let it go," answered Carl, confirming this unbelievable fish tale.

"Well, I'll be!" exclaimed Richard.

Jose, smiling like the devil himself might smile after telling a huge lie, walked back to the end of the pier. Carl was chuckling to himself again, giving Richard the feeling that he had been had. Richard wanted to go over and reconfirm the story with Becky but thought that it might be too attorney-like of him, looking for further corroboration. The story was better left alone, true or not.

"You know, Carl, this place is paradise," said Richard. "This fishing pier, these beaches, the island. No wonder you choose to live down here. Why wouldn't anyone be happy living on a wonderful island like this?"

That was when Carl decided to tell Richard the Nestor story. This story wasn't about fishing, or about someone losing a rod and reel over the side. This was a story about paradise, and it was a sad story.

Richard had remained silent for half an hour after Carl had completed his tale of greed and money. It was Carl who decided to break the silence.

"Richard, paradise is where you make it. Not all the sunny days, nor all the beaches in the world can make a person happy," stated Carl. "Not all the things we think we need, not all the money we make, none of that matters. Happiness comes from within us, Richard, from a place that can only be defined by our hearts and our souls, and not by the landscapes that surround us."

The morning moved along but the school of redfish never returned. Just before noon Richard reeled in his rods and told Carl that it was time for him to be heading back to see what Helen and the boys were up to. Carl asked if he would be back tomorrow morning for some more fishing. Richard told Carl that he would, but Richard knew it wouldn't be for the fishing, it would be for the honor of standing beside this old fishing guide, listening to the wind in the lines and his wonderful stories.

Two

Richard couldn't sleep. The walls of the bedroom kept closing in on him like an oceanfront vise. He felt clammy and claustrophobic. The liquid crystal display on the clock radio kept flashing 3:14 a.m., then 3:15 a.m., then on to 3:36 a.m. and beyond. In the darkness of the condominium, it flashed as brightly as a cheap neon motel room sign on the seedy side of town. It was impossible to sleep. Richard kept turning his oversized body from side to side, trying to find a comfortable position on the mattress, fearful that he was going to awaken Helen in his restlessness.

Richard finally decided to get up and sit out on the porch, overlooking the pitch-dark waters of the Gulf of Mexico at night. He could hear the surf pounding in the steady wind but he could not see the whitecaps. He felt afraid.

This unspoken fear had been building within him all day. He wanted to put a name to it, to attribute it to something tangible, like the fear of an approaching thunderstorm or the fear of falling. He knew intuitively that it went far deeper. He was avoiding himself. He didn't want to do any further probing into his uneasy feeling. It was not a safe place for him to go.

When he got back from his morning of fishing with Carl, Richard had two things to show for it: a 24-inch redfish which he was going to fillet and have for dinner and a silent fear that he didn't want to face. He decided to fillet the fish first and keep himself busy enough to avoid the other issue for as long as possible.

He went up to see Helen and the boys. The boys were watching cable TV. He told them that after he was finished cleaning this redfish, they were all going to take a drive through J.N. "Ding" Darling National Wildlife Refuge. The tide was already dropping. With the flats exposed, the bird viewing would be great in the late afternoon. He held the redfish up high and asked his boys, "Do either of you know what this is?"

"It's a smelly fish," answered Helen sarcastically.

"But what kind of fish is it?" continued Richard, un-amused.

"Is it a trout?" Tyler queried, obviously guessing.

"I think it looks like a redfish dad, is it a redfish?" replied James, always the last one to answer, but always the one to have thought his answer out.

"You got it right James, it's a redfish. And we are going to have it for dinner tonight."

"Yuk!" said Tyler.

"Come on now Tyler, you'll love it," added Richard as he looked through the kitchen drawers in search of something that he could use for a fillet knife. The condominium was a rental unit, and typically ill equipped. The best he could come up with was an old, dull butcher knife. It will have to do, thought Richard as he headed downstairs toward the dumpster.

By the garbage he was lucky enough to find an old 2 x 6 that the dumpster used to sit up on. He took it and set it right on top of the dumpster and set to work on filleting his redfish. It had been about five years since he had last cleaned a fish. It did not go well. Between the dull blade of the knife and his duller skills as a fishmonger, he massacred the redfish. What should have been four boneless fillets were reduced to two hacked up pieces of meat with plenty of bones. It would have to do. Besides, thought Richard, the boys don't like fish anyway.

He threw the carcass and entrails into the dumpster, wondering when they would come to empty this stinking thing. He headed back upstairs for a quick shower and a sandwich. After lunch, while the two boys watched a rerun of *Bewitched*, Richard and Helen packed up a few snacks, some sodas, and some insect repellent. Then Richard told the boys in no uncertain terms that it was time to leave. The boys hated missing the rest of *Bewitched*.

It was after two by the time they passed through the gate at "Ding" Darling. The tide was falling. The viewing would get better later on, but this would have to do for now, thought Richard. They drove up to the voluntary pay booth and dropped in their envelope. The wind was still whipping about the long, gravel road. The preserve was windblown and dusty. Still, even with the water higher than Richard would have liked it to be, there were plenty of birds to see.

Richard and the boys shared an Audubon guide book that they had brought down with them from Peoria. They would take turns trying to identify the many herons, egrets and storks that were wading around the flats on either side of the drive.

The drive had a curious sulfur odor that seemed to worsen as the tide exposed more of the surrounding flats. Helen found the odor distasteful. It smelled like a bowl of rotting eggs, she thought to herself while trying to appear interested in the wildlife around her.

Tyler, their youngest, was impressed with the anhinga. A large male was perched along the side of the roadway, frozen on a lower branch of a red mangrove tree, drying its long pointed wingspan in the afternoon sun. The field guide book pointed out that they dry like this because they have no natural oils in their feathers to keep them afloat, as do the cormorants and ducks. Being strong swimmers, the notation continued, and able to dive to great depths because of this lack of oil, the anhingas spear their prey, impaling fish on their sharp, thin beaks. Once removed from the water however, they cannot fly. Their wings and bodies become soaked in seawater. They need to stretch out their long, slender wings for hours to allow them to dry.

The black-and-white pin feathers and the graceful lines of the anhinga fascinated Tyler. For a few minutes he forgot what program he would usually be watching in this afternoon time slot. For a few minutes he was enjoying real life.

There were many, many other birds they saw that afternoon. There were mergansers, mallards, sandpipers, and a solitary white pelican. But as the sun stepped down from its midday throne, Richard started to drift off. He became unaware of his surroundings and preoccupied with the conversation that he and Carl had earlier that morning. Richard kept thinking about the Nestor family. What a tragedy. Over money, thought Richard, all over money.

Helen, in rare fashion, actually noticed how distant Richard was. As the four of them walked down a long path in hopes of getting a chance to see an alligator, she asked him what was bothering him. Richard was surprised by her interest. He was glad for it, but surprised. He and Helen had become distant. They no longer were married in the present tense. They had become a convenient tape loop of their own relationship. A Memorex marriage, common in the suburbs of Peoria. Altogether too common throughout the suburbs of America.

They took out whatever tape was appropriate for the moment and played it. Some evenings it was the "dinner party tape," some days it was the "let's take the kids to soccer tape." The list goes on. There was no sense of the here and now any longer between the two of them. Everything was pleasant. Everything was on tape. In the safety of these perpetual tape loops, Richard found it strange that Helen would ask him such a thing. Being in such unfamiliar territory as the present, Richard replied almost methodically, "Oh, nothing really."

They got back to the condo to have dinner. On the way back they picked up some pizza slices for the boys and decided to feed the children first, then shuffle them off to the back-up cable television in the master bedroom, hook up their Nintendo 64, and have a quiet dinner together. They had picked up some spices at the local grocery and they were going to have 'blackened redfish.'

Between Richard's mutilated fillets and Helen's nonexistent flair for cooking, they ate something for dinner, but it was difficult to describe. It was a sort of spicy overcooked fish with bones in it. They both ate it out of a sense of obligation to each other. Richard told Helen that it tasted great. Helen commented to Richard on how fantastic it was to be eating fresh fish that he had caught. Both of them secretly wished that they had ordered more pizza.

After dinner, they all settled in to watch the tube for a while, and comment on their day during the muted commercials. Helen asked if Richard was going to head out to the pier again in the morning. He told her that he thought he would. He might not stay at the pier as long as he had today. He didn't tell her about the story Carl had told him earlier about the Nestors. It wasn't that he didn't want to tell her, because he did. It was more of a situation where he was still too tied up with the story himself. He wasn't ready to share the story with anyone just yet.

Richard and Helen and the boys turned out the lights at around 10:30. Just after the local news and weather. The alarm was set for 6:15 a.m. and Richard was looking forward to visiting with Carl again at the pier.

But Richard Evans woke up at 3:14 in the morning and couldn't get back to sleep. There were too many thoughts swimming around in his head. Now he was sitting on the porch, listening to an ocean that he could not see, with his thoughts as restless as the surf breaking against the shoreline in the darkness beyond him. He had poured himself a double over ice, but even the Scotch couldn't numb his racing thoughts.

He realized that money had become everything for him. Money was how he had come to measure his life's worth. He had managed to make plenty of it in the marble-faced war rooms of divorce courts. He had played so many husbands against wives, wives against husbands that he had become a master at creating animosity. It was the other party that was guilty of the indiscretion, the emotional abuse, the infidelity. He could work over the best of relationships to a point of restraining orders and long, bitter custody battles. All this at three hundred and ninety dollars per hour.

Listening to Carl talking about the ocean, telling his tall tales of fish that he landed and even taller tales of fish that had broken off, or jumped free, seemed more important to him now than did his substantial portfolio of stocks, bonds, and retirement plans. When did I change? he kept asking himself. When did I lose sight of what it was I was after? Where are my dreams?

He thought back to when he had first entered law school. At that time, more than anything else in the world, he wanted to teach law to students just like himself. He recalled his favorite professor, Dr. Adams. How he used to count the hours to when he could get back into his class. How he used to sit up front, listening to Dr. Adams describe the beauty and the dignity of law. How law separated us from all other creatures. How civilizations flourished and grew because of law. Laws that governed and ruled people. Laws that established justice and equality, fairness and freedom.

There wasn't any beauty or dignity left in the law that Richard practiced. It was a primal, ugly law that kept him in the office each night until eight. It was down to who was responsible for paying off the overdrawn VISA bill in the final settlement. It was about who got the Jaguar and who settled for the Ford. It was a long, endless screaming match between two members of the opposite sex who now despised each other. Secret bank accounts, lovers, scandals, and abuse, the cigarette burns, bruises, Prozac, and jealous rages - they all ran through Richard's sleepless thoughts like a river of sewage. That was the river that kept him alive. He wondered what Dr. Adams would be thinking about his star pupil if he could see him today.

To see him sitting there, chain smoking Camels on a chaise lounge that was straining beneath the load of his huge body, looking out into the darkness, wondering why? Attorney Richard Evans, Dr. Adams' star student. The way they fought over that estate, the Nestor kids, reminded him of the way they fight over the assets. They fight like animals until that day when the judge slams down that gavel and it's settled. When both parties feel like they have screwed over the other party and have been screwed over with equal fervor. All the time with Richard's first-class meter running. That is who I am, thought Richard, a Goddamned scavenger in a river of human sewage. He took another long, hard sip of Scotch and shook his head in disbelief.

It wasn't until four thirty that he fell back to sleep. He had looked in on his boys, sleeping peacefully in the spare bedroom. He couldn't change now and let them down. Besides, he had an easy case to wrap up next week that would net him another eleven grand. Life was good, he repeated quietly to himself as he finally fell back to sleep. His life was good.

Three

Carl didn't feel like cooking. He felt like having a drink. As the fishing grew slack and the sun lumbered off toward the west, he packed up his gear in the wagon and decided to head up to Tween Waters Inn to have a bump with some of his old fishing guide friends. He figured that he would meet up with Rusty, Crazy Captain Ray and Tony at the No-see-um Tiki bar. They usually pulled back into the barn with their charters around 5:00. After cleaning up their catch and their boat, they always managed to find a barstool at the Tiki bar around 6:00 or 6:30. The timing was ideal, thought Carl.

The drive up to Captiva was long and uneventful. Carl got stuck behind some tourist from South Carolina who drove 27 miles per hour all the way down San-Cap Road. "No one drives the speed limit on San-Cap except these tourons," Carl kept mumbling to himself as he crawled along. "Tourons!"

The traffic coming off the Island was too steady to dare any attempt at passing. There wasn't anything else to do but put up with it. He listened inattentively to the radio and thought about how many times in his life he had made this drive. More than he could imagine. Still, it wasn't a bad drive.

As he passed between the two islands, Carl counted the snook fishermen at the Blind Pass bridge. There were seven. By midnight there would be twenty. The snook fishing at Blind Pass is always best during the night, he reflected. Everybody knows that.

He finally pulled into Tweenies around a quarter after six. He locked up the wagon safe and sound and worked his way through the cottages and buildings from the parking lot to the bar. He was looking forward to an ice-cold rum and Coke, with just a twist of lemon.

"Well, what the hell has the cat dragged in!" said Rusty upon seeing Carl approaching.

"That ain't Carl now, is it?" added Crazy Ray.

"Where in God's earth have you been, ya old salt?" Rusty asked.

"Fishin', just like you two old sorry sons-a-bitches," answered Carl. He was as glad to see his old friends as they were to see him.

"What can I get you, Carl?" said Crazy Ray.

"I'll have a nice tall rum and Coke, with just a twist of lemon," answered Carl, speaking to both Ray and to the bartender who had come over to take the order.

Crazy Ray was the younger of the two guides at the bar. He was a yuppie guide. Ray wore expensive shorts and pleated shirts with redfish and snook embroidered just above the pocket. Like many of the new, young guides, he looked great. Ocean Wave sunglasses, leather deck shoes, and a haircut that belonged more to a photo shoot out of *Gentleman's Quarterly* than a back issue of Florida Sportsman.

Crazy Ray had a brand new, expensive flats boat that he took his customers out in. His tackle matched the rest of his image. Fine, graphite rods, platinum series reels, and name-brand tackle from start to finish. He had been guiding out of Tween Waters for four years. The old guides at Tweenies would have ousted him long ago except for one decisive factor: Crazy Ray was good.

His family owned a couple of gulf-front properties on Captiva and it was common knowledge that Crazy Ray didn't have to work. He came from money. Big money. Crazy Ray was generous enough to spread his money around. It helped to make up for the fact that he was a little rich kid. None of that really mattered to the old-time guides up on Captiva. Theirs wasn't an easy club to gain admission into, and money didn't help.

What made Crazy Ray a member of the club was his passion for fishing. Year after year he was in the running at the Cracker. The Cracker was a local tournament that only the best anglers were invited to participate in. Ray had won it two years ago. The Cracker was a bitch of a tournament to win. That afternoon two years back, when he flopped down his forty-two-inch snook and took the lead for good, Crazy Ray was in.

His real name was Ray Dee, but over the few years he had been fishing, he had become known only as Crazy Captain Ray. He would tell his customers the most outrageous fishing lies possible.

He would do it with such a straight face and honest-to-goodness that most of his first-time customers would believe him. When they got off the charter and started repeating these outrageous tales to the rest of the staff and regulars at the No-see-um Bar, the listeners would unexpectedly burst out laughing. By next season his charters would be onto him.

They were ridiculous stories. Stories about catching yellowfin tuna in the back bay, about a shark that ate one of his anglers, about the time he had to wrestle a snook out of an alligator's jaws and worse. Crazy Ray was like that. He often complained that the earth should have two moons instead of one.

"Just imagine the ripping tides we'd have with two moons!" he would tell his customers out on one of his charters. "Wow, wouldn't that be fantastic!"

One of his recent favorites was fishing for dinosaurs. He had watched a Discovery Channel special a few years ago that really caught his attention. It was about what the oceans were like during the Jurassic period. The time of the great dinosaurs.

"There was some big fish back then," he would start in. "Real monsters! Just imagine what it would be like hooking into a forty-five- foot ichthyosaurus! Or one of those long-necked elasmosauruses? They look like Nellie up in Loch Ness. You know, up in Scotland. Wouldn't that be great?"

Nobody thought it would be all that great. The other guides thought the whole idea insane. What would you use for bait? Half a tarpon? What about the reels? They would have to be the size of fifty-gallon oil drums, with matching rods the size of small telephone poles. And the hooks, the hooks would have to be bigger than the largest flying gaffs available.

"But just think of the runs you'd get as that eighty-five-foot tylosaurus spooled ya."

Crazy Ray had worked the whole thing out. Armor-plated flats boats to protect against their whipping tails. Tails that were as long as a Bertram Sportfish. Harpoons to finish them off. Even his own special BBQ sauce to use once you got your thirty-pound steaks back to the grill. Crazy Ray. Fishing for dinosaurs. He was ready for it, should the opportunity ever arise.

Crazy Captain Ray was divorced. He was married for about a year to a beautiful waitress he had met at the Crow's Nest. They fell madly in love. When the chemistry of the romance and the honeymoon fever wore off, they found out that they didn't have much in common. She hated to fish, and knowing how much money his family had, tried to talk him out of his guiding career. It didn't work. She talked her way out of a marriage. If Crazy Ray were asked to choose between his wife and his flats boat...well, everyone but his ex-wife knew the answer. She knows the answer now.

Rusty, the other guide sitting at the bar, was the real McCoy. His face was rough, like it had been acid-etched from years of sunlight and wind. He had cracked, deep wrinkles that gave him a look way beyond his age. His hands were like paws. Hands with big, thick fingers and skin like tanned leather. He wore old, ragged T-shirts with faded prints from tournaments that he had won. Won year after year. The Caloosa, the Grand Slam, and the coveted Cracker. Last year's Cracker in fact, though the T-shirt from it already looked ten years old. Tournaments for tarpon, redfish, trout, and the elusive snook. Monied tournaments with plenty of side bets and calcuttas going. Tournaments where the anglers fish for keeps. Where the guides fish for their reputations as well as their pocket books.

It was rumored that Rusty could actually smell the snook. It was said that he could find a school of redfish in the Arctic Ocean. He was a great fisherman and a greater drunk. No one, in all of Lee County, could drink more, or catch more fish than Rusty. You could tell in a glance that challenging either record would be useless. He had a long, deep scar on his right hand where a shark had once grabbed it while he was trying to revive a big snook during the off season. The shark made off with both the snook and a good-sized chunk of Rusty's right hand. He took it in stride. He got it stitched back up, and was out fishing the next morning. He was drinking with his left hand the next afternoon at the No-see-um Bar.

Rusty had just turned fifty-seven. He looked to be in his seventies. He was thin and muscular and looked like a mountain man. A mountain man with a casting reel instead of an ax, and he knew how to cast that rod.

"How'd you two do today in all this wind?" asked Carl.

"It was a pain in the ass, Carl, but I managed to find my folks a big old school of redfish just off of Demere Key. We loaded up on them and had us a ball," said Rusty. He was already slurring his words.

"I did OK, but one of my people got pretty seasick, so I was back at the dock around three," said Ray.

The rum and Coke tasted better than he had imagined, thought Carl. Lots of ice, with a long sweating glass, dripping in the failing sunlight. There is nothing quite like it after a hard day of fishing.

"You said you've been fishing, Carl? Where's that, I thought you'd sold your boat." Rusty inquired.

"I've been fishing off the old pier at the east end of Sanibel. I love it. We've got a bunch of regulars and it's always a stitch watching the tourists make a mess of things. We got into some big ocean-run reds today that really busted us up. With the tide change coming, I expect we'll be getting into some old linesiders in the next few mornings," said Carl. "By the way, where's Tony?"

"He might not make it today, his wife's been on him about drinking up all his profits at the bar. You know how she can get," said Rusty.

"Well, his wife's right, ain't she?" Carl commented, trying to get under their skin a bit.

"Damn straight she's right, but that still ain't reason to make him stop coming to the Tiki bar now and again to share some fishing stories with his friends," added Rusty. Rusty missed Tony. They had been drinking together for years.

Tony wasn't a very good guide. Never had been. Never would be. He was just a good ole' boy who did the best he could. He was also a drunk. That was why Rusty was angry with Tony's wife, Judy. She had put the cuffs back on him for a spell.

Rusty figured that Tony would be back drinking within a week or so, after Judy cooled down and a few of the broken items around the house had been fixed. The bizarre dynamics of their relationship hadn't changed in eight years. Not since Tony stopped tending bar and started guiding. There was no reason to think that it would change now. Next week, thought Rusty to himself. Tony will be back here next week.

All three of them - Carl, Crazy Ray and Rusty got down to

the serious business of drinking and swapping fish tales. Every time Carl reached for his wallet, either Ray or Rusty would quickly shout to the bartender to just put it on their respective tabs. Their weekly tabs came damn close to their net profits after their expenses for bait, gas, boat payments and food. That suited them fine. They were alike in that they didn't fish for the money. They fished for the love of the sea. They were modern day whalers. They were Portuguese fishermen, with old, brightly painted wooden boats putting out to sea for schools of tuna far beyond the sight of land. They were immortal.

The conversation wandered around like a derelict vessel without a rudder. The fish stories got more and more unbelievable as the tab ran up like an electric meter at a light bulb factory. Crazy Ray even started in on his dinosaur fishing again.

Some of the old stories were being retold. Told with the same fervor they were told with on the day they had happened. It was the rum. Rusty went on again about the shark hitting his snook, all the blood and one of his customers fainting at the sight of it. Ray talked about winning the Cracker with that forty-two-inch linesider he took out of his secret hole.

"Secret hole my ---," said Rusty. He was starting to get ornery. Rusty could be a mean ass drunk. "I saw you catch that fish in Redfish Pass that morning. There ain't shit that's secret about Redfish Pass!"

They carried on like three school kids at recess. Carl was getting drunk. He was doing it with very little dignity. Rusty and Ray had left dignity behind years ago. For them it was just another useless run for the pennant, another ball game that no one was watching.

About an hour later, with a somber tone to his voice, Rusty unexpectedly turned to Carl and said, "Tell me the truth now, Carl, how you getting along since Marie's passed away?"

The question took Carl off guard. He didn't know what to say. He was feeling a sublime combination of strong rum and hearty laughter. This question slammed into him as if he'd run hard aground going thirty-five across a dead-calm sea. He stopped and reflected for the longest time.

What can I possibly say? Carl thought to himself. Can I tell them how much I miss her? Can I say that I miss her more than anyone or anything imaginable? That I miss her every minute, every hour? That my life is now a play without a script, without meaning, without her?

That, for them, it would be like going out to their boats tomorrow morning only to find that someone has taken away the ocean. That you're unable to fish again. Stuck out there on the damp mud of the bay, looking at a world without water. Worse. That you would never see or smell that blue, blue ocean again. That was what it was like for me now, a world without water. A world without Marie.

Carl realized that he was taking too long to respond. Just before Rusty could start regretting asking, Carl hedged and said, "Thanks for asking, Rusty. I'm getting along just fine."

"If you ever need some company, Carl, just give me, or Ray, or Tony a call. We'll be glad to come down and see ya," said Rusty in a rare display of emotion. Rusty was drunker than Carl. He was becoming that kind of teary-eyed drunk that old salts melt into when the hour is late and the booze has worked its way to their souls. You could see the tears well in his eyes and slowly trickle into the deep crevices of his sun-carved face. Rusty had always admired and respected Carl. The tears were real.

It was time to break up the party. All three of them knew it. "Let me leave the tip," insisted Carl.

They both agreed, knowing that it would be insulting to Carl if they didn't allow him to spend a few of his bucks at the bar. Carl left a five spot and said his farewells. All three of them stumbled back to their vehicles and headed their separate ways. Rusty lived on the western end of Sanibel and Ray was staying in one of his parents' properties on Captiva. They were all legally drunk, but all three of them knew the local cops on a first name basis. Unless they drove like idiots, they were in no real danger of getting into trouble.

Carl drove home listening to his favorite station, the public radio. They were playing a piece by Saint Seans. Carl loved Saint Seans. His music was delicate. Peaceable. Carl noticed that he was swerving around a bit. He did his best to keep the car in the middle of his lane as he hurried down San-Cap Road toward his home on the east end of the island. There were no tourons in front of him this time, so he quickly sped up to 45. No one ever got ticketed for going 45 on that road, even though the posted limit was 35. It was local knowledge. He was glad the touron from the Carolinas wasn't in front of him now. He would have tried to pass even if the traffic were bumper to bumper. Carl was ready for anything.

When he got home, he was hungry. He made himself a turkey sandwich and turned on the TV to catch up on the news. The news was more of the same, but he watched it until he finished his sandwich. It was 11:30. He was tired and drunk. After washing up he got in bed to lie down for the night. He double checked the alarm to make sure that it was set for 5:30 a.m. It was. It always was.

He fell fast asleep in a sleep without dreams, or memories of Marie, or tall tales of fish being caught off foreign shores. When the alarm went off at 5:30 he rolled over, turned off the terrible pipe organ music the DJ had chosen for no one else in the world but Carl, and fell back to sleep. He was hung over. He knew when he reached over and hit that alarm that he was going to be late getting to the pier this morning. He didn't give a damn if he was. His head hurt something awful.

The Fourth Morning

One

Richard arrived at the pier around 7:00. He looked bad. He had finally got back to sleep at 5:00 a.m. Even at that, it was an unsettled, disjointed sleep. But he wanted to come down to the pier again to be with Carl. He wanted to listen to him tell his tales of fishing, of life and death and the people of this small, beautiful village by the sea. The sound of Carl's voice drew him back. A deep and rhythmic voice, like the sound of all things human.

Richard was surprised to find that Carl wasn't there. They had made plans to rendezvous, just like the day before. As he hiked up the wooden planks of the pier, it came as a bit of a shock to find Carl absent. Perhaps he was running late? Maybe he had gone back to his house to get something he had forgotten? Jose, Ralph and some of the other pier gang members and a handful of tourists were already fishing. Perhaps they had seen Carl earlier.

Richard walked over to Jose. "Jose, have you seen Carl this morning?"

"No, Richard, he hasn't been here yet. Were you supposed to meet him or something?"

"Yes, I brought the sandwiches this morning and he was supposed to bring the Cokes. I wonder if anything has happened to him?"

"One of my buddies said he saw his station wagon up at Tween Waters last night. He's probably hung over. Carl has a bunch of old guide buddies he likes to drink with up there. They can drink more liquid than the fish they catch. No doubt he'll be here later, looking pretty bad for it at that."

"I don't have any bait to use without him here to net it for me,

Jose. He always has it in his livewell by the time I arrive. Would you have any extra minnows or shrimp I could have until he shows up?"

"No problem, Ricky, just pull up my bait bucket and grab yourself some shrimp. They had some jumbo shrimp today at Fisherman's World, so I decided to give them a try for a change. Just help yourself, I've got plenty. Freddie threw in an extra half dozen for free."

Richard walked over to Jose's bait bucket. I hate being called Ricky, he thought to himself. I've always hated that name.

It wasn't one of those little yellow plastic bait buckets like the tourists use. It was a large white five-gallon paint can with hundreds of tiny drill holes in it, just like Carl's. I wonder how long it took Jose to drill all those holes? thought Richard to himself as he pulled the heavy bucket up onto the pier.

Richard noticed that instead of hanging off the side of the pier, the bucket was now hanging almost straight down. The tide change Carl was talking about was beginning. In a few more days, the morning tide would turn to an outgoing tide. The snook would be back.

With his limited tackle and his single fishing rod, Richard rigged the best he could. He was not expecting to catch anything, but thought that he might look stupid if he just stood there, waiting for a hung over Carl to show.

The wind had died and the air was calmer. It was colder than it had been all week. The air was dry. The sun was already well on its journey to zenith. It was going to be a perfect day. It was going to be a chamber of commerce day. The cold front that had been approaching slipped through Ft. Myers during the night. It had made it to Naples and stalled out there. No one could have ordered better weather. Richard had noted there were no stringers next to the bait buckets tied off the side of the pier. No stringers, no fish. Carl had told him that ocean fishing was done at the mercy of the tides. With the tide this morning running lazy, the fishing took on that same sense of apathy. When the tide turned on, the fishing would turn on as well. Until then, fishing was merely a function of habit. The only thing to do was to stand there, watching the light wind ripple across the water, and wait for Carl to appear. This is exactly what Richard did.

Carl stumbled in around 8:00. He looked a bit peaked and

hung over, but he had a smile on his face. A big smile.

"How are you feeling?" asked Richard as he approached. "You look like hell."

"Who told you?" said Carl, half laughing as he reached down for his cast net.

"Jose had some friends who saw your car up at Tween Waters last night. Your bloodshot eyes tell the rest. Did you have fun?"

"We had a ball," answered Carl. "Now let me see if I can still cast this damn thing." Carl picked up his six-foot cast net and headed back toward the sand.

Of course he could. Over the decades he had thrown these cast nets a thousand times. He could cast it blindfolded in a gale. There had been plenty of other mornings when he stood there, on the bow of his boat, hung over and tired, trying to look good for his customers. Carl could throw a cast net in a force five hurricane. Being hung over was not much of a challenge, he thought to himself as he readied the net and started walking up the beach.

Well, on this morning, it was more of a challenge than he had expected. With his sense of balance still suffering from the effects of too much rum, it took him a dozen throws to finally capture a net full of bait. A few of the early casts didn't even open. The heavy lead sinkers that line the perimeter of the cast net plunked into the ocean like a stone. Carl wasn't embarrassed. To him, it was funny. He laughed.

Twenty minutes later, they managed to get all the pilchards baited up and soaking in the sea. The four rods were looking good. It was almost nine o'clock. The tide was now pouring out. The change had come too late in the morning for the big snook to bite. Snook like a falling tide at dawn, long before the sun makes a thirty-pound leader look like rope under water. The big snook are too wise for midday fishing.

With the arrival of the first real cold front, the water had chilled. Every fall, when that happens, the schools of Spanish mackerel reappear. They migrate down from the cooling waters near the big bend area of Florida by the millions. On calm days like this, when the saltwater's flowing strong and clear, they show up by the hundreds at the fishing pier. Today was one of those days. You could see flashes of them as they darted up and through the schools of small scaled sardines and glass minnows that had formed in the eddies of the wooden pilings. The minnows danced on the surface like a rain squall made of life.

Earlier in the morning Becky had managed to land a large grouper. She and Paul had arrived while Carl was busy wrestling with his cast net. On her very first cast out to her deep hole she got a tremendous strike. Setting the hook with that long spinning rod like an old Carolina cracker fishing the surf at Cape Hatteras, she imbedded the forged hook deep into that grouper. The big fish ran her up and down the pier in the near slack current. After a great fight that lasted over five minutes, Paul managed to stop smoking just long enough to net the fish. It was twenty-nine inches long. Eleven pounds.

Carl, perhaps because he was still a bit tipsy, was in a very talkative mood. Shortly after Becky brought in the grouper, Carl started telling Richard a classic fish story.

"About six months ago, during the spring, we were all fishing here quietly when Becky hooked into the biggest grouper of her life."

"Oh yeah, how big was it?" Richard inquired. He was delighted to find Carl in such a talkative mood.

"I'll get to that part in a moment. First, let me tell you what happened. Becky and Paul had already brought in two or three nice blacks from their favorite hole when her big old spinning rod really took a bend. Like she always does, Becky leaned back into that bite and slammed her hook into the fish. To her surprise, the fish did not respond. She lowered that rod tip a second time and brought it back with as forceful a jerk as she could without shattering the rod in two. The fish on the other end, annoyed by all of this, decided that it was time to find another place to eat. He started swimming off.

"You have to understand here that the fish was still attached to Becky's line. Her big spinning reel started losing line. The line wasn't screaming off, like it does when a big tarpon or a shark hits, but it was singing away at a fairly good pace. Everyone guessed what she had hooked up with right from the start."

"What was it?"

"It was a jewfish. We didn't confirm that until later, but Jose, Ralph and I suspected it right from the start. Becky was in shock.

She had never encountered a fish whose head she could not turn by using her 30 lb. test line and the sheer leverage of that long, nine-foot rod of hers. This fish was not turning. It was just swimming away. Luckily, it was swimming up the beach.

"Becky soon realized that whatever was on the other end, if she stood her ground on the end of the pier and hoped to turn it around, she would lose the fish. Over half of her line was gone and there was no change in either the direction or the tempo of the fish's run. What could she do?"

"Well...," said Richard.

"She did what you have to do at a pier when you get a monster on that you cannot stop. You get off the dock and follow it. I have done this many, many times out to sea in my boat, especially during the tarpon runs in the spring. That's when the big sharks and monster tarpon can take you on journeys that last for miles. On a boat it's easy, but from a fishing pier, it's far more difficult.

"Becky threw open her bail and started walking back to the beach as fast as she could. The pier was crowded with tourists and anglers that morning. As Becky walked back to the beach, she had to pass her rod and reel over and under, below and above about twenty rods before she was able to stand on the beach. With the bail open, there were only a dozen wraps of line left on her big Penn 750 when she stepped on that sand. She flipped the bail closed, wound in twenty feet of slack, and commenced battling with this brute once again.

"Luck was with her. The big fish had just swam up and along the beach. He had stayed about 75 yards offshore, following the contour of the beach in a deep trough that runs up and around the island for half a mile."

Carl had used his arms to graphically show the outline of this trough to Richard. He pointed to where it ran, and Richard estimated by Carl's description that it must have swum very near the condominium complex where he was staying.

"So Becky started running up the beach, following her big fish, with skinny old Paul behind her holding the long-handled net up high, like it was some sort of medieval banner or something. Both of them pursuing this sea monster back out toward the Gulf. Becky soon recovered more than half of her line. She was putting near constant pressure on this stubborn creature all the while. When they both disappeared behind the corner of the point, all of us decided that this was just too good a battle to miss. Leaving only Ralph behind to watch our gear for us, Jose, Chip, Andrew and Sonny, as well as a few tourists, all ran back down off the pier to catch up with Becky and the big fish.

"By the time we caught up with her, Becky was a block down the beach. She was still working that long powerful spinning rod in noble, but futile, attempts to turn this big fish's head. Although she hadn't managed to stop or turn him yet, she was starting to slow him down some. She was just as determined to bring in this fish as the fish was determined to drag her out to sea. It was a world-class battle and we were all getting a real charge out of it.

"After twenty minutes on the beach, Becky was tired. Even Paul, who had been carrying around the long pier net, was getting tired. The fight was now a half-hour long and neither party was willing to give an inch. It reminded me of one of those arm wrestling competitions where no one is willing to concede. Both opponents were equally matched. Sweat kept pouring off of Becky while the big fish grew weary against the constant strain of her fishing line.

"The stalemate lasted another fifteen minutes. Two blocks further up the sandy beach the stalemate broke. The fight by this time had picked up scores of onlookers, beachcombers, sunbathers and joggers. There were fifty people behind Becky and her doubled-over rod, behind Paul and his fishnet flag. It was a curious and odd looking group that headed along the beach that morning.

"Of course, everyone was guessing as to what this woman had caught. Was it a big nurse shark? Could it be a manta ray? A big snook? Tarpon? Jewfish? What was it? The tourists made the most outrageous guesses of all, coming up with things like yellowfin tuna, or a blue marlin. Even a giant squid was mentioned. We all kept quiet, but we all figured it was a jewfish.

"The concern at this point was twofold: Would Becky be able to hold out much longer, and would the 60 lb. leader she used eventually wear through? If the fish was hooked in the lip, where only the hook was touching the mouth of the fish and not the leader, the leader would make it. After forty minutes, I was convinced it was lip hooked. But Becky was falling apart. Her legs were sore, her arms were shaking and her nerves were unraveled. She was exhausted. All of us could tell that she only had a limited amount of time left in her before she would begin to crumble.

"I have seen it happen before. Mostly during the tarpon season. Strong, healthy men reaching over to cut the line because their backs are so sore and their arms too numb to hang on any longer. Big fish can do that to an angler, they can exhaust a healthy man in no time.

"That's just when the fish decided to turn. In a sudden change of fortune, the rod slackened up, and Becky gained a few turns of line. The entire pier gang let out a tremendous shout of relief. The surrounding tourists were perplexed by this cheer. But what did they know?

"The pier gang knew that the big fish had conceded, that he had decided to let his powerful arm fall back down to the table in defeat. Becky was going to win!

"Over the next ten minutes the fight continued, but it soon became obvious to everyone that the big fish had surrendered. Slowly but surely, Becky gained more line on the goliath. Now you could see the shape of this monster in the water, about 25 yards off the beach. As it was pulled closer and closer to the beach, it was easy to see that it was hitting the bottom. With every passing wave you could see either the dorsal fin or its huge round tail coming out of the water. The small brown spots and yellowish tint confirmed what we had long suspected. It was a jewfish.

"Judging by its length and girth, it weighed way over 300 pounds. Becky didn't weigh half of that. It was too big to beach. Besides, it would have been very harmful to the fish had Becky chosen to try and drag it up on shore. Paul looked like an idiot with his tiny net next to this fish the size of a Volkswagen. He couldn't have fit the tail into Ralph's pier net.

"What happened next was that Jose, who had been wearing nothing more than a pair of shorts and his sandals, took off his gold chains, took out his wallet and handed both of them to me. He waded in to grab a hold of this big fish for Becky.

"About the closest she could drag the fish with her 30 lb. line was thirty or forty feet from shore. At that point, a good third of this fish was sticking up out of the water. It looked like a beached whale.

"Did she end up keeping it?"

"No, you can't keep jewfish in Florida anymore. You could have ten years ago, but the scuba divers ended all that. It wasn't the spear fishing that did it. A diver would have to be crazy to spear a jewfish. It was when they started using power-heads that the jewfish population started falling. For the divers, these largest members of the grouper family were like sitting ducks. They just swam up to them, putting that shotgun shell-loaded bang stick to their heads and blew them away. Since they taste like grouper, the local restaurants were always ready to buy them off of the divers at a buck or two per pound. The divers started paying for their dive trips by taking a jewfish back home with them.

"With that kind of pressure, it didn't take long for the jewfish population to collapse. Knowing that the fish was becoming endangered, the people in the fisheries division decided to ban all harvesting, including hook and line. In the last few years, the fish have started to make a strong comeback. They are caught and released much more often these days.

"Jose knew that it was illegal for Becky to keep this big grouper, but he wanted to take a hold of it to prove that Becky had actually won the battle. Becky was glad to see Jose wade out there, grab the leader and hang onto this big, yellowish sea monster for her. She handed the rod over to Paul. She was standing there on the beach, utterly exhausted and shaking, not thirty feet from her opponent. Jose insisted that she come out and stand next to him with her catch.

"One of the other members of the pier gang, I think it was Chip, produced a small camera. As the fifty or sixty spectators all cheered and clapped, Becky waded out to the waist-deep water to stand beside her fish. Chip took a couple of shots amidst the smiles and salutations. Jose handed Becky his stainless steel hook removers, and with a good strong tug, Becky pulled her forged hook out. The fish was exhausted. Becky tossed the hook up in the air in an act of final celebration. Everyone was delighted. A small woman, not half the weight of this mighty beast, had conquered.

"There was a primal, almost tribal sense of conquest that rippled through the crowd. Strangers smiled at each other. The pier gang hollered out great accolades to Becky. She just stood there, tired and blushing, with this six-foot-long grouper bobbing half belly up alongside of her. It was an impressive sight.

"Jose knew what to do. He took a hold of the lower jaw of this big fish and started walking forward through the waist-deep water as fast as he could. He was reviving the fish, forcing the salt water into his mouth and across his gills. He was bringing the fish back to life. Jose was making it breath. He walked his way down the beach nearly 100 feet before the big jewfish started kicking its wide tail again and showing signs of recovering. Upon noting the revival, Jose tossed the big fish forward and as it swam off, its wide tail slapped him across the knees. It didn't hurt Jose in the least. It was a goodbye gesture, a thank you.

"You could follow the dark silhouette of this oversized football-shaped fish until it got about 50 yards out, then it disappeared forever into the depths of the Gulf of Mexico. Becky walked back to shore. The crowd slowly thinned.

"In all the years that Jose and Chip had fished the pier, they have never seen such a noble battle as the one between Becky and that big old jewfish. So every time I see her haul back on the long spinning rod of hers I have to wonder if it might not be another day like the one last spring. That is one of the greatest things about the ocean, the way it can surprise us. The ways it can make that sea trout you were planning to catch suddenly become a sixty-pound cobia. The sea is full of surprises. I guess life is too."

"What a story Carl! What a great story," said Richard.

"Yeah, Richard, it was a memorable fish and a noble fight. For months afterward Becky's catch was the topic of many a conversation down here at the pier and all across the Island. Becky's big fish.

"Becky had a ball with it. She had a good story to tell, and I'll wager my best rod and reel that she still tells it whenever the opportunity arises. She and her husband Paul have been coming down to the pier off an' on for years now. Catching that fish was probably the most exciting thing that has happened to her down here. A good fish story can serve to break up the routine a bit, that's for sure."

Carl took a long, slow sip of his Coke. A minute or two passed before he continued.

"Let's face it, Richard, our lives have a rhythm to them. We're born, raised, we marry, have children of our own, grow old and vanish. For most of us the story is simple. For most of us, we will never discover a new continent, or the cure for cancer, or walk on the moon. Nah. For people like you and me, Richard, life will be a series of little things connected by days and weeks that are even smaller. Like pearls on a long, fragile necklace. The marriage of a friend, the birth of your first child, the passing away of your father, divorce, an accidental death, these are the changes that happen. Small things really, but large enough through our own eyes. Pearls, Richard. Little pearls for the most part, some white, some black. And the string holding them together is our life.

"We sometimes attach more importance to ourselves than we should. It's only natural, I suppose. To our own lives, and the close circle of friends and family that surround us, we are important. But to the great tides of life, we are no more important than those glass minnows hiding behind the eddy of that piling down there."

Carl pointed downward to the uncountable school dashing about below the pier. There was a sorrow in his voice as he spoke. A distant sadness.

Richard listened attentively. He understood perfectly what Carl was trying to say. He had always wondered why his wife, Helen, was so interested in her thrillers and romances, and now he knew why. Because they offered her more than that. They offered her escape. They were her fishing stories. They spoke of spies and murders, intrigue, and betrayals. Buildings were destroyed, men and women were tortured and killed, briefcases full of money passed between sweaty palms while life hung in the balance. Why wouldn't Helen be interested?

What was her real life like? Richard unexpectedly asked himself. She was a rich suburban woman married to an overweight divorce attorney with two kids who were spoiled rotten. Nothing else ever happened. Maybe a bad vacation in a Winnebago once in a blue moon. Maybe a special wedding invitation, or a graduation to look forward to, but for the most part, just ordinary people, living ordinary lives. There were briefcases full of money, but they had direct deposit and American Express to make the transfers with. No spies or couriers were involved. Just statements. Bills and statements. Why would Helen not want to vanish into her collection of dime novels?

Richard realized that he was getting uncomfortable again thinking about it. There were too many issues that hit close to home. He wanted to change the subject. Find something easier to discuss.

"What's the biggest fish you've ever seen caught off the pier, Carl?"

"Hooked? I've seen some unbelievable fish on the line down here. One evening a bunch of beer drinking rednecks from North Ft. Myers hooked into a fourteen-foot sawfish. They had all come down to the pier that night to fish for summer sharks. These guys were tackled up for big fish. That old sawfish, and he must have weighed half a ton, gave them more than they bargained for. They eventually saw every yard of their 100 lb. test line pulled off their 6/0 reels and head straight out to sea. That sawfish came up just once, and that was it.

"I've seen some big hammerheads, and once, quite by accident I'm sure, one of the regulars hooked a porpoise. He was fishing for a big snook with a whole live mullet and this dolphin swam right over and took the bait. It was the only time I've seen a mammal hooked up. It didn't last long. The three-hundred pound dolphin just swam off with a vengeance and this guy's line broke immediately.

"There have been lots of big cobias brought to the pier, some damn near 100 pounds, some big barracuda, and some huge black drum taken. But the best fight I'd ever saw was the one between Becky and that jewfish. It would be a hard fight to beat!"

Just then a run of Spanish mackerel made a sweep through the waters surrounding the pier. Baits were inhaled or cut cleanly in two by the razor sharp teeth of the mackerel. Lines were zinging off the spools and voices were once again raised in a chorus of excitement and panic. These were good-sized Spanish mackerel. Carl and Richard had each hooked up with one of those little speedsters. They were having a ball bringing their long, skinny mackerel in.

Spanish mackerel are beautiful fish. They have a dark back and flashy, silvery sides that are covered with small dots that run the length of their body. They are very long for their weight and, once hooked, they streak through the saltwater erratically in an attempt to regain their freedom. Spanish mackerel are very fast but they tire quickly. They have neither the tenacity nor the brute strength of redfish or snook.

Rather than bother with the net, Carl told Richard to just hoist the small fish up and flop them back on the dock. With their sharp, pointed fins and their row of razor sharp teeth, they can quickly tear up a good net, so it's easier to just hoist them on the dock. Carl never liked Spanish mackerel and Richard wasn't in the mood to massacre any more fillets this week, so they both knew that they were going to release them.

Once the fish was on the dock Carl reached for his hook outs and warned Richard to wait until he had finished releasing his fish before he tried to get the hook out of the other one.

"These damn things have teeth, Richard, and they're sharp as needles!" Carl yelled, warning him to be careful.

It didn't really take a warning to keep Richard from getting too close to those gnashing teeth. Richard was used to things wanting to take a piece out him. Like the plaintiff's husband or the opposing divorce attorney. He knew how to keep his distance. Ralph and Jose were having a ball at the end of the pier and even Becky, fishing with a big pinfish in the grouper hole, had managed to hook up a large Spanish.

It was a scene to behold. All the tourists getting their lines cut off or their hooks cleaned, and the regulars all hooked up and acting crazy. The mackerel, frantic and hungry, rocketing through the schools of bait that lay sheltered behind the pilings as the bay water moved back out to sea. A calm, gorgeous fall morning in south Florida, full of life, sunlight, and excitement.

After a while the bite tapered off. Carl and Richard brought in and released a total of five fish. Richard had caught three, Carl only two. Richard was silently proud of the fact that he had actually out fished Carl for once. Things were settling back to the normal pace of an occasional sheepshead strike or a tourist trying to untangle a nightmare of a backlash.

Carl kept rubbing his left shoulder. It was obvious to Richard that it was bothering him.

"Is it your shoulder bothering you again?" Richard asked.

"Yeah, it's my shoulder again. Every time I finish catching a fish it wants to want to act up on me. It goes numb. I should have it looked at I guess."

"Yes, you should."

Carl continued, "That's one thing about getting old, Richard. Just like an old spinning reel, the gears inside start to wear out. The anti-reverse goes, the handle turns harder and harder, all gummed up with salt spray, and there are days when you're tempted to just toss the damn reel back into the ocean.

"It's tough, getting old," Carl went on. "Your legs hurt sometimes, you pull a muscle in your arm or strain your back and what used to take a couple of days to heal now takes weeks. Everything falls apart. I'm not complaining, mind you, I'm just telling it like it is."

"My wife Helen sounds just like you, Carl. She's been after me for almost a year to pay for her to have a tummy tuck and a boob job. She says that her breasts are starting to sag. Like everyone else, she's just trying to ward off the telltale signs of aging. Look at me. Shit, I must be at least eighty pounds too heavy, and I know damn well that this smoking is going to kill me. But in my job there is so much stress that I'd probably go quicker without my two packs a day," said Richard.

"Be careful about letting your wife undergo that surgery, Richard. It's never as sure a thing as they lead you to believe. You might be better off just telling her that growing old happens. It reminds me of two things, a joke I heard last week, and what happened to Rosanne," said Carl, about to launch into another tale.

"Let's hear the joke first, Carl, then you can tell me what happened to Rosanne."

"Well, this older gal was walking home from church one Sunday morning when she thought she heard a voice. 'Claire... CLAIRE!' coming down from the sky. With that, she looked up sheepishly and said, 'Is that you, God?' God answered in his all-powerful voice, 'YES CLAIRE, IT IS I. I HAVE COME TO TELL YOU THAT YOU WILL LIVE 30 MORE YEARS!'

"With that single message, the voice disappeared. Claire was thrilled. She had been having some serious health problems but now that God had told her that she was going to live 30 more years she decided it was time to fix herself up for a long and wonderful future.

"She went out and had a boob job, a tummy tuck, and a facelift. She had more plastic put into her than a new car. She had her teeth redone, her cellulite suctioned, and her hair dyed bleach blonde. Finally, she had a manicure, a pedicure, and went out and bought a brand-new wardrobe to match her brand-new self."

"Yes, and then what happened?"

"Just as she was walking out of Saks Fifth Avenue, a bus came by and hit her head on. She died instantly. When she finally made it through the pearly gates, she headed straight to God and asked him what the deal was. She said, 'What's going on here God? Last month you told me that I was going to live another 30 years and this morning I get hit and killed by a bus. What's the story here?'

"God looked at her and asked, 'Claire?'

" 'Of course it's Claire,' she replied.

" 'Sorry Claire, I just didn't recognize you.'"

Richard laughed. Not a big hearty laugh, but more of a chuckle. It was a good joke, he thought. He didn't think Helen would find it all that funny. He wanted to hear the next tale, the one about Rosanne.

"What happened to Rosanne?" asked Richard.

Carl told Richard about Rosanne, Mrs. Rosanne Swenson. Rosanne lived just down the street from Carl in a new, very expensive canal-front home. By all appearances, Rosanne had everything. She was happily married to a retired contractor who had done very well for himself. Her daughter was engaged to a wealthy businessman from Cincinnati. She drove a big white Cadillac, had plenty of bridge partners and enjoyed good health. Rosanne was 63 years young.

About five years back, Rosanne decided that her smile wasn't what it used to be. She still had a pretty smile, but over time Rosanne's teeth had become discolored and worn. "It's called 'getting old'," Carl added with a chuckle. One of her bridge partners had told her about dental implants. How much better and more natural they were than false teeth. She made an appointment with a specialist in Ft. Myers. After the initial consultation with the doctor, she elected to go with the implants. Within a few months she was going about the meticulous business of having her own teeth pulled and replaced with these new implants. Her smile was going to look like a million dollars.

The process took about a year. When all of the surgery was

completed, her beautiful, youthful smile was back. There was no doubt that her new implants looked great. The trouble was, in the process of pulling all of her lower teeth and putting these replacement teeth into her lower jaw, the nerves had become inflamed. The pain became excruciating. She had her new teeth, but the pain that they came with was relentless.

To alleviate the pain for a while, at least until the nerve endings became accustomed to the implants, her dentist gave her a prescription for Percodan. Percodan is a powerful and addictive pain killer, Carl explained. The Percodan worked. It helped alleviate the pain, the swelling eventually went down and the nerve endings retreated. Everything appeared to be going Rosanne's way. Seeing that she was better, her dentist stopped the prescription for the pain killer.

His decision to take her off of Percodan didn't go over well with Rosanne. She insisted that there was still a lot of pain. She needed her Percodan to work through it. Her dentist became concerned and told her that he felt that the teeth and the jaw looked fine and that she might have accidentally developed an addiction to the pain killer. She told him to go to hell. With her money and connections, she quickly found another dentist who was sympathetic to her problem. She filed a law suit against the first dentist for malpractice. She insisted that he had incorrectly put her implants in and had caused the pain in the first place.

The next dentist kept monitoring the nerves and the lower jaw and noticed that they didn't seem to be inflamed. After three months, he withdrew her prescription to Percodan. She fired him. She went out and found another dentist who was more sympathetic to her plight.

By this time, for those of us who knew her, it was obvious that Mrs. Swenson was a junkie. She kept bouncing from doctors, to dentists, to whomever she could find in her endless search to keep that prescription bottle filled. She wasn't feeling any pain any longer and she liked it. In fact, Rosanne wasn't feeling anything. During the time that this went on, her husband had passed away from an unexpected stroke. Her life was now in a state of steady decline. Under the influence of this drug she had become addicted to, Rosanne was no longer herself. When the effect of the drugs wore off, she became irritable and irrational. Her bridge partners started to forget to include her in their games. Her daughter and her new son-in-law rarely visited. Rosanne told them all to go to hell. She withdrew further and further into herself and into the painless life inside her medicine chest. She vanished into the world of painkillers. Nothing else mattered. Finally, the last dentist on her list of sources cut her off. He saw what had happened. He told her that she was addicted to painkillers and informed her in no uncertain terms that she needed treatment.

Her daughter was contacted and the arrangements were made for Rosanne to stay at a drug rehab facility in Naples. She had to break the cycle of addiction. She stayed at the center for nine months. When Rosanne got out everything appeared to be like it used to be. She missed her husband, but she kept busy with the bridge club and she became involved with the island's conservation foundation. She had her smile back, her beautiful new teeth and her addiction appeared to be behind her.

But Rosanne had changed. Her daughter could sense it. Whereas before the addiction, Rosanne was able to take things as they came, she was now easily irritated and upset by the smallest incidents. She was moody and pensive, always suspicious of hidden agendas and motives. Because of this attitude, when her daughter informed her that she and her husband had decided to buy a place on Marathon, instead of Sanibel, she completely lost it.

"How could you do this to me?!" Shouted Rosanne to her daughter. "You know how I can't stand the Keys. You promised me that you would move to Sanibel. Don't you know how lonely I am?"

They got into a tremendous fight that afternoon. Her daughter decided that she didn't care if she ever spoke with Rosanne again. About a week later, the pain in her lower jaw came back. Soon after that, Rosanne found a new dentist. She explained to him that her lower jaw had a terrible inflammation, and after examining her, and listening to her go on and on about the suffering she was in, he prescribed a painkiller for the problem. The painkiller was Percodan.

Everything started to slide again. Within a few months the bridge club had put Rosanne back on their "not to be invited" list. After the fight, her daughter never called. She really had no way of knowing that her mom was back to being a junkie. Life for Rosanne became ever more isolated. She hardly ever came out of the house. She grew thin and pale, looking like a ghost when she walked out every morning to pick up the newspaper from the front yard. She had all the money she would ever need, all the things she could ever want, and yet she had nothing.

Six months later she picked up her .38 caliber pistol, squeezed that cold steel barrel between her beautiful white implants, and blew the back of her head off. One of the neighbors called the Sanibel Police when they noticed the newspapers piling up in the driveway. There was a note leaving some money to her sister and an empty bottle of Percodan on the kitchen table.

"Vanity is a strange animal, Richard. Your wife can get her breasts done, and you can have your liposuction, but know what you're getting into. We all fall apart, we all ache and crumble with time. Although we can forestall it by staying healthy and living well, time always wins. Life comes to us with a death sentence. It doesn't have to be fatalistic, but it has to be acknowledged. Denying your own mortality just doesn't work."

"Did her daughter ever speak with her before the suicide?" Richard asked.

"No, she never did. She did come back to Sanibel to make all the arrangements for the funeral. She made sure that Rosanne's sister got the money she promised her in the suicide note. Oddly enough, she didn't pay it off all at once, which she easily could have done. Instead, Rosanne's daughter, Anna, is still trickling the money to Rosanne's sister. I think that the reason for doing it that way is that Anna wants to keep some contact with her mother's family. This is the only way she knows how to do it," concluded Carl.

About that time a school of Spanish mackerel reappeared at the fishing pier. It was a madhouse once again, with everyone getting cut off, hooked up or tangled with some unsuspecting tourist. You could see the bright silver flashes of these slender fish as they sliced and cut through the schools of baitfish that hid behind the eddies formed on the back side of the pier pilings.

The rhythm of the sea is all there is that makes sense anymore, thought Carl to himself as the morning slowly, magically transformed itself into afternoon. Richard and he parted ways once more, promising to meet again tomorrow, when the tides would finish turning and the snook would be on the prowl. It had been a good day of fishing and a great day of stories. It had been a wonderful fourth morning.

Two

Richard left the pier at one o'clock. He didn't feel like going straight home so he decided just to drive around the back streets of the island for a while. He kept thinking about Carl's latest story. He needed some time to sort through things before having to deal with Helen and the boys. He needed some space.

The myriad little, dusty island roads are a good place to wander. Tiny streets that linger and wind through the heart of the island. Like oversized paths, they wind through rows of sabal palms and Australian pines. Narrow roads of shell and sand. Inviting places to get lost in. Getting lost suited the mood Richard was in perfectly.

Carl did this to him. Carl's voice and the stories he told unraveled the fabric of Richard's private mythology. It was an uncomfortable feeling, but Richard invited it. He was glad that his well-rehearsed life could become disturbed, shaken by the stories of this old fisherman from Davenport, Iowa. The slow, melodic voice that Carl spoke in reverberated through his thoughts like a deep, peaceful echo. Richard knew that it was truth he was hearing from this old man, and he was not familiar with the sound of truth.

Richard was familiar with the sound of lies. Husbands and wives lashing out at each other across highly polished tables. Neither story was ever true. Lies and more lies, like some pathological fairy tale where everything goes badly. Evil places, where love is methodically sacrificed to the pathetic process of divorce. "Divorce," he mumbled to himself as the car took him down a crooked lane named Cardium. He was beginning to hate the sound of that word.

It was hard for him to imagine that any of his clients had ever loved each other. That they once walked down an aisle together, with children throwing rose petals and mothers weeping in the pews. Images of them cutting the wedding cake, of photo albums gathering dust in the attic and exchanging vows. Vows now being reduced to rubble in this junkyard of malice. But divorce meant money to him. Big money.

Richard had learned to look past the tears in the eyes of the children involved. "They'll get over it," he had grown accustomed to saying to himself. Deep inside, Richard knew damned well that they'd never get over it. That the children were the ones who suffered the most. He knew that those children were the war babies of divorce. That they alone endured the chunks of emotional shrapnel that ripped through their tender hearts. The children of divorce. Never understanding why their mother and father had to go their separate ways, never understanding the anger. Sleepless nights full of scary dreams, tumbling grades and years of counseling. They'll get over it. "Bullshit," he said aloud as he turned down yet another neighborhood lane.

At the end of that lane, he found himself turning the van around and heading back to the condo. Everything on the island seemed greener than it did even yesterday. Richard wasn't feeling well.

When he got home, he sat at the kitchen counter. The boys were playing Nintendo 64 in the living room. They had the volume turned up loud. The sound of laser bombs, alien intruders, and cosmic missiles exploding inside that television contrasted sharply with the last few hours Richard had spent at the fishing pier. Instead of getting angry and telling the boys to turn down the volume, Richard laughed to himself. It is the story of my life, he thought.

Over the din of the video game, he told Helen the tale of Rosanne and her daughter. Helen didn't get it.

"Why couldn't Rosanne have simply gone back for more treatments? The story doesn't make any sense to me," said Helen.

Richard was frustrated. He interjected the idea that this was the same as her getting a boob job.

"Don't start in, Richard. You just don't want to spend the $20,000 it would cost to have the work done. Don't hand me this ridiculous story about some old bag who happens to get hooked on painkillers as an excuse for not getting my breast implants, because I don't buy it!"

"Don't you see the connection, Helen?"

"No, I don't."

"It's like Carl said, 'We can't avoid growing old, we have to accept what time does to us.'"

"Well Richard, I can avoid having my breasts sag. And I will. Half the ladies at the club have had some kind of cosmetic surgery and they're all doing fine. Eileen Fitzsimmons just had a perfect tummy tuck and she's yet to become some pathetic junkie. Maybe you should take a look in the mirror yourself, Richard. You could stand a treatment of liposuction."

"What's the use, Helen?"

Their conversation was like that, without impasse. Richard felt like taking another walk. He got up quietly and walked out the front door of the condominium. He was surprised by the fact that he wasn't angry. He took his walk alone. He left Helen back in the condo with her future implants and her two boys destroying space creatures designed by computer geeks from L.A.

Nothing was making sense. Richard walked down to the beach. He just stood there, looking at the breaking surf while trying to understand what it was saying to him. He turned to the west, walking slowly toward the setting sun. The sun never actually sets, Richard thought to himself as he headed down the beach. Instead, the world turns. His world was turning.

Three

Carl left the fishing pier earlier than he had all week. Between Richard and himself, they had ended up catching over a dozen Spanish mackerel. Carl was tired. The hangover had stayed with him all day. As the sun disappeared toward the west, he packed up his fishing gear and headed home. There was some yard work he needed to do and he thought he could get it done before the daylight was gone.

When he got home, he put all his gear away in the garage and walked out to check the mail. Apart from the usual onslaught of junk mail and bills, he found a hand-addressed letter from Marie's sister, June. It had been a long time since he had heard from June. He walked back inside, sat down in his favorite chair, and opened the letter.

In the envelope was a sympathy card and a two-page letter. The card was one of your typical drugstore sympathy cards with the usual greeting on it. On the bottom June had hand written, "Dear Carl, I wish the best to you and I want you to know that my thoughts and prayers are with you on Friday. That is the anniversary of Marie's departure from us one year ago. Love, June."

Carl started to cry. He had forgotten the date Marie had passed away. He knew why he had forgotten. He was still in denial. He didn't want to accept the painful truth that he could never, ever come home to make small talk with her again. That their life together in this place of stone and oceans, this place of pleasure and pain, was over. Everything was left to memories. To the items that once belonged to her. Her clothes still hung in the walk-in closet. Her jewelry still sat upon her dresser. Like lonely keepsakes, Carl could neither part with them nor look at them.

Instead, he waited. He waited for Marie to come home again some afternoon to change her clothes and go out and work in the yard. To reprimand him for setting his coffee cup down on her dresser or just smile at him once more. To ask him how the fishing had gone that day. Carl knew better, but it never stopped him from feeling the way he did. It never stopped him from hoping.

The letter that June had enclosed with her card was just as somber. Her husband's brother had recently passed away from liver failure. Carl remembered Stan from past family get-togethers. He was a kind and loving drunk. It couldn't have been much of a surprise to anyone that his liver finally gave out. He hadn't been sober for more than a day in the last twenty years.

June mentioned briefly how it was going between her and her husband Andy. She brought him up to date on what their three grown children were up to. June asked him to call her on Friday if he had a chance. She asked Carl to come up and see them over the holidays. It was a nice letter. As Carl set it down after reading it a second time, he was glad that June had reminded him. Carl liked June, and this letter reminded him of what a good sister Marie had.

Carl went into the bedroom to change into his yard-work clothes. It was already twilight, and he wanted to get started on the lawn. He couldn't let it go another week. The neighbors would start to complain.

He wasn't in the mood for it, but he went on to get out the hedge trimmers, the leaf rake, and all the two-cycle devices designed to make your yard look manicured. He worked at it for almost an hour. Carl was glad when the sun went down. It let him use the darkness as a good excuse to knock off early. He would take care of the rest of it in the next few days. He put the tools back in the other corner of the garage, opposite his fishing gear.

After half-finishing the yard work he opened a can of tuna fish, mixed it with some salad dressing and made a sandwich. Normally he would have had something warm for dinner, but because of the lingering remnants of his hangover, Carl wasn't in the mood to cook. While he slowly ate his sandwich, he flipped on the television to watch the evening news on CNN. The news was the same.

A plane had crashed somewhere in Ethiopia killing everyone on board. There were some sex scandals in Washington and the Pope was back in the hospital. The leading economic indicators were up for the third month in a row and some poor souls were nabbed in a welfare fraud case in Newark. Everything changes while everything remains the same, thought Carl to himself while watching the footage unroll on his twenty-seven-inch color TV.

Eventually, he fell asleep in his easy chair like he had many, many nights before. The TV was still on when he woke up at around 3:00 in the morning. The person inside the TV was repeating the stories that Carl had been listening to at 7:30, just before he fell asleep. The world was falling apart and coming together at the same time, just like it always had. Planes were crashing, famous people were dying and although it was three in the morning, the person inside the television was wide awake. Perhaps this station is on a tape loop, thought Carl as he got up to turn the TV off. He had a glass of warm milk, brushed his teeth, went into the bedroom and fell asleep.

He dreamed of Marie and the life they had together back in Davenport, before moving to Florida. His children were little. They were swinging on a high rope swing. As they swung out over the river, they would let go of the rope. They would fall into the water, only to come up laughing a moment later. These were good dreams. Dreams of Iowa in the warmth of summertime. Fields of corn, the rolling Mississippi and afternoon thunderstorms. Good dreams.

The Fifth Morning

One

Carl had forgotten to set his alarm. For the first time in months, 5:30 came and went and Carl's alarm didn't go off. He woke up at 8:15 a.m. and realized that after turning his clock radio off yesterday he had forgotten to reset it. He had only his hangover to thank. Although no one was present to make note of it, Carl was embarrassed. He remembered Richard. He must be down there by now, waiting for him at the pier. This was the morning that the tide was going to be shifting to an outgoing. Carl knew Richard was excited about the chance of catching a snook. They had even talked about running over to the Bait Box to buy some pinfish.

When Carl got out of bed, he noticed that his shoulder was still bothering him. The pain had now caused a slight numbness that ran all the way down his left arm. I must have pulled a muscle doing that yard work last night, he thought to himself. He went outside to pick up the morning paper. Then he came back inside to fix himself some coffee and breakfast. He wasn't feeling well. It wasn't because he had gotten drunk with his fishing buddies two nights ago. The hangover was gone. Carl was just tired and sore, like an old dog.

After breakfast he considered staying home for the day. After thinking about it for a while and reading the morning's editorials, he realized that it would be unfair to Richard. It would be selfish. He would take some aspirin for his shoulder, load up his gear, and head down to the pier. Catching a snook today is unlikely, he thought to himself while loading up the wagon. I won't even make it down there until nine. That's way too bright for snook.

Richard was worried. He had arrived at the fishing pier at 6:30 a.m. Ralph and Jose were already there. Chip arrived a few minutes later. Noticing that Carl wasn't there yet, Chip had cast netted enough bait for both of them. He invited Richard to use whatever he wanted until Carl showed. Chip went to his usual spot on the dock and started fishing. He wanted to hook up a big snook. The tide was going out and the conditions were right.

It was a perfect Thursday morning. There wasn't a cloud in the sky and the winds of the cold front that came through earlier in the week had now wrapped themselves around Florida. They were coming up from the southeast. When they blew up from the south, they were warm winds, heated by the air that rose above the Everglades. Winds that swept across the sawgrass and cypress hammocks as the sun rose over Miami. Richard had grown to love these mornings at the rickety pier. Away from the office. Away from the game.

Just after seven, Richard heard an unusual buzzing noise coming from the boardwalk. He hadn't heard this noise before. Perhaps it was someone from the city spraying for insects? It wasn't loud enough to be a leaf blower. The noise grew closer. Richard looked down to the end of the pier and discovered the source of the buzzing. There was a young man driving up in an electric wheel chair. He had a fishing rod in his hand. On his lap was a small red tackle box.

"Well, what the hell!" Chip shouted to the newcomer.

Ralph and Jose quickly turned to see whom Chip was hollering to. Ralph put down his rod and started sprinting down the pier toward this man in the wheelchair.

"Gary, it's great to see you. How've ya been?" Ralph asked.

"I've been fine, Ralph. I was looking over my tide chart and I noticed that this morning is looking pretty good for those old linesiders. I thought that I might come down and give it a go," said Gary.

"It's been too damn long, Gary," added Chip, who, out of character, had left his rod unattended to come down to greet Gary.

"Can we give you a hand?" asked Ralph.

"Sure can," replied Gary.

Chip grabbed the fishing pole and the tackle box from Gary. Gary got up and stood while Ralph lifted the wheelchair up over the small step onto the pier itself. Then Gary stepped up onto the dock, holding firmly onto the railing, and started to make his way toward the end of the pier. Richard was surprised to see that he could walk. With the help of his two friends and the sturdy railing, Gary made his way down to the end of the T-dock. He went to the south side of the dock. After putting down the pole and tackle box, Chip ran back to fetch the wheelchair. Richard thought that it was odd that he hadn't just ridden down the length of the pier in his electric wheelchair. It would have been easier.

"Can I get you a pinfish?" Ralph asked.

"That'd be great, Ralph."

Over the next few minutes, Richard watched from his vantage point two-thirds of the way up the pier as the three anglers dropped everything to help Gary get fixed up to fish. They attached the leader, the sinker and tied on the hook. Chip checked his drag and made sure that Gary was comfortable in the wheelchair. Chip checked and rechecked everything, making sure that it was positioned just right. Ralph and Gary started making small talk as Ralph switched from his favorite location on the north end of the pier to a spot right beside Gary.

Richard surmised that Gary must have been a regular member of the pier gang. No one had introduced Richard to him as Gary hobbled by. It was understandable, thought Richard. They were all so elated to see Gary that the thought probably never occurred to them. Besides, Carl wasn't there to help Richard understand the relationships involved. Obviously, Gary was familiar to everyone in the pier gang.

By this time Jose and Chip were back at their stations. Ralph and the young man in the electric wheelchair were busy fishing. As if there is such a thing as being busy at fishing. A few tourists and a couple of locals had now arrived at the pier. There were a dozen anglers leaning over the long, sun-dried and splintered railing. The sun was just coming up over the condominiums along Ft. Myers Beach. There was this feeling of a gorgeous day in paradise. Not quite as cool as yesterday morning. Perfect, thought Richard, just perfect.

Richard was preoccupied with wondering what could be delaying Carl. As a result, he hardly noticed when his line got slammed. His thoughts were elsewhere. He lost the fish. It was a snook. There wasn't any nibbling or warning when a snook hit, like you have with a catfish or a mangrove snapper. It was a quick and powerful strike. Richard knew that to hook up a big snook you have to react immediately, setting the hook instantly or risk losing the fish. He hadn't reacted quickly enough. Richard was only mildly disappointed. He was wondering about Carl and he was worried.

It was more than the thoughts of Carl that were rolling through his mind. The entire week had been difficult for him. He was thinking about everything. He was reflecting on his job, on his family, and on his life. He had come down here to relax and to recharge himself for the next onslaught of divorces, discoveries, and depositions. Instead he found himself not wanting to go back. He looked in the mirror last night after coming back from his long walk on the beach. Maybe it was Helen's cruel comment about liposuction that inspired him to do so. He was disappointed at what he saw in that mirror, let down by who was standing there staring back at him.

He hadn't really noticed how fat he had become. Richard Evans took off his extra, extra large T-shirt and his stretch-banded shorts so he could get a good look. Standing there like that, in his white, size 46 Jockey-style underwear, he looked absurd. His thighs were huge, looking like pale, white tree trunks. His belly completely hid the elastic of his shorts. His breasts, from all the fat and the lack of exercise, looked like those of an old woman. A fat old woman. His skin was white and ghostly, and his obesity made his entire body look soft and puffy, like he was sculpted out of marshmallows.

The only places he had any color at all were his arms, neck, and face. There was a little tan on his lower legs, below the hem of the shorts he wore every day down to the pier, but the best of the tan was on his arms and face. The tan looked good, he thought to himself. The light golden colors took away from the white, marble-like tones of the fat. He went over to the scale to weigh himself. The scale in the bathroom of the condominium went up to 250 pounds. The needle went there immediately and stopped. He knew that he was closer to 300 pounds.

He thought back to the year he had graduated from law school. He weighed 205 that year. He had always been heavy, but nothing like this. Nothing like this pale mountain looking at itself in the mirror. Had anyone ever told him he would look like this in twenty years, he would have laughed at them. He would have insisted that it wasn't possible. It was possible, he now admitted. He looked awful.

That and the smoking. When he graduated from law school, Richard didn't smoke. He had started smoking three years after joining the family law firm he was still practicing with. The stress had become too much for him to take. The cigarettes helped to ease that stress. For the first few years he had a ten-cigarette-a-day limit. He increased it to fifteen a day after "Cunningham vs. Cunningham." That was the one where she abducted the children and tried to flee the county. They arrested Mrs. Cunningham at Kennedy International. Mrs. Cunningham and the three children were all brought back to Peoria.

Mrs. Cunningham didn't want to face up to her alcoholism any more than the reality that her husband was better suited to take care of their children. It was an awful case, thought Richard. He was glad he had won. Mrs. Cunningham would never be allowed to see her children again. Richard wondered who had lost. He knew who had lost from the moment the custody order was handed down from the bench. The children had lost. And they were never allowed an attorney to defend or even mention their interests. They lost by default. They lost their mother, whom they loved regardless of all her faults.

That was when he decided that it would be OK to smoke a pack a day. Three months later, all of his self-imposed restrictions were removed. There were weeks when he knew he was pushing three packs a day. He didn't keep track. He didn't want to know.

Over the past few days, with Carl spinning his tales, and the air on this island so fresh and wonderful, Richard was back to under a pack a day. It wouldn't last. As soon as he got back to the office on Monday, he knew he would shoot back up to three, four packs a day. A walking incinerator for R.J. Reynolds, he thought to himself. Damn lucky I own a thousand shares of their stock, he added silently.

He knew that his chain smoking was uncontrollable. He could see the stack of files sitting on his desk right now. New files in the right-hand stack, old files on the left. Lies, betrayal, adultery and malice distributed evenly between them. Files that Richard converted into billing hours. Thousands and thousands of them.

The chain smoking was affecting his breathing. He had developed that heavy, labored panting common to overweight people. Between the obesity and the smoking, Richard sounded like a locomotive. His doctor was furious. His doctor had warned him a thousand times over that should he continue on his present path, he would be lucky to see 50.

Richard Evans, Attorney at Law, stood there in that mirror like an upright beluga whale, and realized that his doctor was right. He just didn't have the guts to do anything about it.

Richard's train of thought was unexpectedly interrupted by the sound of seagulls. The gulls were about a mile off the end of the pier. They were all screaming and hovering about, diving over a school of Spanish mackerel. Richard stood there watching them for the longest time. They were free.

For some reason, the pier was full of pelicans this morning. There had always been pelicans at the pier, but not like this morning. There were at least twenty of them loafing around. Pelicans are stupid looking birds, thought Richard to himself as he watched one of the juveniles sit there on the wooden two-by-four railing not six feet from him. And they shit everywhere, he added to that thought.

Almost all of the pelicans were juveniles, dull brown and stupid. The older pelicans had yellow heads and white necks. Aside from being gangly and awkward on land, the mature pelicans were pretty, in a way. The younger pelicans were not. Two or three of them were busy trying to eat a sheepshead that was hanging on the end of one of the tourist's stringers in the water. The birds couldn't understand that the fish was connected to a stringer, which in turn was connected to the railing of the pier. The two birds kept picking at it with the small hook at the very end of their upper beaks, lifting it out of the water in a futile attempt to swallow the fish. The tourist who had caught it eventually had to take the poor sheepshead up and lay it on the deck of the pier. It looked terrible there, slowly drying out in the sun.

There were about ten more pelicans up on the roof of the small covered section of the pier. They were sitting up there looking like a flock of miss-fashioned ducks. Their big webbed feet were sticking out over the edge of the roof as though they were all wearing flippers. The design of these birds is wrong, thought Richard. Their beaks are too big for their body, their wings look like they should fit on a bird about twice as large, and when they dive it's as though they've just been shot.

Pelicans were designed by a committee, concluded Richard. A volunteer committee at that.

The only time they really look good is when they form that perfect flying V formation in the very early morning as they all leave their roost and head back out to sea. They look like prehistoric geese. With their enormous wings beating in rhythm, they are a glorious sight to behold as the sun rises over Ft. Myers Beach. Those are the mature, graceful adults flying out into the open ocean. They don't try to beg and steal their food down here at the fishing pier. Those birds are headed far out into the Gulf where they can feed themselves and live noble, honorable lives.

These shit-brown punks that hang out at the fishing pier are an entirely different class of pelicans. They get tangled in your line, try to dive into your bait bucket, beg for scraps of anything, and shit everywhere. These are welfare pelicans, thought Richard, derelicts. Typical committee work.

"I wonder who handles their divorce work?" he mumbled to himself in a rare moment of self-humor.

With those thoughts running through his head, Richard took his rod and shooed off five of them that had settled down on the railing not three feet from him. He didn't know why he bothered to do it. All they did was to take off, make one big circle and land on the railing behind him. He knew if he shooed them off of that spot they would just come back and land next to him again. These birds were born without brains. Because it was Sanibel, and someone would probably turn him in if he kept harassing these stupid birds, Richard decided to let them be. They didn't deserve the protection they had on Sanibel. If a tourist behaved this way at the fishing pier, you could have him arrested, thought Richard. These birds get off without so much as a reprimand.

He let it go at that. Richard was still wondering what might have happened to Carl when he heard Ralph let out one hell of a hoot. Gary was hooked up with a snook.

Richard had set up on the south side of the dock, to take advantage of the falling tide, so he enjoyed a clear view of the battle. Immediately after striking, the big fish rose quickly to the surface, shaking its head from side to side in a futile attempt to throw the hook. It was a linesider all right, a snook. And a big one at that.

Ralph helped Gary to stand up. It was easy enough for Gary

to set the hook while seated, but to fight the fish he needed to be standing up.

"Pull my wheel chair back Ralph. Get me some room to move."

Ralph grabbed hold of the heavy, motorized wheel chair, and pulled it back to the center of the pier. He then came back up to help Gary out in any way he could.

Gary was holding his spinning rod taut in his right hand and using the railing of the pier and his left hand to help support himself. Catching a good-sized snook is hard enough. Being crippled added infinitely to the challenge. Richard was impressed.

Every so often Richard could see Gary lean forward enough to allow him to shift his weight to the railing and free up his left hand to reel. Luckily, the snook ran down current, keeping away from the razor-sharp pilings underneath the pier. Jose and Chip had set down their rods to join Ralph as Gary's personal cheering section.

"Hang onto him, Gary," said Chip. "He's a beauty!"

"Keep that rod tip up," added Jose. Advice was always easy when it was someone else holding onto the rod.

The fish was growing tired. After a few spectacular leaps and long runs, the big linesider was being cranked back to the pier. Ralph had run over to get the long-handled net. Gary, equally worn out, looked a rare combination of wobbly and thrilled. The fight had lasted ten minutes. It was obvious to Richard that Gary wasn't used to standing that long.

When the snook finally made it within netting range, Ralph leaned over and scooped him up. The snook was too tired to make a dash for the pilings. It had made a poor decision early in the fight, and that decision was to try and run downstream with the outgoing current. Had it ducked under the pier immediately after being hooked, the outcome would have been different. The snook had lost. With the snook now flopping around helplessly in the dark green mesh of the net, Ralph set it down and ran back for Gary's wheelchair. Gary gave a sigh of relief as he settled back into it.

"What a fish!" cried Jose.

"Give me five," said Chip, as he went up to Gary and slapped his right hand.

It was a scene of great celebration. Richard couldn't resist joining in. He set down his rod. Using a small piece of rope that some other angler had left tied to the top railing of the dock, he secured the rod to make sure it didn't get pulled into the sea if he got a strike. He walked over to the entourage at the south side of the T-dock and approached Gary.

"Hi, I'm Richard. I just want to tell you that you handled that snook magnificently."

"Thanks. It was just lucky that the old linesider didn't head under the pier on its first run. I was just lucky, I guess."

"Hold her up for a picture, Gary," said Ralph. He had worked the big snook out of the net, removed the hook, and had already given it a good wake-up call with his baseball bat. He didn't hit it hard enough to crush the fish's skull this time. He just knocked it unconscious so it wouldn't flop around when Gary held it up. Ralph had brought along one of those small, disposable point-and-shoot cameras. Gary took hold of the fish, which went nearly twenty pounds, and held it up.

It was a memorable sight. Here was this young man in a wheelchair at the end of a fishing pier, with Chip on his left and Jose on his right, holding up the massive fish he had just caught. The smiles on their faces said everything. It was a proud moment.

Just after Ralph shot the photo, Richard spoke up, "Hey, Ralph, you netted him. Why not hold the net up and stand behind Gary. I'll get a shot with all four of you in the picture."

The tableau was formed. Chip held the rod, Ralph stood behind and held the net, Jose had his right hand on Gary's right shoulder, and Gary held the trophy. Click. Memories immortalized.

"Are you going to keep him or release him?" Ralph asked.

"Did you say deep-fried or baked?" answered Gary.

"Gotcha," said Ralph.

"If you guys don't mind, one snook will be all she wrote for me today. I need to take some time off. These darn fish can tire a good old boy out. Could you please carry the fish back to the car for me, Ralph?"

"You bettcha, Gary."

The two of them headed back down the pier toward the shoreline. Richard wasn't surprised to see Gary leave after catching that fish. He could see that it was hard on him to stand and hang on like that. It was a heroic scene that morning. Ralph was carrying this beautiful fish, its tail dragging on the ground, while Gary placed his rod and tackle box up on his lap as his wheelchair buzzed back to the end of the pier. He was too tired to walk back. It was a fish story worth remembering.

"Hey, Chip, what do you think happened to Carl this morning?" wondered Richard. "He would have loved to have seen that snook Gary just headed out with."

"Who knows, Richard? Maybe he was still hung over from the other night. I'm sure that he will be here later. Carl knows that the tides are ripe for the big snook and he loves to hook up with those twenty- pound linesiders. You can be sure he'll show up sooner or later."

"Does he miss many mornings like this?"

"You'd have to ask Ralph or Jose that question. I usually only come down on Tuesdays. He's always here then. Today I got lucky and a job I was supposed to be doing had some last-minute permit problems. I took the day off. Ralph might be able to tell you."

Richard decided not to bother to ask Ralph. Chip was probably right. Richard was making more of it than mattered. Carl was probably just tired, or had something else come up. There was nothing to worry about. Carl would eventually show up.

Carl finally arrived. It was around 9:30 when he walked down the winding wooden boardwalk to the foot of the Sanibel fishing pier. Richard heard someone coming and looked down to see if it was his new found fishing buddy. It was.

Carl looked old. He seemed tired and weathered, like the gray, cracked wood on the railing of the pier. The lines in his face ran deeper this morning. His thinning hair was grayer. Even his pace was slower than usual. He looked like a tired old man coming to spend another day of his life down at the local fishing pier. There was still that softness in his pale blue eyes. A softness like the color of the sky, or the blue of the ocean. But this morning, even the blue was faded.

He was wearing a faded T-shirt promoting a local restaurant called The Lazy Flamingo, a pair of dark blue shorts, some old leather deck shoes and his oversized hat. Richard realized that Carl had worn the same clothes yesterday. You could still see the splattered blood stains on the T-shirt from the Spanish mackerel the two of them had landed.

Richard didn't like seeing his friend in this light. It stole the magic from Carl. It made his tales seem less vital, less alive. Seeing this tired old man walking slowly up to him made Richard feel uncomfortable.

What was there to learn from this old man? he asked himself. He was just an old retired fishing guide who had nothing better to do with his time. These were unwelcome thoughts for Richard. They were tearing away the mystique that Richard had wrapped around his new friend. With the mystery gone, all that was left was an old fisherman in shorts, a stained and faded T-shirt, wearing a pair of old shoes, who was carrying some fishing gear up the length of a Florida fishing pier. It was a depressing perspective, and Richard wanted it to go away.

"Well, you finally made it," said Richard.

"Finally," replied Carl.

He sounded tired. His shoulder and left arm had been bothering him all morning. He didn't have his usual enthusiasm. Carl had come down to the pier reluctantly this morning, and it showed.

"What kept you?" Richard asked.

"Oh, this darn shoulder is aching again. I didn't sleep well at all last night. I had heartburn or something. When I finally did get to sleep, I forgot to set the alarm. It's just part of getting old. The horseshit part."

"You missed some great action earlier. There was this guy in a wheelchair that showed up and caught a whopper."

"Gary was here?"

"Yeah, I think that was his name."

"Oh damn, I missed him."

"You know him?"

"Everyone on this island knows Gary."

"Well, he caught a big snook this morning around eight o'clock. It was huge. Ralph helped him carry it back to his car. It weighed every bit of twenty pounds. And what a fight! Gary just leaned up against the railing and held on. It was great when Ralph finally netted it for him."

"Gary is a survivor," remarked Carl. "He's learned to survive the hard way."

"What do you mean?"

"I'll tell you the story in a bit. First I want to get a line in the water."

Carl lifted his trusty cast net out of his multi-holed five-gallon bucket and headed back toward shore to find some minnows. He made a few casts without much success. He then walked up the shore to the north a block and dropped the full-moon circle of his cast net on a big school of baitfish. He had more than he could use in a week. He quickly picked out the little ones, being careful to toss them back alive, and kept about four dozen. He flipped them into the empty bucket. They were still jumping around nervously as he walked back to the pier and lowered them down, using the line from the cast net to tie them off. He got his three rods out, handed one to Richard and baited up.

"Good snook tide this morning, but I'm way too late to expect much today," he said while making a perfect cast to the south.

"You're probably right. No one has had a strike in the last half an hour," said Richard. "Now tell me about Gary."

"Gary. Now that's a tale. Gary had it all. It must be four, maybe five years ago when he had the accident. I remember that it was just before Christmas, because the truck was full of presents when they got hit."

"Who got hit?"

"Gary and his fiancé. I think her name was Diane. She left the island about a year later. I can't say that I blame her. It was such a mess."

Carl was not himself. His story was coming out all disjointed. It was not typical for Carl to spin a yarn like this. It was frustrating.

"What was such a mess?"

"Oh, the accident was a mess. Some drunken asshole from

Ft. Myers was driving the wrong way up Summerlin when he ran head on into Gary and his fiancé, Diane. The drunk was driving a 1985 Cadillac and Gary was in his new Toyota pick-up. It was a bad match. The impact pushed the Toyota's engine right into Gary's legs. He went into a coma. His fiancé, Diane, was banged up very badly too. Not nearly as bad as Gary.

"The ambulance arrived about fifteen minutes later and Gary was near dead. They had to use those jaws of life to cut him out of the truck. The drunk driving the Cadillac wasn't even hurt. The cops arrested him for drunk driving and hauled him off. But Gary was hurt badly. It took nearly an hour to cut him out of there. He was a real mess. His right leg had been shattered. Nahhhh, worse than that, his whole life was shattered.

"The EMS workers never thought he'd pull out of the coma. His heart stopped beating three times before they made it back to the hospital. There was blood everywhere. The gifts they had just picked up for their friends and family had all flown into the front seat with the impact and were covered with blood. The gifts were towed off with the truck.

"Gary was in surgery for nine hours. He was still in a coma when he came out but he had stabilized. They kept him in intensive care for three weeks. The blow to the head was so severe that most of the doctors felt that if he ever did come out of the coma, he'd be a vegetable. Everyone on the island was in shock. Gary had everything. He had just finished college up at one of those expensive, fancy schools up East. He had just gotten engaged to his old high school sweetheart, Diane Jensen. The world was his oyster.

"His parents had moved down to Sanibel years ago and long before the city had banned restaurant chains, they had opened a fast food restaurant right on Periwinkle. It was a gold mine. Gary's parents had a fancy home over on the east end of the island that backed up to a canal. They had a big screened pool, a three-car garage and it seemed like Gary was living in a fairy tale.

"That big white Cadillac ended the fairy tale. About six weeks after the accident, Gary miraculously came out of the coma. Diane was there beside him when he did. He remembered her name. Diane had broken her arm and had a number of cuts and bruises, but had only been in the hospital about four days. Except for the cast on her left arm, she was fine the day Gary came to."

"Was he OK?" asked Richard.

"Mentally he was fine, but his legs were a mess. There were skin grafts, bone grafts, operation after operation. The trouble was that there was just too much damage done. Gary would never walk right again. He would have to spend most of the rest of his life in a wheelchair. The drunk, on the other hand, knew all the good ole boys downtown at the courthouse and got off with three years' probation. If Gary would have died, he would have gotten manslaughter. But Gary lived.

"Diane couldn't handle it. Most women couldn't. After a year, they broke off the engagement. Diane felt so bad about all that had happened that she moved back up to Ohio with her sister. She couldn't deal with the lifelong commitment of being married to an invalid."

"How did Gary handle it? I mean, everything was gone," said Richard.

"I can't answer that question exactly. Only Gary could. But it seems that there are certain people who, no matter what their predicament, they always choose life. They have this inner core that survives. It's a perspective, an energy that keeps them strong amidst the worst of circumstances. Nobody really knows if they have that courage or not until they are faced with real adversity. I'm not talking about the little things here. I'm talking about the kind of adversity that involves the jaws of life. Real challenge, real hardship. The kind of situation where your fiancé leaves you, you're crippled for life, and everything you have ever planned for yourself is gone. Like Roosevelt must have felt like after he came down with polio.

"Gary just kept picking himself back up again and again. Now he sits tall in his wheelchair. He used to be one of the best fishermen you'd ever seen. He could thread a needle with his four-pound tippet on his fly rod, land a hundred-pound tarpon in ten minutes flat and throw a twelve-foot cast net better than anyone I've ever known.

"Even though he can't do any of those things physically any longer, he can do greater stuff inside. Because he's alive. He's a thousand times more appreciative than most people for what it means to live. Gary has been to the edge of death and back. He doesn't feel sorry for himself, or feel bad about Diane leaving him, or even blame the drunken bastard that ran into him. He just does the best he can and lives every day to the fullest. More people should do that."

Just then one of Carl's rod tips started dancing. Carl reached over, took up the rod and waited. It was too soon to tell what might be playing with it on the other end. It might be a catfish, or a mangrove snapper, but it was too soon to know. Carl held his rod steady. Poised like some cobra about to strike. The fish grabbed the minnow firmly and swam off. Carl snapped the long rod back flawlessly and set the hook. It was something large but it didn't rise to the surface.

"What's on, Carl?"

"I don't know, Richard. This one's got me fooled. It ain't a snook though. Snook almost always come up to the surface when you strike them. This fish is staying deep. It's not running as fast as either a snook or redfish either, but it's too damn strong for a catfish. I don't know what the hell it is."

"Should I get the net?"

"In a minute."

The fish stayed deep. It hung tight to the bottom just below the pilings of the pier but never dashed toward them. It might be a gag grouper, thought Carl. He wasn't sure. As he slowly worked it up to the surface, he finally saw what it was. It was a black drum.

"You can get the net now," he told Richard.

Richard ran over and picked up Ralph's long-handled pier net. Richard had never used such a long net before. It was awkward to handle on the pier. The handle was too long. If he wasn't careful with it, he could easily hit someone clear across the width of the pier with the oversized handle. He worked his way carefully back to Carl, holding the net high above his head.

By the time he got back to Carl the black drum was lying on its side, exhausted from the battle.

"What in the world is that?" questioned Richard while lowering the net.

"It's a black drum. Ugly as sin, isn't it," said Carl.

Black drum are ugly. They have huge heads and thick, prehistoric-looking scales. Their mouths point down, like a sucker or a carp, and just behind their mouths they have a patch of short, fleshy whiskers that resemble small, white worms. They are short and thick, with a large head and shoulders tapering quickly to a wide tail-fin. They look ancient. Medieval.

Richard engulfed the ten-pound fish in the net and started lifting it up toward the dock. Instead of pulling the net straight up, hauling up the long handle hand over hand like Ralph or Jose do, Richard lifted the net straight out and starting pulling it in. About the time he had brought the netted drum level with the railing, with ten feet of aluminum handle hanging straight out over the water, it buckled. The leveraged weight of the fish was too much for that long stretch of light aluminum to handle. The fish, the net, and over half the handle went plummeting back down to the water. Carl's line parted on impact. The big drum thrashed about in the mesh of the landing net for a few minutes, worked itself free and swam off. The net sank. Richard felt like sinking along with it.

Ralph and Jose were laughing. Little did Richard know that they had witnessed this same mistake a dozen times before. Tourists and locals alike had made the same idiotic scoop with the pier net only to watch it buckle before their eyes. They were used to catching fish from boats or from docks that sit lower to the water. That is how you net fish in a boat, you put the net below them, scoop them up, and bring them on board. Not so with a long-handled pier net.

Ralph came over to Richard with a peculiar smile on his face.

"I'm sorry, Ralph. I owe you the cost of a new net," said Richard. Turning to Carl, he added, "and I'm sorry about losing that drum for you."

"Don't worry about the drum. I wasn't going to keep it anyway. But I do think you learned the hard way on how not to net fish from a pier," said Carl.

"I think so," added Ralph.

"How much do I owe you, Ralph?"

"Forty bucks will replace it."

Richard dug out his wallet and handed Ralph two twenties. Richard felt like crawling under one of the two benches that were on either side of the small covered section of the pier. He wanted to disappear. He was far too big to fit under either of those benches and he soon just got back to fishing and keeping quiet. Fifteen minutes later, Carl broke the silence.

"I kept one drum in my life. It was a long time ago," started Carl.

Richard didn't respond, but Carl continued anyway.

"We were fishing near the causeway, using shrimp to catch Spanish mackerel on a charter I had. One of my customers set up on what he thought was a Spanish, but turned out to be a fifty-pound black drum. If you think that ten-pounder we just released was homely, you should see a fifty-pounder. They are absolutely disgusting. They get darker and darker as they age. Those white whiskers grow much longer. When you finally get them on board they make this loud, thumping sound, just like someone is pounding a drum inside of them.

"Well, it turns out that my charter was from up East - Maryland if I recall. Back up that way they eat them. So we gaffed this huge fish and brought it back to the dock with us to clean.

"I have never filleted a more difficult fish in my life. The scales on this thing were like cast iron. They were all but impossible to cut through. Each scale was bigger than a silver dollar. After an hour I had two thick slabs of dark red meat still attached to the skin on the fillet table. It was full of rib bones. I worked the meat from the skin and took out all the rib bones. There must have been twenty pounds of black drum on that cleaning table. It looked like chunks of rump roast.

"In that same amount of time, back when I was cleaning fish for my charters, I could have cleaned twenty big snook, or forty sea trout. This drum was like cleaning a sea monster. From that moment on I told every customer who caught a black drum on my charters that they were inedible in these waters. I said that they ate calico crabs, and that calico crabs had a toxin in them that could be passed through to people if they ate a local black drum."

"Was it true?"

"Not in the least. Grouper eat calico crabs all day long and people eat grouper every day. I just never wanted to clean another black drum again. And I never did."

Carl and Richard both re-baited their lines and got back to fishing. It was noon. Richard had promised to take Helen and the boys up to the Mucky Duck on Captiva for lunch, so he knew that he only had a few more minutes to fish. He wanted to get back and touch a minute more on Gary's story.

"Carl, isn't it amazing that they could save Gary like that?"

"Yeah, it's amazing. Thirty years ago Gary would never have survived an accident like that. There were no air-bags protecting his upper body, no machines to monitor his every breath at the hospital. He would have died at the scene. But Gary's young and strong. He wanted to survive.

"I wouldn't want that. Maybe five years ago I would have wanted that. But not now. When my time comes, I don't want to be kept alive like Gary was. There's a time to live and there is a time to die. We've lost sight of that. That's one of the things I regret about what I went through with my wife. After the first round of cancer, the mastectomy and all the chemo, Marie and I should have learned. It was hard to watch. The chemicals they use to kill the cancer cells nearly killed her. Then, after two years of remission, we received the news that the cancer had spread. That it had metastasized, the doctors told us. Right then and there, the afternoon after the confirmation by her doctor, we both should have jumped on a plane and flown away for a year.

"But we didn't. We thought that if we could beat it once we could beat it again. Only this time it was worse. In the end it was hard to say what took her, the cancer or the treatments. There was the radiation, the chemo and the operations. Marie didn't die in the end. She was tortured to death by those men in white uniforms with fancy initials after their name. She was murdered by a string of broken promises. It was the worst two years of my life.

"There's something wrong with it all. We've created a world where getting old and dying are viewed with disgust. A world where we're supposed to keep these wrinkles from forming around our eyes and our teeth from turning yellow. Every day on the television there's a new cream out there, or a better treadmill, or a dietary supplement that keeps aging at bay. We're a country in denial about growing old. We're even more in denial about dying.

"I just don't understand it. Aging is as inevitable as the tides. It isn't something we can forestall, or avoid, or ignore. It happens to everyone. It is how life completes itself."

Richard was still quiet, listening attentively.

"When I finally go, I don't want to be kept alive by some damn machine somewhere. Breathing through a tube, eating through a tube and pissing through a tube. Why would anyone want that kind of life? I've seen it. Not just with Marie but with friends of mine. I've talked to them, laying there in those sterile rooms blinking once for yes and twice for no. It's bullshit.

"We live our lives, make the best decisions we can, give what we have and, more importantly, what we've learned over the years, to our children, grow old and die. Now what the hell is so wrong with that? Why does everyone make it so complicated? I like what I've done. I like the fact that I quit my job back in Davenport. I've loved my years out here on the ocean fishing. My kids are off and married now, raising families of their own up in Atlanta and over in the Carolinas and I'm glad for them.

"Sure, I'm not rich or some world-famous guide, or a celebrity or anything. I'm just Carl, the old fart from Sanibel who spends almost every day of his life down here at the pier with Ralph, Chip, Jose and the boys. Ain't that good enough?"

"It's good enough, Carl."

The sun climbed to the roof of the sky and hung there for just a moment, bearing witness to their conversation. No one in the world knew it, but it hesitated for just an instant on its ceaseless journey. The world had stood still in the sheer simplicity of it all. It was a moment in the sun.

Richard told Carl that he really had to be going. It had been a great morning of fishing. Richard hadn't caught a fish.

Two

Helen was in a terrible mood as Richard walked through the door into the condominium. The boys had been fighting all morning. They didn't fight often, but when they did, there was always hell to pay. It had started over which program they wanted to watch. The insane thing about the disagreement was that there were two televisions in the condominium. They could have each watched the show they wanted to, without needing to get into a fight. That's not the way James and Tyler worked. They were spoiled.

They each wanted to watch their favorite program on the big TV, and not on the little 13-inch color TV in the master bedroom. Tyler grabbed the remote and wouldn't let James have it. Then came the kicking, fighting, and the inevitable swearing and carrying on. Helen was doing what she could to contain them, but they paid little attention to her.

Richard walked in to see that the condo was a mess. James had managed to get the remote from Tyler in the wrestling match for it and had now locked himself in the guest bathroom. You could hear Tyler crying from the guest bedroom. There were cushions and pillows tossed about everywhere. Clear evidence of a spat.

Helen was in a dreadful state when she started in with her husband. "It's about time you came home, Richard! Your going out and fishing every single morning has ruined our vacation. I'm sick and tired of it and so are the boys," she stated emphatically.

"Have the boys been fighting again?" He knew that it was the root of her problem. He could see that he had better use some of his legal skills if he planned on making it through this trial.

"I think the answer to that is rather obvious, Richard," answered Helen sarcastically. "James has locked himself in the bathroom for the last hour and Tyler is in the guest bedroom crying with a bloody nose. You had better go have a talking to both of them.

They are totally out of control."

The boys had been out of control their entire lives. It wasn't anything new to Richard. He never really had any time to spend with them and, lacking the time, he had compensated for it by getting them everything imaginable. He had bought them more toys and gadgets each year than most children would own in a lifetime. Of course they liked the mountains of things their dad had got for them: the Nintendo, the pool table, the electric race car set - but in their hearts they would have traded every present they owned for some time with their father. For them, any time at all would be quality time.

Because Richard never spent any time with his boys, situations like this were especially trying for him. Richard rarely spoke with his kids when they were behaving. When they fought like this, he felt awkward and inept at how to patch things back together. He walked over to Tyler first, determined to give it a try.

"Tyler, you should know better. You're the older brother and you should set a better example...," said Richard in a weak, worn monologue with no impact.

"James started it," accused Tyler. There were tears in his eyes. Tyler had always been the more emotional of the two. Although he was both larger and older, James won most of the skirmishes. James was tougher. He was made out of a stronger emotional fabric.

"I don't really care who started it, Tyler. I just want you both to apologize to each other and end it," said Richard.

"OK."

Tyler went over to the bathroom door and said that he was sorry. Through the hollow bathroom door James could hear him say it clearly, but he pretended that he didn't hear him.

"What did you say, Tyler?" asked James.

"I'm sorry."

"What?"

"I SAID I'M SORRY, YOU SHITHEAD!"

They started up again. Richard didn't know what to do. He got angry. That was his fall-back position, to get angry. When a three-hundred- pound attorney gets angry, kids listen up.

"That's enough from both of you. And Tyler, you watch your mouth or I'll rinse it out with dish soap. Your mother and I had plans to take everyone up to lunch at the Mucky Duck this afternoon and we're leaving you two at home." Walking over to the locked bathroom door, Richard continued, "I'll give you to the count of three to unlock this door and come out, James. If you don't, I'll kick it in and take the cost of repairing it out of your hide!"

"One..., two...," click. The door unlocked and opened and a sheepish James emerged. Tyler ran up and grabbed the changer from him.

"Not so fast Tyler, give me that changer," said Richard.

Tyler handed it over. He knew his father was upset. His face was red and there was that quiver in his voice. His voice had that vibrato it had when he was really, really angry. Richard took the changer from Tyler, walked over to the master bedroom, picked up his locking briefcase, dropped it inside and slammed it shut. No one, except Richard, knew the combination. For now at least, it was over.

You could still operate the television manually but the thought of doing so had never occurred to either of the boys. Their entire lives were defined by joysticks, computer mice, and remote controls. They weren't about to operate a television manually. In fact, neither of them knew that such a thing could be done.

Richard, Helen, and the boys got ready to drive up to Captiva. Tyler and James, still sulking from the fight, were quiet for the long ride up to the Mucky Duck. Because they didn't arrive at the restaurant until two o'clock, they were seated immediately. That was good. Richard hated waiting. He hated it with a passion. Especially waiting to eat.

The proprietor of the Mucky Duck, Waldo, came around to their table and did his usual shtick. He pretended to spill some coffee on them, squirted them with the fake mustard dispenser, and ran through his well-rehearsed string of corny jokes. Tourist-oriented patter, entertaining for the most part. None of them laughed. Tyler and James just sat there and stared at him. The only thing funny about the scene was the total absence of humor. Waldo might as well have been doing his comedy routine at the local morgue. He would have had a better reception.

Lunch was fine. Helen had the barbecued shrimp and Richard had a crunchy grouper sandwich. He was glad that he hadn't been the one to fillet the grouper. It was boneless and over an inch thick. The boys had what they always had. Regardless of the menu, the restaurant, or the ethnic orientation, they each had a hot dog with melted American cheese on it and an order of fries. If the restaurant didn't have hot dogs, cheeseburgers worked. Lacking cheeseburgers, which rarely happened, grilled cheese sandwiches were the default settings.

Both Tyler and James never experimented or tasted anything else. It would have been useless to ask them to taste the grouper sandwich or the shrimp. It had been so long since they had asked the boys to try something new that the thought of it never occurred to either parent. When it came to food, the boys ruled, and ruled with iron fists.

They all drove back to the condo in a better mood. By the time they arrived at their apartment Waldo's humorous routine would have worked. It was too late. Waldo was counting the receipts by now and getting ready for the early bird special. Waldo didn't care if the Evans family thought he was funny or not. Their tab was $64.15. That was how Waldo had fun. He was laughing all the way to the bank.

"What do you say we go for a swim?" said Richard.

Helen and the boys all looked at each other as if they had just heard their father ask them if they wanted to go for a swim. That was impossible. They were all too stunned to verify or acknowledge his request. Helen finally broke the silence.

"Did you just say 'go for a swim?' " repeated Helen somewhat sheepishly.

"Sure, why not? It's hot out and I could use a cool down," answered Richard.

Something was wrong, thought Helen. Something had been going on down at that fishing pier that just didn't add up. Richard had not gone swimming with his boys since their infant swimming lessons. Richard hated swimming. He disliked exposing his immense body to anyone and he abhorred the smell and taste of chlorine. His request to go swimming this afternoon with his family had the same odds as Tyler and James giving up TV for a month. Those odds were nil.

"Sounds great, Dad!" said James enthusiastically.

"Sure Dad, I'll get my swimming trunks on," added Tyler.

Helen still wasn't sure. The whole week Richard had been acting out of character. At times she even liked him, an emotion that was utterly foreign to her as well. Now this swimming nonsense. This was the enigma that broke the camel's back.

"Just give me a few minutes to get my suit on," said Helen unexpectedly. She said it in such a way that it was as though someone else had spoken the words through her. She didn't expect to say yes. She didn't know what she was going to say. There was no stock answer to Richard's request. She had double checked her vast collection of tape-looped responses only to come up empty handed. Richard had never asked to go swimming with his family before. There wasn't a single phrase in her vast repertoire of stock responses that would work for the moment. They were all going swimming.

It was a sight to behold. Richard, the walrus, and his happy family all heading down to the pool together. The boys took their swimming accessories along, which amounted to a complete collection of pool toys. They had snorkels, masks, fins, diving batons, inflatable alligators, high-powered squirt guns called Super-soakers and remote control electric motor boats that cost $139.95 each. Both of the remote controls were broken.

Standing next to the deep end of the pool, Richard debated with himself over whether or not he should jump in. It had been twenty years since he had jumped into a pool. Twenty years and one hundred and thirty-five pounds ago. There was no one at the pool except the four of them, so there was no one there to laugh at him.

"You're not thinking about jumping in, are you Richard?" Helen inquired. She knew he was. He was standing there, like a fat suicide jumper on the 30th floor with that glint in his eye. Richard was ready to flatten some yellow cab three hundred feet down below him. Parked on Wall Street, innocently waiting for a stock broker to get in.

"I sure am."

"Don't do it yet Dad, let me and James get in the pool first," said Tyler.

"Why?"

"We want to play tidal wave," Tyler answered.

"Yeah, TIDAL WAVE!" shouted James as he jumped in.

Richard waited until the boys got into position on either side of him on the deep end of the pool. They were ready.

"Count down from ten," requested Tyler.

"Ten-nine-eight-seven-six-five-four-three-two...ONE!"

Richard hit the water with the same impact as the giant meteor that hit the earth sixty million years ago. The tidal wave almost pushed the kids out of the pool. Some of the water made it up and over the rim of the pool and washed up on the pool deck. It was steaming as it hit the hot concrete. Richard never touched bottom. His enormous excess of fat had kept him too buoyant to reach the bottom. He hit the water and stayed there, like he had jumped into a bowl of aquamarine Jell-O.

Tyler and James had a ball playing in the great waves that reverberated around the pool like aftershocks to a killer quake. Tsunamis. Great fun. Helen was smiling. She had not seen this side of Richard since just after their marriage. For a moment she remembered that Richard, and for an instant, felt as if she could love him again. It was a side of Richard, that crazy, childlike side, that she adored. For a brief moment under an autumn sun, poolside at some obscure condominium on Sanibel Island, Helen had a genuine feeling toward her husband again. It made her feel confused.

Helen had once loved Richard. But so much had changed over the years that her feelings toward him had faded like a pair of college jeans. He had changed. His dream of teaching law, his crazy, flippant side, all of that had been slowly, methodically killed in the war rooms and hallways of divorce court. She wanted to love Richard again. She wanted to have him back, but until this one exceptional afternoon, she had never thought it possible. Was it possible? she kept thinking to herself while she watched the three of them play together.

"Do it again, Dad, please do it again?" asked James.

"Just one more time and that's it."

Richard swam to the stairs at the shallow end of the pool. There was a ladder at the deep end of the pool but Richard knew better. He looked at it briefly as he swam by and decided to not take the chance. First, if he tried to pull himself up, the metal bars next to the ladder might rip right off. Second, he probably couldn't fit between those metal posts anyway. They were too narrow. And lastly, he might not have the arm strength to yank himself up at all. The last factor bothered Richard the most. It would be embarrassing.

He made it to the stairs at the far side and lumbered out of the pool. Then, again to the complete surprise of Helen, he kind of ran back to the deep end of the pool. Watching him run was entertaining. He waddled, with the rolls of fat tumbling about his waistline. He looked like a Japanese sumo wrestler with a weight problem.

Richard didn't care. He was usually so self-conscious about his obesity that he rarely took off his T-shirt, let alone jump into a swimming pool. But there he was, "Ten...nine...eight... GER-ONIMO!!!"

The second splash was even better. Richard had catapulted himself into a "quasi-cannonball" position. The splash went so far as to hit Helen, and she was relaxing on a chaise lounge halfway down the pool, twenty feet from impact. James, laughing as hard as he was, had accidently taken a mouth full of water and was laughing and coughing at the same time. Tyler couldn't remember the last time he had this much fun with his father.

"That's enough for now, boys. Your old man is tired and I just want to swim for a while," said Richard.

"Are you coming in, Mom?"

"In a little bit, James. I'm going to try to get some sun for now. I want a tan when we get back home to show off at the club on Sunday. I've only got one more day to get it."

The boys went down to the shallow end of the pool to play with their Super-soaker squirt guns. Richard stayed off by himself in the deep end. He let himself relax and float in the water. He was amazed at how easily he floated. The buoyant nature of all his fat behaved like some blubbery life vest. He could just lie there on his back, breathing slowly, gazing up at the clear blue sky above. It felt wonderful.

He imagined for a minute what it must be like to be a fish. He let all the air out of his lungs. He slowly sank. When he got a foot below the surface, he opened his eyes. Normally, he hated to open his eyes in the chlorinated water of the pool, but today was different. With a foot of water between him and the blue sky everything appeared different. The sky bent and twisted with each passing ripple. With the refraction of the water he could see the palm trees and sea grapes that surrounded the pool. It was as though he was looking up through fish-eye lenses.

It was the weightlessness that he noticed the most. He was floating. Gravity had abandoned him. He was floating comfortably in this lukewarm water without a trace of discomfort. He wasn't sweating, or breathing heavily from the chore of walking. He wasn't cold, or afraid. He was free.

He gave himself a little kick and came back up to the surface for a breath of air. Once he caught his wind again, he let all the air in his lungs out for a second time and sank toward the bottom. He wondered what a school of creatures that looked like him might be. Small whales? Elephant seals? Manatees? He was having fun with his obesity. He stayed down a little longer than the time before, growing more at ease in this liquid world.

The afternoon vanished into sunset. Helen spent most of her time on the chaise lounge, perfecting her tan. She came in and swam a few laps in the pool to cool off once. That was enough. The boys played with their toys and did so without any further arguments.

As for Richard, he became a fish. A large fish whose habitat was about a foot below the surface of a well-maintained pool on the east end of Sanibel. In this new found environment, the world was making sense to him again. As he exhaled, his rotund body would slowly drift toward the bottom of the clear, aquamarine pool. His tired feet would touch the bottom of the pool. He could feel the water encasing him, wrapping around him like some comforting, liquid blanket. It made him feel confident and secure.

Slowly, he shut down all the higher functions of his thinking. It was as though he were in a trance. Suspended in this eighty-five-degree water, floating up and down on every inhale, every exhale, Richard momentarily returned to the center of life. It was a primal place. It was the place from whence everything begins and ends. He could hear his beating heart as he sank toward the bottom. He could see the light of life itself, even when his eyes were closed. This is it, he thought to himself. This moment in time and water, in all of its simplicity, this is it. He never knew that it could be this simple.

Three

Carl left the fishing pier around four that afternoon. He was through. He and Ralph had become entangled in a heated conversation about fishing regulations. Ralph hated fishing regulations. Ralph would have loved to use his small baseball bat on the skull of the local Florida Marine Patrol officers if he could. Repeatedly.

Ralph argued that nature could take care of itself. "It doesn't need those goddamned meddlesome bureaucrats screwing things up." Ralph was old school. He felt that you shouldn't have to measure anything and your limit should equal the carrying capacity of the back of your pickup truck. Your limit should be measured in metric tons, not in inches.

Carl couldn't have disagreed more. Carl was a long-standing member of the Florida Conservation Association (the FCA), the Sanibel and Captiva Conservation Foundation, and the Sanibel Fishing Club. Over the years he had donated charters to every conservation charity fund raiser imaginable. Carl believed that people are inherently selfish. If allowed, most men would take home more than their fair share. They would harvest more than the species could reproduce. He had seen it happen again and again over the decades he had been fishing.

He had seen what happened to the redfish schools after that chef from New Orleans, chef Prudhomme, popularized blackened redfish. The commercial fishing captains, who had long regarded redfish as worthless, started to purse seine them by the thousands. Within three years, the redfish population collapsed. Over the endless flats of Pine Island Sound, where he could once find schools of juvenile redfish searching for crabs and grass shrimp, Carl and his charters found nothing. The limit before the spicy seasoning mix became popularized was easy to remember. There was no limit. After the decimation by the commercial netters, the fishery had to be closed for a year. Now the limit was one each and no commercial harvesting was allowed.

The redfish schools slowly came back. The flats once again shone with those big bronze tails and large schools of them prowl the skinny waters. Ralph was wrong about conservation. Carl and he were polar opposites in this debate, and it wasn't the first or the last time that the two of them would have this disagreement.

Realizing that no matter how long they argued, there wouldn't be any resolution, Carl grew weary of the debate. He decided to head home. They parted company and the issue was dropped. Despite their opposing camps with regard to conservation, they liked each other. They were both fishermen. That was enough of a common bond to keep their friendship alive. The rest was just opinion.

Carl had never seen Ralph take an undersized fish or go home with more than his limit. Ralph was upset with the principle of conservation. Ironically, he practiced it better than a lot of conservationists Carl had known over the years. Typical.

Carl headed straight home. He had taken out some hamburger from the freezer before going to the pier in the morning and he wanted to get it back into the refrigerator as soon as he could. His attention to sanitary details had lapsed since Marie had passed away. Lapsed to the point where he sometimes felt lucky to still be alive. He would leave out half a sandwich for an afternoon and gobble it up without thinking, mayonnaise and all. He did get a stomach bug a few times from his careless habits, but he was a tough old codger, and he pulled through just fine.

He put away his rods and reels, took a hot shower, and read the newspaper. The world was in exactly the same shape it was yesterday. There was a big political scandal involving the campaign fund raising of some Alabama senator, the Atlanta Braves were in the pennant race again this year, and the Centers for Disease Control had just issued a health warning about carrots. Carrots, pondered Carl? What the hell could be wrong with carrots? The world was just as mad as it was yesterday.

Carl took the hamburger back out of the fridge and cooked up a couple of small cheeseburgers for himself. When he took the plastic wrapping off, he noted that the burger looked exceptionally brown.

"Maybe I left it out too long?" He mumbled to himself nervously. "I'll just cook it a little longer today."

He cooked his burgers to death. When he made the fifth or sixth flip of his two burgers they resembled charcoal briquettes. They tasted like beef jerky. Carl didn't mind. He smothered each patty with Heinz 57 and ate both of them, washing them down with an ice-cold can of Budweiser.

Since Marie had passed away, eating had lost its charm. He had always enjoyed sitting down to dinner with Marie and talking over the day. Laughing about some dumb charter member who had gotten fishing line tangled in her hair. Or telling Marie about some Midwestern angler who was in shock after seeing a ten-foot bull shark bite his trophy snook in two. Funny things that had happened on the boat or stories from Marie about odds and ends.

Marie would tell Carl that Sally Porter was finally going to file for divorce from that drunken bum of a husband of hers. Or that the Conservation Foundation was planning a big garage sale next Saturday to raise money for their new land acquisitions. Marie had volunteered to help out with the sale. Marie always volunteered to help.

Now the sound of her voice, the joy of her laughter, was gone. It was just the sound of an empty kitchen with one person having dinner. The rattle of the plate as you leaned your fork against the edge to have a drink of water. The sound of setting the water glass back down on the table. The sound of chewing. Noises in the distance, cars heading down Periwinkle, the splashes of mullet and porpoises in the canal behind him. Lonely sounds. He missed Marie intensely.

He did the dishes by hand after dinner. He used the dishwasher only once or twice since her passing. There were never enough dishes to make running it worthwhile. It was Marie's dishwasher. She had picked it out about a month before the cancer overcame her. Carl knew that she wanted to buy a new one to make things easier for him after she was gone. Marie knew that her death was near. Like some hand-delivered message from a marathon runner, her death was long in coming. The runner was tired when he finally handed her the message. She read it without self-pity. It was just the way things happen. Marie accepted her death with the eloquence of a saint. She was a saint.

Carl seldom used the dishwasher Marie had picked out for him. Nothing was easy since her death. A dishwasher didn't change any of that. It was never about yard work or house work or the like. It was about loving someone so completely that when the other person died, a part of you died along with them. It was about missing someone more than anything imaginable. About an emptiness so vast that only the eternity of space rivaled it. It was about a marriage. About a commitment to each other that could not, would not cease with this rude interruption of mortality.

It was about love. Great love. Landscapes of the human heart where only a few dare to go. Carl and Marie had gone there, and they were glad that they had. In knowing that great gladness, in appreciating where it was that they had traveled together, Carl drew the strength he needed to carry on without her.

Carl looked over at the brand new dishwasher and became saddened. Oh God, how he missed her. How it hurt for him to get up every morning without her. To no longer be able to yell at her for using up all the hot water in the shower, or kiss her each day just before he went down to the Sanibel Marina to pick up his charters. How every day without her was longer now. Like the clock had gained six more hours, and every week had two more days to it. How time stretched out like a bad movie he had seen before but had to stay and watch anyway. Watch again and again and again.

These were his feeling as he took his last sip of his Budweiser, which had now grown warm and flat. The world was not the same without her. It never would be.

Just then the phone rang. He went over and picked it up.

"Hi Dad, it's Anne. How you doing?" Carl knew immediately who it was on the other end. His daughter's voice sounded so like Marie's. There could be no mistaking it.

"I'm just fine, Anne. How are Art and the kids?"

"They're doing great, Dad. Art just got a promotion and the firm has never been busier. You know the kids, they're just regular kids. No trouble. But it's you that I'm worried about, Dad. What have you been doing to keep yourself busy?"

"I'm still fishing down at the pier, Anne. The snook are biting, the big fall reds are passing through every so often, and I'm having a ball."

Anne knew better. She knew that he missed mom immensely. This was his usual stonewalling, and she knew that he would never confess his real feelings to her. Her father was like that. The pain was his cross alone to bear. He never thought that it needed to be something the two children should concern themselves with. Reluctantly, Anne respected his decision to carry his burden alone. It hurt her to do so.

"How's your shoulder doing?"

"Well, it's been bothering me some the last few days, but tonight it doesn't seem to hurt too much. It's OK I guess."

"You know that you should have that looked at, Dad."

"It's like all the other aches and pains I'm having. It's called 'getting old,' Anne. I don't think I need a doctor to tell me that I'm getting old, sweetheart. I'll be just fine."

"How's the yard looking?"

The yard was looking pretty grim and Carl knew it. Anne knew it as well, even though she was too far away for a visual verification. Anne knew it because Marie had always done the yard work. With Marie gone for a year now, Anne knew that the yard would look abandoned. Carl was too stubborn to hire a yard service to replace the fine job Marie had done. His daughter knew how he hated doing yard work. She knew the yard languished under the careless hands of neglect.

"The yard looks great!" said Carl enthusiastically. Carl was lying.

"I'll bet." Anne was acknowledging the lie.

"No really, Anne, everything's just fine. I've been fishing with this big divorce attorney from Peoria all week and we've been having a heck of a time. He's been losing just about everything to the pilings, but he's a nice enough fellow and fun to talk to."

"I suppose you've told him your catfish story."

"Sure 'nough have."

"You love that story, Dad. How many times have you told it now?"

"More times than I can count on both hands."

"Way more than that. Are you still thinking about our offer for you to move up here to Atlanta with us? It'd be wonderful for the kids to have their grandfather around. There's some good bass fishing in these parts and you wouldn't have to eat those awful TV dinners all the time."

"Excuse me, little lady," Carl said sarcastically. "I happen to like TV dinners. Have you ever tried the Salisbury Steak Supreme? Deeeelicious. Besides, I just don't want to be a burden to you all. I'm getting along just fine and you know how I feel about leaving the ocean. This old expanse of salty brine is the only woman in my life now. I'd be hard pressed to walk out on her just to live in some fancy suburb in Atlanta."

"Dad."

"Well it's true. This is where I belong. And until that day comes when I can't put on my own pants in the morning, this is where I'm going to stay."

Anne knew that it was impossible to get Carl to change his mind about moving in with them. Still, she felt that she had to try. If for no other reason than letting him know that the invitation was always there. "Well, Dad, just let me know if there's anything you need from us. You're still coming up for Christmas, right?"

"Wouldn't miss it for the world."

"See you later, Dad, I've got to get these kids started for bed."

"Bye, Anne. Love ya much."

"Love you too, Dad."

The phone clicked down on the receiver in the small concrete block house on King's Crown Drive on Sanibel Island. Everything returned to silence. Carl went over to his easy chair and rested.

Anne went into the living room and told the kids to start picking their toys up and get ready for bed.

"Seven o'clock comes mighty early!" she said. She said that every night. The kids paid no attention to her. Anne would need to go get their father. When dad roared, the cubs listened up. Some things never change.

Anne kept thinking about her father long after the phone was put back on the hook. She loved her father. In her eyes, he had been the perfect father. Always coming home around six o'clock, smelling like fish. Picking her up and spinning her around. Always threatening to use both of his kids for shark bait if they misbehaved. Never meaning it. Showering off before dinner and helping with the homework.

Every summer they would take long trips together. Since there was never enough money to fly, they would drive. They drove to New Orleans, to Charleston, and to Washington, D.C. They would spend hours and hours in the car playing word games. Playing that game where you find all the letters of the alphabet in the road signs. Q was always the hardest. Q.

She was concerned about him. Living alone in that big house. Being there on Sanibel without Mom. She was worried about him getting older, about growing older. She knew that he wouldn't come up to live with them. He didn't want to be an imposition. She would see him around Christmas. Christmas was only a few months away, and Anne looked forward to it.

"Come on kids, it's time to brush your teeth." She was hoping Dad would come out of the den soon and lend her a hand. He did.

Carl rested in his easy chair for half an hour. He didn't do anything and just rested. After a bit he decided to call his old friend Dan back up in Davenport. The conversation with his daughter put him in a telephone mood. He enjoyed talking to Dan, and what better time to do so than the present?

First Carl went over to the fridge and grabbed a second beer. It was Miller time. He had finished off his last Budweiser. Most beers taste about the same, he thought to himself as he cracked the ice-cold can. Then Carl went to his telephone directory and looked up Dan's number. Long distance. It seemed as though everyone close to him was now long distance. He punched in the numbers on his touch-tone phone and settled back into his easy chair.

Carl reached him on the first call. Dan was glad to hear from him. It had been only a week or so but it didn't matter. They talked for an hour. They talked about the grandkids, about Dan's recent fishing trip back up to Leech Lake. This time he took his wife, Yolanda. They talked about friends who had died, friends who were taken ill, and friends they had not heard from in years.

They brought up Michael Rey again, their dew-worm catching friend some sixty years ago. He was about to be released from prison.

It was a good thing that he was going to be released. It would be terrible to have to die in prison. It was a long telephone conversation, an extended exercise in friendship.

It was a conversation between two old men that stretched across nearly two thousand miles of fiber optics and electronic switches. It was a good conversation, full of hearty laughter and cloudy recollections. All the little things that make up a person's life: their lovers, their jobs, their hobbies, their children and in turn grandchildren, their losses, their journeys, their joys and sorrows. Nothing and everything out of the ordinary. Just a slow, beautiful tide that flows across seventy-some years of grass flats and ends quietly. A life recalled in some other telephone conversation by two of their other friends remembering them. Simple tales, exquisite in their sheer simplicity. The way life really is.

After an hour they both ran out of interesting topics to cover and their aging voices grew tired. Carl had gotten up to take another Miller out of the refrigerator and Dan was clearly enjoying his whiskey back in Davenport. They might as well have been sitting right next to each other at the local tavern. They were.

When Carl hung up it was late. He was tired. He cleaned up the kitchen a bit, noting how loud the silence was. The dishes and the pots and pans seemed to reverberate with every passing contact. It was as though he was washing them in an immense cave. The echo was endless. Carl was tired of living alone. Very tired.

He brushed his cracked and stained teeth and went to bed. As he slept, he dreamed that he was way, way out in the ocean. He could not see any land and he didn't know which direction to go. His boat was beautiful. It was the color of polished copper. The steering wheel was silver. Although he was lost at sea, he was not at all afraid. High above him was a flock of seagulls. Land must be nearby, he thought to himself in his dream. Land must be nearby.

The Sixth Morning

One

"Wind from the north, no anglers go forth.
Wind from the west, the fishing is best.
Wind from the east, fish bite the least.
Wind from the south, blows the bait in their mouth."

Anonymous Author

The wind was from the south. The wind was steady at ten knots and the snook were everywhere. They were on a major feed. The anglers on the dock and the motley members of the pier gang knew it. As they put their feet on the long wooden pier, they all could sense it. Anticipate it. There was a fishy smell in the wind, an electrical charge to the air.

Jose and Ralph were the first to arrive that Friday. The sun was having its first cup of coffee somewhere off the Grand Bahamas Bank when they stepped up on the dock. It was still dark, with only a passing hint of morning in the sky. The stars were out. One by one, the closest star, the sun, would delete them. The planet Mercury would be the last to disappear.

"This is going to be a good morning for fishing, Ralph," said Jose.

"I know."

Both of them knew. They transferred their pinfish from their yellow-and-white minnow buckets into their five-gallon buckets drilled with holes and lowered them over the south side of the dock. The tide was ripping out. The instant the buckets hit the water, they were dragged toward the open waters of the Gulf. Only the white nylon line held them there, tied fast to the rickety railing. The tide was so strong that those lines looked as though they might break under the strain.

But they held. Inside the bucket the pinfish fought the hundreds of tiny eddies and currents created by the seawater rushing in through the uncountable drill holes. The water was rich with oxygen. Their pinfish could keep hardy for days in a current like this.

Ralph pulled up the bucket and got two fresh baits out for himself and Jose. Jose had already taken his shirt off. They were ready. Just as the two of them were throwing their lines in the water, Carl showed up. He looked rested and awake. Like the other anglers, Carl sensed the bite. He put his gear down next to the three-foot section of dock that seemed like home to him now. He dug his cast net out and went down the beach to look for baits.

Before he made it back to the end of the dock, he heard the heavy footsteps of Richard approaching. The thumping of this big man rang out clearly as he walked down that snakelike boardwalk toward the pier. Carl decided to have Richard join him cast-netting this morning. Maybe I should teach that attorney how to throw a cast net, he thought to himself.

"Good morning, Richard!" Carl hollered over to Richard as he wobbled up the boardwalk.

"Oh, hi, Carl," said Richard. Richard had been looking down. He had been wondering how they manage to keep the cracks between the wooden planks so even with all these bends in this boardwalk. Good carpenters, he thought to himself as he walked up slowly. Damn good carpenters. His mind was a thousand miles from the office.

The buttonwood and sea grapes that ran beside the boardwalk were swaying back and forth in the breeze. The air was still dry, but less dry than the last few mornings. It was picking up moisture from its long run across the blue waters of the Gulf. The last time that air had rushed over land was when it had blown across the streets of Key West one hundred and thirty miles to the south of Sanibel. Breezes that whipped down Duval Street and across Highway 1, picking up the faint scent of jerked chicken and confederate jasmine as it did. Wind that whipped past drunks passed out on Whitehead Street and young ladies on holiday smelling like rum runners and excessive perfume. Ladies who were lying next to young men on holiday in quaint bed and breakfasts whose walls had witnessed a thousand sins.

But the scents of Key West had long since vanished from

the air. Now the wind smelled like the ocean. It smelled like salt air. There was a distinct fishy odor hanging in the wind. No one knew where that fishy odor came from, it was just there.

"Do you want to learn how to toss a cast net, Richard?"

"Hey, that'd be great."

"It's not as easy as it looks. Come on, put your stuff down and follow me."

Richard set his tackle and small cooler on one of the wooden benches under the covered section of the pier and went down on the sand beside Carl. They walked down the beach toward the south. Carl started to explain the art of finding schools of bait off the beach. "The white baits tend to like to hang in the eddy side of the pier. If the tide is coming in, the cast netting is best to the north, toward the causeway. If the tide is moving out, the bait will be stacked to the south, toward the lighthouse just around the corner." It was a simple rule. It made sense.

Carl quickly spotted the telltale sign of a school of minnows dancing on the surface, about ten feet off the beach. The water along this shoreline dropped quickly. Whereas in other sections of the beach along Sanibel an angler might walk a hundred feet out to get waist deep, here it was over your head just ten feet from the shoreline. The strong currents that ran back and forth every day carved away the sand faster than the rolling waves could replace it. Carl felt it might be a tough cast, but he thought he could probably reach them.

"See them over there?" Carl asked.

"See what?" Richard replied.

"The bait over there, don't you see it?"

"No."

Carl put his left arm around Richard's wide shoulder, and using his right hand, which was still holding the heavy cast net, he lifted up his arm and pointed to the school of bait just off the beach. "Right there, Richard, it looks like rain falling on the water. That's a school of bait."

Richard saw them, but it wasn't easy. The wind was coming up from the south and the tide was rushing out against it. As they met, the sea became choppy and unpredictable. The two opposing forces had created waves known as "standing men." These were tall, steep waves that never moved. They just stood there, like hostages held by these two powerful forces of nature. The wind from one direction and the sea from another. Dangerous waves, full of current and energy. Difficult to read.

When it was calm, these schools of white bait were easy to spot. Here, amid all the chop and current, it took a trained eye to see them. Carl could see them. Richard struggled with it.

"Oh yes, I see them now. I'll tell you though, Carl, if you weren't pointing to them, I would never have found them in all these waves."

"Now, here's how we cast in this wind....," Carl said. He went on to explain that in a breeze you always try to cast downwind. Throwing a cast net into the wind was hard. The wind would overwhelm the open net and cause it to either open poorly or to not open at all. Carl and Richard walked a few feet south along the beach until the school was between them and the pier.

With such a small net, Carl preferred to spin rather than fold the net to make his cast. Spinning was easier. He took a piece of the lead line in his teeth, grabbed the net an arm's length up with his right hand, and held the balance of the net and line in his left hand. He told Richard to stand back a bit and he gave the net a big twirl. The net flew open and landed just shy of the school. It quickly settled to the bottom.

Carl carefully pulled it in. There were a dozen small shiners flopping around inside of it. Carl lifted up the net and dumped them into his five-gallon plastic bucket, the one without the holes drilled in it. A few of the shiners missed the bucket and fell on the sand. The sand stuck to their little white bodies, covering them in seconds. Carl tossed them back into the ocean. He knew that if he tried to put them in the livewell after that, they would die.

"Your turn, Richard," he said. He took the looped line off of his left hand and handed the net to Richard.

"I don't think so, Carl," said Richard. "I don't think I can throw this thing."

"Sure you can, Richard. It's like anything new, it just takes some time and some practice and before long, you know how to do it. Before long, you're the pro."

Carl went through the entire process with Richard while the sun lifted its huge yellow eye up over the back of Ft. Myers Beach. Finally, after a little prodding, Richard agreed to give it a toss. The sun looked upon both of them with more than a little curiosity that morning. They made such an unlikely pair.

It was a scene worth photographing. The first slanted shafts of sunlight were hitting the beach just as this three-hundred-pound attorney did a clumsy pirouette with a six-foot cast net in his hand. He let go of the net just as the sun stood atop one of the low-rise condominiums on the beach. The net fell like a bucketful of stones being dumped into the ocean. It hadn't opened at all.

"Damn!!!" swore Richard.

"Well, I think we've got some work to do," added Carl.

"Don't make me do that again, Carl. It's embarrassing," said Richard as he dragged the wet net back in. There were no minnows in it. The only bait he had found on that cast was killed instantly by the clump of falling lead sinkers.

"One more time, Richard. Give it one more throw. This time, be sure to keep your right arm out further."

Richard held the net as instructed. He readied himself for a second cast. This time as his rotund body spun around, the little net, as if by magic, opened beautifully. It fell directly on a school of whitebaits. Both of them were amazed. Richard let the net sink for a few seconds and quickly hauled the hand line back in. The net was teeming with jittery whitebaits. Richard had done it. He had made his first successful cast. He felt great. He felt like he had just won a million-dollar settlement. He felt better than when he had secured a ten-year restraining order.

The old man had taught him something. He had taught him how to throw a cast net. Carl helped him dump the minnows into the bucket. Many of them fell on the sand. He quickly tried to pick all of them up and flip them back into the sea, but he missed a few. Right after the two of them started walking back toward the fishing pier a great white egret walked up to the spot where their bucket was sitting. The egret cocked its head to the side and stared down at the beach. One of the sand-covered minnows twitched. WHAM! The egret nailed him like a bolt of lightning. One after another the egret ate what was left on the beach. Nothing was ever wasted along this stretch of sand.

Carl transplanted the minnows from one bucket to the other, from the one that held water to the one that didn't. As he poured them into his other bucket, the water drained out through the drill holes. Once completed, he sealed the lid on tightly and tied it off to the railing.

The bucket quickly rushed out with the fast-flowing tide and the line became taut. Carl and Richard readied their four rods. Carl tied on the leaders and attached some three-quarter-ounce sinkers. The tide was stronger than it had been of late. He knew that they would need the extra weight to keep their baits near the bottom. Should they go with lighter sinkers, the small minnows would lift up too high into the rushing tide and the big snook would swim right under them.

"It's going to be a good morning," said Carl.

"Do you think so?"

"I know so."

The sun was now up and running, preparing for its marathon journey across peninsular Florida. At the end of the day it would dive back into the refreshing waters of the Gulf of Mexico. At the moment, the sunlight was pouring down on the world, clear and brilliant. Carl picked up one of the baits they had kept in the five-gallon pail, impaled it right in front of the dorsal fin and sent it down current. With the weight of the heavy sinker, it quickly sank.

Carl was very methodical when it came to angling. Over the years he had learned that if you do certain things religiously, you catch fish. Before he tossed his lines in, he checked each drag carefully. Not too tight, causing the line to part, and not too loose, enabling the fish to pull out line too easily. That created slack. Once the line became slack, it was easy for the snook to shake the hook out. Carl grabbed a section of line and pulled. It came off the reel smoothly. He did this every time he made a cast, even though no one had changed the settings. That was how it was done.

He checked the end of the line and leader for nicks or fraying. Finally, he took the point of each hook and ran it over his thumbnail. If it was sharp, it would scratch the surface of the nail without effort. If it didn't scratch the fingernail easily, he took out his hook-hone and sharpened the hook until it did. Everything had to be right.

The wind was pushing up from the south at a steady pace. The air was saturated with humidity, but because of the breeze, it didn't feel uncomfortable. By mid-afternoon it will be hot, thought Carl. But in this slanted light of the morning sun, it was ideal.

Richard and Carl started their morning conversation slowly. Richard was feeling overly confident, almost boastful about his toss of the cast net. He had lit up a Camel after the rods were set, and he had that smug look about him. Carl knew it was luck, but didn't want to break Richard's bubble. Richard wouldn't stop going on about it so Carl finally decided to set him straight.

"Richard, that second cast didn't have anything at all to do with you suddenly becoming a great cast-netter. It was a lucky throw. Sometimes we just get lucky. Your second toss was charmed."

"No way, Carl. I've got that cast netting thing down."

"Five bucks."

"Five bucks for what?"

"Five bucks say that you could not make another cast like that in three..., no, make that six more tries."

"You're on."

Richard didn't gamble much. Still gloating from his earlier toss, he knew that he could win this bet. He reached down and grabbed the net.

"Where are the minnows, Carl? Can you see them?"

"We don't need any more minnows, Richard, so you don't have to bother finding them. If we put any more in the bucket, they'll only die. Just walk up the beach a bit and make your casts. If the net opens once more like it did on your second cast, I owe you a five spot. If not, dig out your wallet."

Richard walked down to the end of the pier and headed south, against the wind. He had remembered what Carl had told him about not casting into the breeze. After twenty paces he turned around and angled himself to throw the net between the beach and the pier. The net would be going straight downwind.

He grabbed the lead line and checked to make sure that the balance of the net was not tangled and that it would unfurl readily. Then he reached down with his right hand a full arm's length and started his twirl. Being as large as he was, from a distance he looked a little like the planet Jupiter spinning on the beach.

The net flew away from his body and landed in the shape of a banana. At the widest point the opening wasn't more than a foot. Richard didn't say a thing. Carl chuckled quietly to himself.

"One down!" Carl hollered over to him.

Richard pulled the wet net back, straightened it out again and readied himself for his second throw. He spun around and released the net, hoping for the same charm as his second throw earlier in the morning. The net became tangled. As it hit the water, it was anything but opened.

The third cast was a larger banana. The fourth was as if he had just taken the net, put it in the five-gallon bucket and thrown the bucket and all in the ocean. It was a belly flop of a toss. The fifth and sixth casts were variations on a bad theme. None of them stood a chance of catching any minnows had there been any around. All of them were horrid.

By this time Richard was wheezing. These few minutes of exercise had winded him. He didn't have the strength to try it again, double or nothing notwithstanding. He wanted to, just to prove Carl wrong. Instead, he sat on the beach next to the net, reached into his shirt pocket, pulled out another Camel, and lit up. He looked over at Carl with more than enough humility, knowing he had lost.

Carl smiled.

Richard sat there for five minutes, smoking two camels back to back. He then picked up the net, dropped it into the white plastic bucket and came back to the dock.

"It's called the learning curve," said Carl. "It takes years to be able to throw a cast net as well as you did on your second toss. You might get lucky now and then. You might make a good throw before your time, but that's all it is, luck. As you get better at it, the lucky throws show up more often. Eventually it reverses; you throw the net perfectly almost all of the time and only when you have an occasional unlucky toss do you lose out. Learning something new, changing - it takes time. Time, perseverance, and practice. In a couple of hundred throws, you'll be able to make a cast like the one you did a few minutes ago every time. But for now, you owe me some money."

Richard dug out his wallet and mixed in amid his stack of hundreds was a five-dollar bill. He took out the five-dollar bill in a manner that Carl could see the hundreds clearly. Carl took the five spot and smiled. He had seen all the hundreds. Carl wasn't impressed. Carl had chartered plenty of rich folks in his day. Being rich didn't mean shit to Carl Johnson. Never had and never would. Throwing a cast net well - now that was something a man could be proud of.

They both got back to fishing. Ralph and Jose were now joined by Becky and her skinny husband, Paul. Chip had telephoned Ralph last night to let him know that he wasn't going to be making it down today. He had to work. He was pissed about it, too.

A few tourists and locals had dropped in to wet a line. All totaled, there were probably a dozen people on the dock when Jose got his first big strike. It was one hell of a strike.

Jose and Ralph had been watching Richard throwing the cast net. It was a spectacle. Ralph was doing his Howard Cosell imitation throughout Richard's performance. Jose was the crowd. Ralph kept saying it was like watching Humpty Dumpty at the ballet with a fishnet in his arms. Every time the net landed in the ocean, twisted, banana shaped, and sinking like a stone, they both would laugh. They turned away as they did, so as not to embarrass Richard. It wasn't that as much as they knew that it offended Carl when they made fun of tourons. They could see that Carl had been laughing as well, though not as blatantly.

After watching Richard strike out, Ralph and Jose got onto a conversation about the first few times they tried throwing a cast net. What a chore. Then they settled back to drinking some beers and watching the earth wake up. They never waited until noon to crack open a beer. "It's noon somewhere, goddamn it," Ralph was fond of saying. Ralph still had his shirt on, but it wouldn't be on much longer.

Both anglers were startled by the power of their first strike. Jose's stiff pier rod doubled over when the big linesider struck. Had he not carefully tied it to the railing with an old shoelace, it would have been pulled up and over that railing. As fast as any gunslinger could have reached for his six-shooter, Jose reached for his fishing rod. Although the snook had hooked himself with his intense strike, Jose reared back on the rod and slammed the big fish back. In an instant, feeling the sting of that hook, the snook rose to the surface, shaking its thunderous head.

It was a twenty-pounder! The line screamed out, voices rose, and the locals and tourists alike abandoned their rods to watch the battle. Although it was a large snook, Jose, using 50-lb. test line and 80-lb. leader, quickly turned it. He had it back to the edge of the pier in no time. The snook made several dashes for the pilings but the rod was not being held by an amateur. The rod was in the hands of the leading skins player on the dock. Every time the snook made for the pilings, Jose extended the rod out and powered the fish back into open water.

Ralph got out the brand-new net, courtesy of Richard, reached over with its long handle, and engulfed the fish. It was over. The crowd applauded and one by one went up to admire this beautiful creature, now entangled in the dark-green mesh of the landing net. Ralph went over to get his billy club. The snook had lost.

Carl and Richard watched the battle but decided not to leave their post. They were continuing their conversation about learning curves and cast netting. It was good enough to watch the fight from the side lines. Besides, once netted, Richard knew that Ralph's bloody club was soon to follow. It was a scene in the movie he could live without.

Just as Ralph was smashing the skull of Jose's snook, Richard's line was smashed. Richard grabbed hold of the rod and struck back. For the briefest moment, he could feel the power of the fish on the other end of his line. When he yanked the rod tip up to set the hook, the line parted.

There was nothing to be done. There was a strike, a set, a broken line, and it was over.

"What happened?" questioned Richard. "What did I do wrong?"

Carl reached over and checked Richard's drag. Maybe it was set too tightly, he thought. Upon wrapping a section of it in his cracked and leathery hand, he pulled firmly. The drag came out smooth and easy, without undue effort.

"I don't know what happened. Your drag is set perfectly."

"I paid a lot of money for this line. The kid down at the Bait

Box said it was the best brand they had. Shit like this shouldn't happen!" said Richard angrily.

"That's why they call it fishing and not catching, Richard."

"But I don't get it. Has this ever happened to you?"

"More times than you could imagine. Sometimes there's a flaw in the line. Sometimes it's a nick, where the line rubbed against this old splintered railing wrong. Sometimes it's because you set the hook at the same instant the fish decides to streak away from you. Sometimes it's the knot. Who knows?

"Everything appears perfect: the right leader, the right drag, the best line and perfect knots, and none of it matters. The line breaks and the fish swims off. It just happens. You did everything right. There isn't anyone responsible and you can't always blame your equipment when it happens. The fish breaks off. Things sometimes just happen.

"The right thing to do is to re-rig and get your bait back out there. Maybe we'll get another strike."

"Wow! That was one hell of a strike!"

Richard reached into his shirt pocket for his pack of camels. He took a fresh one out and lit up. He thought that he would take a moment to enjoy a cigarette before he took the time to retie everything and get his second rod back out. He looked over to Jose and Ralph. Jose was holding up his trophy and Ralph had his cheap disposable camera out. He was stepping back to frame the photo, parting the crowd that had gathered to admire the fish. It was a great photo-op, thought Richard. The rising sun in the background and this huge black-and- gold fish held up high by a delighted Cuban-American on the fishing pier on Sanibel Island on an early fall morning. Nothing could be better than this moment. Nothing in all of the world.

Just as Richard tossed his butt into the sea, Carl's favorite rod got slammed. Just like Jose's hit, and Richard's hit moments before, it was a snook. Big snook don't nibble, or play with baits. They see the minnow, note that it's swimming poorly, or that it's injured, and they inhale it. Once inhaled they swim off. When they feel the foreign and unknown resistance from the line, they swim harder.

Carl grabbed the rod and raised it high above his head. He let the rod tip fall toward the horizon as he felt the thin line slowly tighten. Once the line became taut, Carl reared back on the rod and set the hook. He did so with a calculated, sweeping motion that was athletic in its stride. It was like watching a well-trained runner or a dancer perform. It was the way a hook is set.

Surprisingly, the fish didn't jump. It just started taking out line, heading toward the open waters of the gulf.

"What is it? Is it a snook? Do you think it's a big snook?" asked Richard anxiously.

"Yeah, it feels like a snook all right. A damned big one."

The line flew off the reel like it was connected to an electric line spooling machine stuck in reverse. Carl looked down and watched the diameter of his 14-lb. test spool shrinking right before his eyes. He knew that if the snook didn't stop his run soon he would expose his clinch knot at the very end of the spool in seconds. Once down to that knot, something would have to give. The forgiveness of the slipping drag would vanish. It would be the strength of the fish against the strength of the line. Carl had seen it a thousand times before. The knot would give, or the line would snap.

"Richard," Carl said with a nervous certainty, "if this fish doesn't stop running soon, it's over."

Richard looked down and saw the spool spinning like a tiny centrifuge.

"Can't you tighten the drag down?"

"No. If I tighten it at all, it will break."

"Can we run down the beach with it?"

"There isn't time."

Just then, the spool hesitated. It didn't stop spinning completely, but it slowed. There couldn't have been more than ten wraps left until it reached the tie-off knot at the end of the spool. In the distance, over a hundred yards down current, the big snook rose and jumped. Jose, Ralph, Ruth and everyone else gathered at the pier that morning stood in awe over what they witnessed. A colossal linesider cleared the water and flipped itself, end over end, and landed with a tremendous splash back into the ocean. No one there, including Carl, had ever seen a snook as big as this fish was.

Carl knew this fish. It wasn't the same fish, but he, or one of his charters, had hooked into this fish before. No one had ever landed him. This was an old, smart linesider who had been hooked many times in the past. He knew how to get himself free. He could spool you, or jump until the leader became tangled in his razor-sharp gill plates. He knew how to run under the barnacle-encrusted pilings or dash under the hull of the boat, wrapping the line in the sharp edges of the stainless steel propeller. This was a great fish, and he would fight long and hard. Carl thought all these things to himself as he stood there, tethered to this fish with a thin fiberglass rod, a well-oiled reel and a stretch of monofilament not much thicker than a strand of his greying hair.

"Oh my God, Carl! Did you see how big that snook is?"

"Yes."

It was all he could say. He saw how big the fish was. He knew that it had to be thirty, maybe forty pounds. Maybe fifty. He knew that this would be a fish that had been hooked before. It was a fish that had grown wise and powerful in the open ocean. A fish that had busted many a line, chased down a thousand full-grown mullet in the back bay and spent a lifetime avoiding sharks and porpoises. It was a snook that had survived deep winter freezes and hurricane tides. Carl knew that he had only the slimmest of chances to ever land him. It was rare that Carl's scaled sardine would even trick such a wise old fish into biting. It was rarer still that Carl would ever end up holding this fish in his tough, weathered hands.

He had fished three decades in these waters and he had never landed a snook this size. He had seen hundreds of them. When the deep freezes make their way to the very tip of Florida, during the coldest of winters up north, these big linesiders cannot handle the falling temperatures. As the water temperature drops, they come into the canals looking for warm pockets of water to lie still and survive in. That's when you can see scores of these enormous snook.

They sit there like big black logs, barely swimming, slowly flaring their gill plates in and out, in and out. Waiting. Waiting for the sun to touch the Tropic of Capricorn and head back north. Waiting for the spring, for the water to warm. Waiting for the bait to come back up on the flats and the mullet to school up thick in the tidal creeks. Waiting to feed and live again.

Carl had seen many a linesider this size beneath the docked boats at the Sanibel Marina before he would head out with his customers to catch sheepshead and sea trout in the middle of winter. Some of them were nearly six feet long. His customers would always stand there and ask if they could go someplace where they might be able to catch one of these. He would tell them that if there was such a place, he would go there himself.

"No one knows where to catch snook this size," he would tell them. Some say you can find them under the docks off Punta Rassa, and to haul them away from the pilings of those docks you need a hundred-pound test line and one-hundred-and-fifty-pound leaders. Even at that, he would tell his customers, most of them break away, wrapping that hundred-pound test around the old pilings.

When they are like this, he would add, hiding below these boats, barely moving, they are only shadows of their real selves. They are cold now, huddled here to keep from freezing to death in the open waters of the bay. If the wind kicks up and the cold continues for much longer, they will start to die. They are subtropical fish, and their metabolism cannot handle water temperatures below fifty-six degrees. You can reach over and gaff them and they will not put up a fight. They won't chase or eat anything when they are cold like this. As cold as a mountain climber near the top of Everest. "As cold as hell might be," he would add as he fired up his engines and headed out through the sea-walled canal toward the bay.

Carl thought all of this as the big snook rose again, this time coming out just far enough to shake his head violently from side to side, rushing not away from the pier, but now fighting back up current. The snook was coming back toward the pier.

The old fishing guide knew that the water wasn't cold now. The water was eighty-four degrees. This snook was fat and strong from a long, warm summer. This snook was powerful, and in less than a minute he could swim up-current and return to the pilings he dashed out from when he inhaled Carl's scaled sardine. If this snook got anywhere near the pilings of this fishing pier, the fight would end. No amount of leaning out could hope to turn a snook this size. With 14-lb. test line, an angler cannot stop a fish than can easily break 40- lb. test. If the big fish made it back to the pier, Carl would lose him.

Carl knew instinctively what he would need to do if he had any hope at all to land this fish. In the next few seconds, he would have to get off the fishing pier. Then, he could run down the beach, toward the lighthouse. From that vantage point he could try to pull the fish away from the pilings. Using every ounce of his line test, and the rushing outgoing current, he stood a chance of turning this big snook. A very slim chance.

To get to the beach Carl would have to pass his rod around the three posts that held up the covered section of the pier, while keeping his line tight to the fish. Because the snook was swimming toward him, he would have to keep reeling constantly. Reeling would take up the slack. It was a near impossible feat.

There were four people fishing between him and the end of the dock. Two were just bringing in their line, but the others were still fishing. If Carl's line became tangled with theirs, the snook would have yet another opportunity to get free.

"Richard," Carl tried to get his attention, never daring to turn his eyes away from where his big fish was.

"Yes, Carl," answered Richard.

"Ask those folks down there, to our right...," Carl gestured with his left hand, "ask them to bring in their lines for a moment. Tell them I have to get off the pier to fight this snook from the beach."

Richard hurriedly ran down and explained. All of the anglers had seen the size of this snook. They understood and willingly obliged. The lines were brought in and the leaning rods were all quickly untied and moved to the other side of the pier. Carl carefully made his way toward the beach. Richard offered to help him pass the rod around the four-by-four posts, but Carl insisted that he needed to do this alone. Carl knew that the rules were that no one, other than the angler, can handle the rod at any time during the fight. That was how Carl wanted to play this fish. It was the fish of a lifetime.

Within a minute, Carl had managed to reach the beach. The big fish, fighting the strong outgoing tide, was within twenty feet of the southern end of the T at the end of the pier. That was the closest point at which the snook could intersect the pilings. This was a fish who knew the pier. He knew the sting of a well-sharpened barb and the pull of that thin monofilament against his power. He knew that the knife-like edges of the pilings were his release. That was where he would go.

Carl ran down the beach fifty feet. He was now down current from the fish. He took the rod tip and moved it down toward the sand, with the end of his rod pointing south. From this angle he could apply the maximum amount of pressure to turn the head of the snook and break his run toward the pilings. He did one more thing. He reached over with his left hand and tightened the drag on the top of the spinning rod. He gave it a full turn.

There was a hundred feet of line between him and the fish. Carl figured the snook to be more than forty pounds. A thin, clear line of 14-lb. test mono was all that connected them. As he tightened that drag, Carl knew that if there was a nick, a single imperfection, a piece of flotsam in the water that touched against it, the line would part instantly. On the other hand, if Carl did nothing and the big fish reached the pilings, the leader would be shredded against the edges of the organisms living there, the barnacles, clams, and mussels covering the posts. It was a calculated risk. Carl knew he was better off risking it all on the hopes that his line, freshly spooled last week, would hold.

He tightened the drag and he put as much pressure as he could to pull the snook away from the pier. The fish felt the pull. Fighting the falling tide was twice as difficult with this ceaseless pull coming from the hands of the angler. The fish sensed that it was not an ordinary angler who had hooked him. This snook had been hooked before. A dozen times before. He was always able to escape. This fish might decide to run off all the line on the reel, or snap the line when the drag was too tight. He might straighten the hook, or cut the leader. But most of the time, the pilings saved him. The pilings. A careful grid of wooden posts set three feet apart, supporting the weight of the dock. Supporting the weight of thirty anglers, their cast nets and tackle boxes. Supporting the weight of fifty fishing rods and twenty coolers. Old, waterlogged pilings, covered with razor blades. This fish knew that he had to reach the pilings.

Carl exerted the maximum amount of pressure his line could handle. Both of them, the old guide and the snook, stood there for the longest time, holding their ground. The snook turned its wide body and hung there, swimming straight into the current. Unable to swim forward and unwilling to be pulled back down current. Pulled back and away from the freedom of the pilings. The fish had never encountered a fisherman who was smart enough, or quick enough, to do this to him. The fish knew that the angler he was fighting was just as old and wise as he was. The fish, for the first time in its life, grew afraid.

Carl was getting tired. He had been fighting this snook for over ten minutes. He knew it was far from over. As the old man and the snook engaged in their stalemate, the pier emptied. Everyone had brought in their lines. Even Ralph and Jose had reeled in their baits. Ralph had never seen a snook this size played this long before. Jose had hooked several this big over the years but all of them had escaped. Jose knew that the longer Carl could keep him away from the pilings, the more exhausted the snook would become. Swimming against that current with ten pounds of line pressure pulling in the other direction will eventually exhaust a fish. Sooner or later, the snook would break off and swim downstream, toward Naples and the open water of the Gulf. Once this happened, Carl could catch the fish.

One by one, everyone on the pier leaned their rods against the railing, unhooked and tossed back their pinfish and shiners, and came down to the beach to watch Carl fight his snook. Several beachcombers had joined the spectators. The crowd numbered over twenty. Richard was standing right beside Carl.

"Do you have him?"

"No, not until he turns."

"Will he turn?"

"He is the strongest snook I have ever felt, Richard. His size and stamina make it difficult for me to convince him to swim away from that pier. He has been hooked before. This fish knows how the game is played. This is a great fish, Richard, a truly great fish. He does not tire and is as strong as the pilings he wants to reach."

Just then, the snook on the other end of that fine, fine thread started to rise. He had been swimming six or seven feet below the surface, but now you could see the angle of the line coming up. Coming up quickly. The snook exploded like a black-and-gold missile launched from the depths of the ocean. This time he shot straight up and he whipped his dark head from side to side like a tarpon does. He was trying to throw the hook. He was trying to be free.

Carl responded by lowering the rod tip back toward the snook to allow some slack in the line. It was a trick he had learned from years of taking his charters out to fish for tarpon. You bow to the mighty silver king. You bow to this mighty snook as well. With the drag set tight, there was every chance that the fish could snap the line with his violent head shakes. Carl knew this and he would not allow it. The fish landed back in the water with a mighty splash. The crowd applauded and cheered. They didn't cheer for Carl. They cheered for the fish and his magnificent jump.

"He is tiring, Richard. He is an old fish and he is getting tired and I am an old man and I am getting tired. I don't know how much longer I can hold on to him. If he stays here much longer, you may have to take the rod for a while."

"No, no, Carl, I can't take the rod. I don't know how to fight a big fish like this. I will lose him. You have to hang in there, old man. You have to land this fish."

Carl was very tired. The great fish had crashed back into the sea, heading for a brief moment to the south. Then he quickly turned about and ended up in nearly the same position as before. Carl, knowing that the jump took some energy out of the snook, had managed to get two or three turns of the spinning reel in before the fish resumed his position in the current. Now, only ninety feet of line separated them.

Then it happened. The snook turned. He turned his head and his dark eyes toward the beach and broke off to the south. With the current behind him he was going to try to spool the reel. He could not make it to the pilings. This fisherman who had set this hook in his mouth was wise. This fisherman had caught many a snook before. He would not allow this big fish to reach the freedom of the pilings.

Carl reacted like lightning. With the fish running down current Carl knew that his drag setting was too tight. He reached around and backed the setting off a full turn and a half. If it was line that this fish wanted, then Carl would give it to him. The closest pilings to the south were thirty miles away. Let him run, thought Carl to himself. Let the big fish run.

Carl took a few steps toward the point of the Island and stopped. Something was wrong. Inside of himself he felt something go wrong. He didn't know what it was, but he felt it and it frightened him. It was much the same fear that the snook had felt moments ago.

"Richard."

"Yes, Carl, what is it?"

"Richard, the snook is swimming south now, down toward the lighthouse and the beaches. He hasn't the strength to head back up current any longer. He knows that he will not reach the pilings this morning. I am tired of fighting him Richard. I am an old man and I am exhausted. You have to take the rod and land this fish for me. I need to go back to the fishing pier to rest up a minute."

Richard didn't know what to do. He knew that Carl was serious. He could plainly see how tired he was. Carl had started to perspire and grow pale. It had been a long fight already and although the snook was turned, it would be much, much longer before this snook could be landed.

But Richard didn't want to take the rod from Carl. He was afraid that the snook might wear through the leader, or take out all the line. He was afraid of losing this fish for Carl. He didn't want to take on such a responsibility. Carl sensed Richard's apprehensions.

"Don't worry about losing him, Richard. We are only going to release him in the end anyway. We have already won the battle. We have taught this old fish that we can keep him from the pilings. He knows that he has been beaten. Just take the rod and let me rest. When you land him, you can bring him over to show him to me before we let him go free."

Carl held out the fishing pole to Richard. Ralph and Jose were amazed. They had never seen Carl tire before. They had seen him wrestle every sea creature imaginable and never once had they seen him hand a rod off to anyone. This morning, looking at the beads of perspiration on Carl's face running down those deep creases of age, and his arms, shaking from exhaustion, they saw Carl for who he really was. He was an old man. He was an old man who was almost eighty. On old man who fished at the pier every day because it was better than staying at home in a house no longer graced with the presence of the only woman he had ever loved, Marie. Carl was just a tired old sea captain. He needed the help.

Nervously, Richard took the rod from Carl's aged and wrinkled hand. The crowd cheered exuberantly. Carl turned to them and acknowledged their applause. He then turned back to Richard.

"Do not touch the drag unless he heads back to the pier, which I doubt he will. If he does, though, only tighten the drag one full turn.

Any tighter than that and it will break. He will probably just keep running south and follow the trough along the beach like Becky's big jewfish did last year. Only a snook is much faster. You might have to sprint to keep up with him. Eventually, he will tire himself out. I cannot tell you how long that might take. This is a huge fish and he is very strong. I am going back to sit down on the bench for a while to rest. Bring him back to me when you land him."

"I will," said Richard, holding the long rod tip up high. "Are you going to be all right, Carl?"

"I'll be fine. I just need to rest a minute. When I feel better, I'll come back and catch up with ya'll. The best of luck to you, Richard!"

"Thanks, Carl. I'll need it."

Carl walked slowly back toward the Sanibel fishing pier. No one came with him. They had all seen men like Carl before. They had all seen tired old fishermen before. They all stayed with Richard and the opportunity to see a fifty-inch snook being taken. Carl didn't mind. Were he not so tired himself, he would have stayed on to watch the fight along with them.

When he got back to the pier, everything felt strange. It was a Friday morning with a swift outgoing tide and a beautiful day and there was no one on the pier. Only the rods, reels, and tackle boxes remained. The pier was like a ghost town, deserted and empty. There were no smelly fishermen smoking cigarettes and swapping fishing stories. There was only the sound of the south wind in the empty lines. It was a beautiful sound. A chorus of fishing lines singing in the wind. Like music to Carl.

Carl sat on the bench that lay beneath the short, covered section of the pier. He faced south, looking toward the crowd that was gathered around Richard, Ralph, and Jose. Whatever had gone wrong with him a few minutes ago continued. He was perspiring more than he should be for such a fight. His breath was short and heavy. He could feel his heart racing, beating faster than it should be beating.

Then the pain started. It wasn't an ordinary pain. It wasn't sharp or stinging, like a cut or a burn. It was a deep and silent pain. His chest felt heavy. He wanted to cry out but there was no one left on the pier to cry out to. They were on the beach, following Richard and the big fish. They were a block away now. Against the wind, they would not be able to hear him. Though he wanted to cry out, he kept silent.

The pain increased steadily. The pain kept squeezing in on Carl's chest. It kept gaining weight, growing heavier and heavier as the seconds passed. The pain was overwhelming him. The pain was causing his arms and neck to become numb, his vision blurred. He was having a difficult time keeping his thoughts straight. All Carl knew was that this was bad. He knew that it was death that had come to visit with him and he was afraid.

He was afraid and excited. There was a part of him that looked down the boardwalk in terror, hoping, praying that someone would be arriving late. That some wannabe angler would walk on the pier with a price tag dangling from his K-Mart rod and find him like this. That someone could help him. He couldn't move at all now, the weight on his chest held him there. Held him firmly. The weight kept him from moving.

But there was another part of him that was excited by what was happening. "It's OK," the voice kept saying over and over to him. It was his time. It was a voice that came from a place far deeper than his fears.

Amid the increasing pain, he thought of Marie. He saw her in her favorite Easter dress. It was twenty years ago when she last wore that dress, a bright yellow floral print that she wore like a field of daisies. His daughter was there. So was his son. It was a photo he had taken. He remembered backing up to get the three of them framed in the photograph...it was in front of a beautiful traveler palm...that was it...it was the photo he has up in the dining room, next to the old oak sideboard they brought down from Davenport. It is such a lovely dress, thought Carl, such a lovely dress, as he faded away, unable to think clearly enough to think at all.

Richard didn't dare to touch the drag. The snook was swimming down the trough and turning the corner by the Sanibel lighthouse.

Ralph had run up ahead of the crowd. He was clearing away several beach fishermen to make sure that Richard's fish wouldn't get tangled in anyone's line as he worked it down the beach.

Richard had never experienced a fish like this one. He was nervous and so afraid of doing something wrong. "Don't touch the drag," he kept repeating slowly to himself. "Don't touch the drag." The snook would make rapid, short runs and the line would fly off the spool. Richard would just keep the tip up and let the line peel away. When the fish tired, he would pull the rod tip back and reel in as he pointed the tip back toward the water in a steady pumping action. It was all he knew how to do.

The snook stopped running up the beach at Point Ybel, the very tip of Sanibel. Richard planted himself at the point and decided that he would bring him in. You could still see the end of the pier from this point, but you could no longer see the bench where Carl was sitting. It was a good place to draw the final battle line.

Richard sensed that the snook was conceding. His runs were growing shorter. A few of the times, when Richard was pumping the rod back, the big fish would come up to the surface. The snook would turn sideways and roll, becoming nearly belly up. There was less than fifty feet of line separating these adversaries.

The small crowd had grown since the fight began twenty minutes ago. More and more shell pickers, beach bikers, and power walkers had joined in, swelling the total number of onlookers to over thirty.

When the snook would come up to the surface, they would all ooouuu and ahhhhh at once, as if they were watching a fireworks display. When it ran again, vanishing in the turbid waters of the point, they would all comment on the size of the fish. "It's the biggest snook I've ever seen," kept reverberating like an echo through the crowd.

"Richard, the fish is nearing his end now. It is a time you must be very careful. When the line gets short like it will soon, there is no room for error. If the big fish makes a run when the line is short, there is no give to it. The fish can easily break your line at this point," advised Jose.

"What should I do?"

"You must loosen the drag even more than it is now."

"But Carl told me not to touch the drag."

"Yes, I heard him tell you that, but I know that if he was here, he would tell you to loosen it. He is tired and resting now, but he himself would loosen the drag or risk losing this fish when it is this close in."

Richard thought for a minute and decided that Jose was right. It would be better to keep the drag loose as the fish approached the beach. Earlier in the week Carl had explained why he still fished with monofilament and not all the new, high-tech line Richard had purchased. Carl said it was because monofilament stretches.

"The stretch in the line is forgiving," said Carl. "Like the old parable of the oak and the willow, it is the willow that survives the storm."

But Carl was careful to add that the shorter the distance between you and the fish, the less forgiveness is left in the line. That is when you should back off the drag and let the fish take line if it needs it. Not if there are any pilings around, thought Richard to himself. But Jose is right, this fish is in open water. He is a long way from the cutting edges and the freedom of the pilings.

Richard reached over and took a full turn and a half off the drag setting. He looked back toward the fishing pier and glanced at the pilings under it. There was no way this tired snook could make that long run back to the pier. It was the right thing to do.

Within a few more pumps the snook was in two feet of water. He was now lying sideways, his broad, powerful tail flopping at the surface. The big fish was exhausted, worn out by the pull of the fishing rod and the tired muscles of two anglers.

"Did you bring the net?" yelled Richard to Ralph as he started wading in toward the fish.

"That snook is too big to fit in that little net, Richard. I don't have it with me even if it could fit."

"Well, how am I going to land it? I promised Carl that I would show it to him."

"I'll come out and grab it for you. I can get a hold of it just under the gills for you," said Ralph.

"Don't you dare kill it, Ralph!" insisted Richard in his best attorney's voice.

"I don't have my club with me, Richard, and I know Carl will release it. I promise you that I will not kill it. There is no other way to land this old linesider."

Ralph waded in. He walked past Richard and stood beside the big fish. The water was up to his waist. The waves were still coming up from the south. In this steady chop it was hard for Ralph to keep his balance. Richard was ten feet behind him, holding the long rod tip straight up and steady.

Ralph had to be careful. Snook have razor-sharp gill plates. The edges are serrated and a fish this size, if not grabbed perfectly, could slice Ralph's hand wide open. He had to reach under the fish, coming up from his belly, and slide his fingers up and under the gills. If he did it wrong, or the big fish thrashed at the last second, he risked being cut by the knifelike edges of the gill plates. He reached down and touched the snook.

The big fish could see the shape of a man standing over him, contorted and twisting with each wave washing over his dark eyes. He saw the hand of this strange animal coming toward him. When the hand touched him, the fish summoned every remaining ounce of energy within him and made a final run. He did not want to be captured.

The fish ran with the current, toward the side where Ralph had been standing. When the great snook starting cutting back to the beach, the fishing line came right across Ralph's body. Richard gasped. Surely the line would break. The 14-lb. plastic thread stretched down from Ralph's shoulder to just above his knee. The drag was singing wildly as this brave fish made its last desperate run.

Ralph knew what he must do. If he stood his ground, the rushing line might wear through from the friction it produced as it rubbed against his body. If he backed away, slowly, it still might snag on a button, or his tarnished silver belt buckle. Without a second's hesitation, he held his breath and fell backwards, completely submerging himself in the waist-deep water. He let all the air out of his lungs as he fell to keep sinking. He sank to the bottom, the back of his head hitting the sand and shells three feet below the waves. Just as he hit the bottom, he felt the thin strand of monofilament slip across his face. Luckily, the line had cleared his body without snagging anything.

When he came back up, the crowd went wild. Everyone saw what he had done. The shouts of joy were deafening.

"Are you all right, Ralph?"

"I'm wet, Richard. I'm very, very wet. But I'm all right. That fish does not want to surrender. Do we still have him?"

"Yes."

"Then that is all that matters. Let's try for him again."

The fish had not run far. He had taken out ten, maybe fifteen yards of line at most. Had Ralph not fallen backwards into the sea, it would have been more than enough of a run for the line to break.

Ralph did not know it, but for the big, wise old fish, Ralph had become his last, lonely piling. Now there was no more fight left in him. This time when the big snook came back into the breaking surf, Ralph had no trouble sliding his right hand up under the gills. With the fish gently flopping, Ralph lifted him halfway out of the water and began walking back to the beach.

Richard joined him. He put his thick, pudgy arm around Ralph's shoulder as they both waded up and out of the ocean. Ralph held the big fish up high with his right hand as the crowd applauded. He strained to raise it as high as his shoulder. Becky, remembering her great jewfish fight earlier in the year, hollered the loudest. It was an ecstatic scene. Congratulations were streaming in from all the onlookers.

"Fine fight!"

"Great fish!"

"Great job!"

"Well done!" Accolades and praises poured in from everyone gathered.

The comments mixed together in that sweet, intoxicating chorus of success. They laid the vanquished snook down on the sand and guessed at its size. It was more than four feet long. It had to weigh forty-five pounds. It was the biggest snook Ralph or Jose had ever seen landed. It laid there on the hot sand, gasping for the air it could not find. Afraid.

"We have to get it back to show Carl. We can measure it at the pier," said Richard.

Ralph picked the fish up again, this time holding it in both hands. He was soaking wet. Just then he suddenly remembered that he still had his wallet in his pants pocket. It was soaked. He was angry with himself for doing such a stupid thing. It does not matter, he concluded. It will dry out. He was glad he had taken that dunk to catch this fish and would do the same tomorrow morning if he had to. He could not wait to see the look on Carl's face when he showed him this snook.

Everyone, except for the shellers and the joggers, headed back to the pier. The shellers went back to searching for their junonia. The joggers didn't want their pulse rate to drop off any further. It was just a big fish to them. It was fun for a while.

Richard walked as fast as he could back toward the pier. He couldn't wait to show Carl that he had done it, that he had landed the fish. He had done everything right and he had finished the fight for his good friend. Thirty minutes had passed since Carl had first set the hook on this old linesider. Thirty minutes of excitement and joy.

Ralph lagged behind Richard down the beach. Ralph had been careful to stop and dip the large snook in the saltwater several times along the way, knowing that the fish needed to catch its breath and remain wet. Ralph knew that Carl wouldn't want this big fish to become too stressed and be unable to return to the ocean.

When Richard got within fifty feet of the dock, he knew that something was wrong. Something was terribly wrong. Carl sat slumped over on the bench. His color was gone. His face and arms were the same color as the cracked and faded planks of the fishing pier, an ashen, lifeless grey. Richard dropped Carl's rod on the sand and ran to the pier. His heart was pounding rapidly. His mind was wheeling. This couldn't be happening. It just couldn't be happening! No. No. No!

Richard was the first to arrive back on the pier. He rushed over to Carl. His deep blue eyes were open. His pupils were dilated. He wasn't focusing. Is there still a pulse? Richard reached up to touch his neck and ever so faintly, he could still feel a beating heart. The heartbeat was slow and faint. He put his ear up to Carl's mouth. There were small, sporadic gasps coming out. Carl was still alive. Barely alive.

Richard knew what had happened. He had seen it before. It was during a court case four years ago. They had been married forty years when the wife had an affair with the chaplain at the retirement center they both had moved into. It was a scandalous, terrible case.

Richard was representing the wife, who claimed she had been driven into the relationship by years of emotional neglect. Richard knew it was bullshit. The wife was a selfish old bitch who wanted a change.

Her husband didn't want to grant her the divorce. She was his life. In the middle of the second day of the trial, her husband keeled over from a massive heart attack. The same color skin, the same sporadic breathing. Within ten minutes, despite CPR and nearly immediate medical attention, the husband died. The wife won the divorce. Richard charged her double the going rate because he didn't like her. She paid.

Carl was having a heart attack and every second would count.

"Does anyone know CPR?" shouted Richard to the crowd that was now gathered around this dying fisherman. No one replied. They were all stunned into silence.

"DOES ANYONE HERE KNOW CPR?" Richard yelled for a second time. His voice sounded so frightening that he didn't recognize it when he yelled out. Richard was in shock. This couldn't be happening.

"I do," answered a young woman. "I'm a nurse."

Jose and Richard picked up Carl and laid him on the deck of the pier. Laid him down in the shade, below the covered section of the pier. Carl looked terrible. He looked so old and weathered. So alone. Richard loosened his shirt collar and looked at the young lady standing beside him.

"Try to save him. I left my cell phone in my car this morning. I'm going to head out to the parking lot and dial 911. How close is the nearest ambulance service?"

"They're about three miles away, up by Bailey's supermarket," answered a local.

The nurse got on top of Carl and started performing CPR. Everyone stood silent. On the way back to his car Richard glanced over to the big snook. It was lying in a shallow puddle of freshwater formed by a beach swale, right beside the boardwalk where Ralph had left it. Ralph had thrown it there when he realized what had happened to Carl. It was no longer a great fish thought Richard as he ran to his car. It was something that had hurt his friend. Richard wanted to kill it as he walked past it. He was angry.

As Richard approached the car, he searched his right pocket for his key. His pocket was soaked. It was difficult getting his hand in it to find the car key. Nothing was going right. Carl was sick and he needed help immediately and that damn fish had caused it. That damned fish and this stupid, goddamned fishing. What the hell was the point of it? Why the hell do people go fishing anyway?

Richard finally found the key. With his hand shaking, both from the long battle with the snook and from seeing Carl like that, he unlocked his car door. His cell phone was in the glove box. Like an idiot, he realized that he had locked that as well. It was a habit. Cell phones are expensive. It was taking too damn long. It was taking too long to get to his phone. If Carl does die..., I will know who to blame, he kept thinking to himself amidst an avalanche of fear, anxiety, and anger. Richard was walking the thin white line of panic. His world was crashing in on him. Fishing, fishing for what?

He flipped open the cell phone and pressed power. In the upper right hand his cell phone blinked. Little black dots flashed across the liquid crystal display. The phone was "looking for a signal." Then it flashed to roam. Richard hadn't used his cell phone since coming on the islands. He always brought it along with him anyway. Back in Peoria it was his link to the office. His electronic connection to affidavits and final settlement decrees. Without it he felt naked.

It was taking forever to find a local cell. While the transistors inside the tiny hand-held cell phone searched for a communications tower, he tried to remember whether or not he needed to dial the area code first, or if 911 would work directly on Sanibel. He had used his cell phone only once before to call 911. That was for a minor traffic accident back in Peoria. He wasn't on roam that day. It hardly mattered, as no one had been injured in the accident. He called because the accident was backing up traffic and he was on his way to a deposition. He called because he had been stuck in traffic for fifteen minutes without seeing a cop car. That's damn near a hundred dollars of billing time, he thought as he punched in 911 that afternoon in Peoria.

The cell phone finally set up. The LCD showed that it was ready to dial. The signal was good. Richard decided to punch in 9-1-1 and see if it worked first. Besides, he couldn't remember the area code. He dialed and three numbers and with his thumb. He started to press the SEND button.

He stopped.

He didn't press the SEND key.

For an instant he didn't know why. He just sat there, with his index finger held a quarter of an inch off the SEND button, as though he had been turned to stone. He looked at the clock on the dashboard. It was 8:47 a.m. It was 8:47 a.m. and Richard was frozen in time, unable to dial 911. The man he had grown so fond of lay dying not 100 yards from where he sat.

Why am I doing this? he thought to himself.

He knew why. It was because of their conversation yesterday morning. Just another meandering dialogue while they stood on that wooden fishing pier and the ocean moved below them. It was during a slack tide, thought Richard. A slack tide.

It was when Carl told Richard that he never wanted to go through what Marie had gone through. Through the procedures, the treatments, and the pain. That when Carl went, he wanted to die quickly. He remembered how Carl had looked at him straight away. Richard realized now that it was not just a conversation, it was his dying wish. It was what Carl wanted.

Richard's finger rested delicately against the SEND button. It was the most difficult decision in his life. If I dial and they arrive in time they might still be able to revive him. Depending on how much damage his heart has sustained, he might be all right. He might be able to come down and fish the pier again. If the damage is severe, he might be in a wheel chair, even partially paralyzed. It could take months, even years of rehabilitation. There would be the constant monitoring, the drugs, and the pain. If the blood supply has been cut off to Carl's brain for more than three minutes there could be permanent brain damage. Carl may not ever be able to speak again, to tell his catfish story one last time.

He would remain bedridden, with those awful tubes. Those tubes everywhere. In his arms for feeding, in his nose for breathing, in his penis for urinating. Those god-awful plastic saviors of the modern medical world. No! This wasn't Carl.

What am I going to say? Richard looked down at his car

clock once again, it was 8:50. Eight minutes. Richard remembered the conversations that surrounded the death of the defendant back in Peoria. Eight minutes and there is no saving you. After eight minutes, everything fails. The brain has been deprived of oxygen too long, the heart muscle has deteriorated to a point where those high-voltage paddles can no longer jump-start it. The soul has left the body.

Yes, that's it, reflected Richard. The soul has left the body. Carl can be with her again. Carl can be released. Carl can be with his beautiful wife Marie once more. He can leave behind all those lonely afternoons in that empty house. The sound of eating alone, the memories of when she was still with him. He can float away from all of this and return home. Home to her.

That's what he wants. He wants to be with her. But what if someone is watching me, someone sees me like this? It's murder. Richard looked around the parking lot. There was no one. Everyone went to watch the great fish being caught and now they were all huddled around Carl. They are watching the nurse try to keep him alive. I am all alone in this parking lot and no one will ever know.

I'll just say that my cell phone wasn't working. That it was having trouble picking up a signal. That the batteries were low. I hadn't charged the batteries all week. I'll lie. I've lied before. I've lied about everything. I've lied about where my client was on that Friday afternoon. He couldn't have possibly been in that motel room because he was shooting skeet on the outskirts of town. Every one of his hunting buddies would take the stand and lie too. Armies of lies. Denials, counter claims and counter lies, forgeries, false testimony, perjury and who knows what else. Richard was used to lies. He had lied to himself for so long that he had come to believe that his life was the truth. Lies were his strongest suit.

There were no witnesses to prove him wrong. No evidence to deny his testimony. Even if they saw him, they didn't have a case. He was an attorney, and a damn good one. He could beat this. His cell phone wasn't working right and he tried to call but couldn't. It wasn't his fault. He looked at the dash. It was 8:54. One minute left.

In one minute he would press SEND. The numbers, 911, sat there on his display screen looking for a place to go. They sat there as Carl died. Richard was killing him. Richard smiled. Yes, Carl, I'm killing you. I'm setting you free just like all the big fish you set free. What a wonderful way to die. To die after fighting a mighty snook among all of your friends at your favorite fishing pier. To die quickly. Not without pain, not without regrets, but with your dignity and your self-respect still intact. No tubes. No god-awful tubes in you, Carl.

Then Richard started to cry. He started to cry because he realized how much he had come to love this old salt. The tears were running down his cheeks and falling silently on the cell phone he was holding on his lap. He was going to miss him. Miss him more than he could imagine. He was never going to watch him make that perfect cast, or tie a flawless knot again. He was never going to hear Carl's warm, melodic voice telling one of his tales again, or look once more into his wistful blue eyes. Tales of friendship, and survival, of vanity and greed.

It was over. Carl was gone from this world. The world would be a colder place without him.

Richard wept openly. He tried to remember the last time he had cried. He could not. He must have been a boy. Crying wasn't a part of his practice. There were times when he would look into the eyes of the children his clients would fight over and want to cry. He wanted to cry as his client accepted sole custody . No visitation rights. Ever. Richard wanted to weep as he saw the glances of love those children would pour back across the room to their father. Their father, whom they were not allowed to see again until they were eighteen. Their father, who Richard knew was a good father. That didn't matter. Their mother paid for Richard's services and she prevailed. It was family law. Family law, modern medicine. They both lie.

The clock on the dash board hit 8:56. Richard's shaking finger pressed down on the SEND button. He pressed it so hard that it hurt. An operator picked up the line on the second ring. Richard was right, you don't have to dial the area code. He was always right when it came to facts. Always. That's why he made a half million dollars a year.

"There's a man having a heart attack down at the Sanibel fishing pier. We need an ambulance right away. Please hurry."

"Do you have an address?"

"No, he's on the Sanibel fishing pier, down by the lighthouse."

"Where are you calling from?"

"My cell phone. It wasn't working right. I just got through now."

Richard kicked himself for saying that. How would this operator know how long he had been trying. What difference did it make? Now it was on tape. Still, no proof. I must be feeling guilty, he acknowledged to himself.

"Please hold for a minute while I call the Sanibel EMS and confirm your location with them."

Richard waited for thirty seconds.

"Sir." She got back to him.

"Yes."

"The EMS people are on their way. Try to find someone to administer CPR until they arrive. They should be there in a few minutes."

"Tell them to hurry."

"I will."

Richard pressed END/CLEAR. The signal ended. He got out of the car and walked back toward the pier. He had his cell phone in his hand. He left the power on, hoping that it would run down the battery in the next few minutes, adding credence to his story. It was the legal side of him that was working. It never stopped working. At times he wished it would.

"They're on their way," he said as he approached the crowd.

Ralph looked down at Carl and looked over to Richard. It was a penetrating look, one that seemed to cut right through Richard. "What took so long?" Ralph asked.

"My cellphone. I was having trouble using my cellphone. The batteries are weak. I wasn't able to pick up a clear signal. I finally got through."

Ralph didn't respond. It didn't sound right to him. The nurse was still working on Carl. It was obvious to everyone standing around the inside of the circle that it was over. Carl had stopped breathing five minutes ago. He was lifeless. Ashen and lifeless, lying on the cracked and splintered planks of the pier. The nurse was tired. Her blouse was drenched in sweat. She was unraveled.

Richard reached over and touched her on the shoulder.

"It's over," he said.

"No, I've got to keep trying until they arrive."

"No, you don't. He's dead and you know he's dead. It's over."

The nurse collapsed on top of Carl's body and laid there sobbing. She had tried so hard to save him. She had done everything she could to keep this stranger out of death's hands but she had failed. Exhausted, ashamed and saddened, she knelt over Carl, her head next to his, and cried. No one even knew her name.

There were tears everywhere. Some people along the outside of the circle broke away and started drifting down the beach. Their thoughts were heavy with the knowledge of their own mortality. They didn't know this man. He looked like a nice man. They had heard from someone else that he was the one who had first hooked the big snook.

The snook! Everyone had forgotten about the snook, thought Richard. He quickly shoved his way back out of the crowd and walked back to where he last saw the fish. It was still there, lying in a shallow fresh water puddle. Richard thought it was dead. As he reached over to pick it up, he was surprised to see it move. He looked closely and he could see that its gills were still moving back and forth.

The snook was alive. Richard didn't know that snook are able to survive in fresh and brackish water as well as saltwater. The small pool of water Ralph had dropped the snook in had kept it from drying out in the sun. The puddle had given it just enough air to sustain it.

Richard picked up the huge fish and walked back up the pier toward Carl. The crowd parted as he approached Carl's body. The nurse had gotten up and was being comforted by Jose and Ralph. It was a sadness immense on those wooden planks. Richard looked down at Carl's face. It looked peaceful. His blue eyes were still open.

Richard took the big fish and held it in front of Carl's face. He knew that somewhere, from vantage points the quick will never understand, Carl could see this magnificent linesider.

"We landed him Carl. We caught him. I did touch the drag though. I know you told me not to. But I did." Tears were falling from Richards face as he spoke, falling on the dry wooden deck of the pier, staining a small portion of the plank below him dark. Dark, like when the rains fall. Richard went on.

"Ralph waded in and picked him up and here he is. He's a beauty, Carl. He's a big fish. But I can't stand here and show him to you all day. He's still alive, Carl. You're not alive but I know that you would want to make sure he gets back in the water. So I'm going to release him for you, Carl. You can't release him now, because you've been released. You're free, you wonderful old fisherman. Free."

Richard kept sobbing as he spoke, his voice almost whispering. It was so quiet that every word he said was heard by all who stood there. Heard as clearly as the deepest prayer.

"Say hello to Marie for me. Tell her that I look forward to meeting her someday. Tell her that I'm going to miss you, Carl. I'm going to miss you more than anyone I've ever missed in my life. Goodbye my good friend. Good-bye."

The EMS men were barging in just as Richard finished. They cleared everyone away from the body and started doing all those things that EMS people do. They were taking his pulse, stabbing needles into him and putting him on a stretcher. Richard couldn't watch. He was glad that Carl wasn't around to watch either.

Richard took the big fish back down to the end of the pier and walked down the beach a bit. The snook was heavy. He waded in up over his waist. His cell phone crackled when it hit the salt water. The evidence was destroyed, thought the lawyer inside of him. He set the big fish in the saltwater but it just floated there, lifeless and still. Ralph yelled over to Richard from the pier as they were wheeling Carl back toward the ambulance.

"You've got to revive him, Richard. He needs air. Take and swish him back and forth in the water for a while. That will force some water into his gills. It should revive him."

Richard held it firmly in both hands just under the surface. He rocked the big snook back and forth. He could feel the life flowing back into the fish with every pass. He must have done it a dozen times or more. Then he looked into the dark, black eyes of the fish and he could see that he was coming back into life. He wasn't angry at the fish any longer. It was all meant to be. This was a noble creature.

The fish realized that it was still in the hands of this strange animal called man. With a sudden kick of its wide tail fin, it swam free. It had won after all.

Richard walked back up to the pier and sat across the way

from where Carl was sitting a few moments ago. Carl's body was gone. He could hear the sirens disappearing into the distance. Richard just sat there, thinking of nothing. Sat there with the sun falling on his back and the current pouring out to sea beneath him. The sun felt warm, he thought, warm and wonderful.

"In the event we experience a sudden drop in cabin pressure, the oxygen masks, found directly overhead, will drop down automatically. Place the masks securely over your mouth, putting the elastic band around your head and breathe normally...," the tape-looped message continued, but Richard had stopped paying attention.

Breathe normally. Richard had always thought it was a ridiculous assumption. There's a gaping hole in the fuselage somewhere that's causing the rapid collapse of the cabin pressure. Walkmans, Game Boys, bad food and babies are being sucked out into the thin air of 35,000 feet. Magazines and tiny whiskey bottles are whizzing past your head as a little plastic mask drops in front of you. You're supposed to place it over your mouth, tighten the elastic band until it fits comfortably and breathe normally! More corporate bullshit.

Richard had a window seat. First class. Lots of leg room. A comfortable, reclining seat in dark tan leather. The food was better than it is in coach. You had to qualify that. How much better can airline food be? Still more bullshit. Only this time they serve it to you with silverware bearing the airline's logo.

"You can keep the silverware if you like," said the pretty stewardess to his oldest son, Tyler. Pleeeease, thought Richard.

Helen sat beside him. Tyler and James sat just in front. Tyler was playing a Game Boy. The plane was just about to depart on a windy Saturday morning. It was late in departing. Why can't they just push the whole damn airline schedule back an hour and stop being late? Why can't they, just this once, be on time? Richard wanted to complain to the stewardess but he decided that it was pointless. It's all pointless.

Richard was angry. Over the last twenty hours he had been

angry, sad, elated, depressed, guilt ridden, and suspended. Most of this time he was suspended. Dangling like some insect caught in an ethereal web that was as strong as cable and as elusive as the proof of God. Neither awake nor asleep. So shaken by what had happened at the pier yesterday morning that the world had taken on a flat, one-dimensional quality to it. He is floating through this world in an illusion. It is called shock.

Helen tried to get through to him. She could not. He would lash out at her for no reason. At other times, he would walk over to her, put his head on her shoulder and start weeping. Richard was a mess. Helen had never met Carl, but she was beginning to realize how much he must have meant to Richard. She had never seen him this exposed. In a way, she thanked Carl for doing this to him. At least her husband was real again. He was alive again.

The plane taxied down the runway. Richard looked out the window to the palm trees and the slash pines that stood along the far side of the runway. The wind was still pouring up from the south, moist and tropical. The palm fronds were quivering and whipping about in the steady breeze. It was just past noon, and the sun had put a brilliant glare on the palmettos and cabbage palms. It was surreal. Everything in my life is surreal, he reflected. Everything.

Only death matters. Only death makes sense. Final death. Ultimate death. Painful and certain, like a car slamming head on into a stone wall. Or falling, being sucked out of a hole in this airplane and falling, falling, falling until that final, merciful thud. Death. What a son of a bitch death is. What an indifferent asshole death is! It should have been me lying on those wooden planks. I'm the fool who deserves to die. Not Carl. Damn it to hell, not Carl!

The anger was sweeping back through him like a foul wind. It would pass. Then the sadness would follow. In time, the guilt would resurface again. I should have dialed 911. He might still be alive if I had done the right thing yesterday.

But who can say what the right thing is?

The plane just stood there. Like some roaring animal, ready to tear down that runway and take off. The big jet engines started accelerating while the captain and copilot held the brakes. The cabin air started to smell of burnt kerosene and that strange, mechanical odor that planes smell like just before they take off. The air conditioning was shut off. It was getting stuffy in the cabin, and the air inside smelled thick and industrial. The captain released the brakes and the airplane raced down the runway like an aluminum thoroughbred. It lifted off in seconds.

The air conditioning kicked back on and Richard reached up to adjust those little nozzles that squirt the cool air down on your head. These damned things never work right. Never. They give me a goddamned headache!

It was a nonstop flight to St. Louis, followed by a commuter run back over to Peoria. Richard hated the commuter run. He hated turbo props. He disliked having to hand your carry-on luggage to someone because there wasn't enough room for it in the cabin. Most of all, he hated the stairs. He hated them because he was fat and the guardrails up the staircase were always too narrow. As he walked up the stairs, his oversized body touched both sides of the railing, squeezing him in like a giant marshmallow getting on a plane. As fat as he was, having himself pinched between these two railings made him feel a thousand times fatter.

No one flew to Peoria nonstop. It didn't matter that Richard would have paid an extra thousand dollars a ticket to do so. Peoria was just too small a town. Peoria was a small, Midwestern town "non grata." It was just another pathetic manufacturing town. It was full of Caterpillar plants and Cummings diesels. Full of bowling alleys, corner bars and small town scandals. The divorce rate was holding steady at 53 percent. Peoria was Richard's meal ticket. Family law. Breathe normally. What difference does it make?

Richard was still looking out the window as the airplane climbed. The sadness was coming now. He could feel it beginning deep in his soul and he felt it slowly working its way over him. The sadness was a thick, soft blanket of the deepest, most glorious purple he had ever known. It smothered him. It covered his eyes and put him inside a place of melancholy, a darkness all encompassing. It felt cold and comforting at the same time. Richard didn't mind the sadness. He felt that he owed this sadness to Carl. That Carl had earned it.

He was looking out the window of the plane but he really wasn't looking at anything. He was just trying to avoid having Helen see the tears in his eyes. Without knowing why, he looked down beneath the plane. He wasn't sure at first, but he thought he was looking down on Sanibel. It was Sanibel. The plane was heading to St. Louis and the flight path brought it directly out over the island. They were still low enough for Richard to be able to pick out the pier on the eastern tip of the island. Yes, that's it. It's the fishing pier!

It looks so tiny now, reflected Richard. I wonder if Ralph's using my tackle?

Yesterday, after sitting on the bench across from where Carl had his heart attack for what must have been an hour, Ralph had come up to sit beside him. Ralph said that he and Jose would take the gear back to Carl's house later. They knew Carl never locked the back door so getting into the garage would be easy.

Richard thanked them for being so kind. Then he added that he really didn't want to fish any more today, and since he was leaving tomorrow, they could have all the tackle he had purchased earlier in the week. Most of it was unused, since Carl had been rigging Richard with his old charter gear the entire week. Only the rod and reel he had purchased had felt the wash of salt water on it. Ralph thanked him. Then Ralph and Jose packed up and headed home. They didn't feel like fishing either.

The snook were still hitting hard when they started their cars and drove off alone. It didn't matter. The snook would bite again. Richard got up and left around eleven. He had only his cellphone with him, still leaking water. He felt like a little boy as he walked down that wooden boardwalk to the parking lot for the last time. A lost little boy. He didn't know if he would ever return to the Sanibel fishing pier again.

From a mile in the air the fishing pier looked like a tiny 'T' jutting out from just past the tip of the island. You could see the color changes in the water half a mile from the end of the pier. The tide line formed when the brown waters of the Caloosahatchee mixed with the darker, greenish waters of the Gulf. Richard was too far above the tide lines to see the gulls working along that tide line. He knew that they were. He knew that they were below him, diving and working a pod of baitfish that had formed along the edge of the current. He knew it without seeing it.

He wondered if Ralph or Jose, if Gary or Becky were down there. He wondered if the bite was on. He saw it all so clearly. The tourists with their incessant backlashes and tangles, their pale skin burning under the Florida sun. The locals arriving, walking up the dock with their bright yellow bait buckets. Buckets filled with Bait Box shrimp. He saw the bronze redfish swaying at the end of stringers in the outgoing tide. He saw Becky's skinny husband, Paul, chain smoking. Looking like an escapee from a prison camp. But more than anything else, he still saw Carl.

He saw his bright, sparkling blue eyes. He saw him gazing across the surface of the water, reading its landscape like an artist. Noting the pelicans here, a school of jack crevalles over there. A rusty shrimp boat chugging out into the Gulf for a three-week journey just off Louisiana, a shell collector on the beach, yelling to her friend about the broken lion's paw she just picked up. Carl's world. A world of the sea, the surf and the sand.

He saw the deep, sun-etched lines in Carl's face. Every line telling another tale, another afternoon spent with his charters. Bent rods, broken lines, big fish in dark-green landing nets and smiling faces. Every wrinkle a testament to a man who loved the ocean. A man who chose to live his own life. Not an easy life. A life where a cold week in January might mean you have to cancel all your bookings. Where a blown engine means you're out of work for two weeks running. Not an easy life at all. Just a damn good one.

Richard could hear his voice, deep, rich and melodic. The voice of a storyteller. A voice that could capture you. A voice that would lead you into its tale willingly. Long, idle conversations, as the water of the world poured back and forth beneath the pier. Back and forth. Breath like. The tides of the world. They are the breath of the world.

Richard tried to imagine Marie. He tried to see her working in the yard. Waiting every day for Carl to come back from the sea. Listening to Carl tell her the stories of the day. "A fine catch of sea trout. A big, muscular tarpon that ran so hard he crunched all the gears in his brand-new Penn Senator. Darn, they just don't make reels like they used to, Marie."

They were together now. It was good. There was no reason to feel guilty about it. He felt guilty anyway.

Richard could see the big linesider swimming beneath the pier. Swimming near the bottom, his strength recovered, his muscles and backbone still sore from yesterday morning's battle. But alive again, and riding behind an eddy in the falling tide. Ready. Hungry and poised to lash out and inhale an unsuspecting baitfish. A huge snook. One that will never be landed again.

"Are you OK, Richard?" Helen asked.

The fishing pier was now far behind them. Tears were rolling down Richard's pudgy cheeks and along the edge of his lips. He licked them away. They tasted salty. They tasted like the spray of the ocean. He would never be far from the sea again; if he was, he could just cry for a moment and return, he thought to himself as Helen interrupted.

"No, Helen, I'm not OK. I'm so sad. Carl was such a wonderful person. I'm going to miss him. It is all just so terrible."

"I know."

The plane kept flying toward St. Louis. The stewardesses brought out their little rolling tray of drinks and honey roasted nuts. Richard had a vodka seven. It tasted sweet. The airplane, his wife and his two boys were suspended again. He was in a place of great sorrow. There was nothing mortal that could reach him. The world and everything in it was wrapped in this endless purple cloth. Like a Catholic Church on Good Friday, everything was draped in a rich, sacred purple.

After a long time had passed he looked down again. They must be over Georgia, he thought. Maybe it was Alabama. They were very high. The countryside was divided into large rectangular fields and patches of forest-green woodlands. Some of the fields were still green. Most of them were brown, stripped of their harvest by tractors and complicated machines. Every so often there would be a small town.

Tiny highways, now seemingly thinner than the fishing line Richard was using yesterday, poured in and out of these towns from all directions. The world was an impossible tangle, reflected Richard, like an immense backlash. The world was an endless mess of towns, cities and villages that no one, save God, could hope to untangle. Richard looked down and from his vantage point he could see the tiny houses. They looked like monopoly houses.

They weren't monopoly houses though, and Richard knew

that. Those tiny houses were filled with people. The people in them were not unlike him. They had wives, or girlfriends, children and grandchildren, brothers and sisters. They had jobs, dreams, ambitions and sorrows. They were all connected. Every person below him had decisions to make. Decisions about who they were, what they were doing, and who they wanted to be. They loved others and if they were fortunate enough, they were loved in return. The world made sense to him in a way it never had before.

Every tiny, fragile house below him had its story to tell. Not stories of any grand significance. No kings, queens, or great revelations. Just the stories of ordinary people. Stories of grandpa Clarence dying, or cousin Nancy finally leaving that jerk of a husband she should never have married. Stories of significance to those who told them and, most importantly, to those who lived them.

But that is all the significance there is. It doesn't matter that their lives are small, or that they aren't rich or famous or anything in between. It is so simple in its sublime complexity. We are all alive together, caught up in this monofilament entanglement of highways and phone lines. We are all connected. Each and every one of us is worth as much as the other.

Richard was startled back into the present with these thoughts. He turned away from the thick glass of the airplane window and looked at Helen. She was reading one of those promotional magazines the airlines leave in the back pockets of the seat in front of you.

Helen set the magazine down on her lap and looked back at Richard. His eyes were red and swollen from the river of tears he had shed since coming home from the pier yesterday. He had this look about him, a look she hadn't seen since he first left law school. A look he lost soon after taking the part-time job at the Family Law Firm to raise some money for his post graduate degree in the history of law. A doctorate she had always wanted him to have. Teaching law at Northwestern, or any college in the world for that matter. Having his self-respect back.

It reminded her of whom she once loved. It wasn't the man she was married to. She didn't have any respect for that man at all. Richard started to speak, "Helen...."

"Don't say anything, Richard. You don't have to. I'll call Barbara Holt when we get back home. You've met her at the country club. She's that pretty realtor you remarked about. Remember, the redhead. She's always told me that if we ever decided to sell the house, to call her first."

Richard smiled. He smiled in a way that ended his suspension. He turned back to the window and looked down at the villages seven miles below him. He and his family would be living in one of those tiny houses somewhere in America soon. He and his family. He loved the sound of it.

The End.

The sun rose this morning upon my grave.

It pried open the lid on the coffin of night
To rise like some angel afire.
I was not afraid of it for I am dead.

In a forgotten chapter of Revelations, I found my soul
Stirring beneath its overwhelming light,
Wanting never to change an instant of my self, never to lie.

I saw all. The moment of my death,
The river of tears, the sound of their laughter
As my fabled stories were told and retold.

All life is in transit,
Like the sun that climbs atop the blue shoulders of the sky,
Like the sound of shovels filling this trench I'm forever in.

So we must take each second in earnest.
Breathe the last! Love the most intense!
Stretch our joys, our sorrows until they beg to snap!

We must never let passion fail us. Ever.
Or watch our lives be lost to limbo.
These things I say to you from my sun-drenched grave.

Too many the coward, too many the weak and undecided fools
Surround my rotting body in this eternity of dirt,
Daring never to write this hurried message to the living:

"Venture forth! Today! At once! Put down this peasant's verse!
The sun it flies across the sky with the speed of light,
Catch it while you are filled with life. Revel in it.

"These things I know as tons of soil impound me.
Truths that will never fade. Be off this instant,
With your lovers and your life,
Grab the sunlight and dance
Upon my soon forgotten grave!"

Charles Sobczak,
Winter 1995

This book is dedicated to my little sister, Peggy Hines Sobczak, who left us here alone on October 23, 1996.